THE
LIFEBOAT
ORPHANS

BOOKS BY ELLIE CURZON

A VILLAGE AT WAR SERIES

The Ration Book Baby

The Spitfire Girl

The Wartime Vet

Wartime Wishes for the Land Girls

THE RUNAWAY EVACUEES SERIES

The Lost Orphans

THE
LIFEBOAT
ORPHANS

ELLIE CURZON

Bookouture

Published by Bookouture in 2025

An imprint of Storyfire Ltd.
Carmelite House
50 Victoria Embankment
London EC4Y 0DZ

www.bookouture.com

The authorised representative in the EEA is Hachette Ireland
8 Castlecourt Centre
Dublin 15 D15 XTP3
Ireland
(email: info@hbgi.ie)

ISBN: 978-1-80550-159-6
eBook ISBN: 978-1-80550-158-9

This book is a work of fiction. Whilst some characters and circumstances portrayed by the author are based on real people and historical fact, references to real people, events, establishments, organizations or locales are intended only to provide a sense of authenticity and are used fictitiously. All other characters and all incidents and dialogue are drawn from the author's imagination and are not to be construed as real.

Catherine: to Rick and my family, with love. And to Pippa, for
the inspiration.

Helen: for my partner's grandad and his crewmates, who risked
everything to serve in the merchant navy during the Second
World War.

PROLOGUE

London
Summer 1942

A bomb exploded with an almighty roar nearby and the basement room shook. Connie's whole body tensed. She was always on edge during a bombing raid, no matter how many times she'd heard the sirens go off and the bombs crash to the ground. Nowhere was safe. Life was fragile, all they had was this moment, today.

And in Jasper's underground nightclub, where a candle burned on each table, and couples danced while the piano played, she could leave the horrors of the war behind her for a little while. So she swayed in time to the songs, trying to lose the shivers that ran through her to the music.

Then Jasper, who was as dashing as ever in a chalk-stripe suit with wide lapels, took Connie's trembling hand and helped her onto the stage. The lights caught the threads of silver in his hair and his painted silk tie seemed to gleam. The basement rang with the sound of applause.

Connie knew she didn't look like the other singers, who

were older and more glamorous and wore long silk gowns. She was only fifteen, still growing into herself and unsure where she fitted into the world. Her dark brown hair was neatly bound in plaits and she wore a patched, cotton print dress, with a first aid bag slung over her shoulder. A scar ran down her cheek that she tried and failed to hide with make-up. But what mattered was that she could sing.

As Jasper hopped down off the stage, Connie looked over at Lucien behind the piano. She was too anxious to gaze into the audience right away. She was never sure how they'd react to her until she'd started singing.

'Evenin',' she said. Her voice sounded high-pitched and showed her nerves. She tried again. 'I'd like to sing a song for you, something all you Yanks'll know. We love the fact that you're over here now, helping the fight. This song is called "What a Diff'rence a Day Makes".'

Lucien started to play, and Connie sang the swoony song as she took in the couples dancing close, the customers at tables lit by the flickering candlelight, the people who'd come from the street to shelter.

Whenever the air-raid sirens wailed, Jasper let anyone who needed refuge from the bombs into his club. The basement was safer than running through the streets to Piccadilly Underground station. And everyone was welcome; Jasper never treated anyone differently for who they were, because he knew what it was like to be shunned.

Here, people could forget about rationing and shortages, and the war raging above ground. They could dance to Glenn Miller's music, and listen to Jasper's resident performers sing the songs of Billie Holiday, Vera Lynn, Noël Coward and the Andrews Sisters. And sometimes, they'd get Connie singing too. She'd never been trained, but she had an ear for music and was pitch-perfect even if she'd only heard a song once.

The club had also become a second home to Connie and

her friends, a place where they were always welcome. They were the Blitz Kids, a small group of runaway evacuees who had escaped the abusive farmers they'd been billeted with, only to find their homes destroyed and their parents dead.

Back in London, despite the danger they wanted to help other people who were at risk of losing their homes and families like they had. The bombs didn't fall every night now, but there were still lots of things that Connie and her friends could do to help their fellow Londoners. As Churchill had said, his voice speaking through the radio, 'You do your worst and we will do our best.'

There were Victory Gardens to tend, so that people in the city could get fresh vegetables. There were clothes to patch and clothes to knit. They helped out at the Jewish soup kitchen in Whitechapel, where they had once been fed when they'd had nothing, and they helped people who'd been bombed out to find anything they might need. It was amazing what a bit of London knowledge could do if they were tracking down saucepans and curtains to help someone start again.

There was work to do on bombsites, clearing the rubble, although they always ended up covered in dust and dirt. And sometimes all they needed to do was hold someone's hand, because they were lonely and afraid, and needed a friend.

There were American servicemen to welcome, and Ned had appointed himself their guide to London. For a donation rendered even more generous by his wide-eyed tales of being an orphan, the little boy would show the servicemen the city that he loved, from the gates of Buckingham Palace to the secret poker schools of the East End – and, of course, the pubs where the best beer and prettiest girls could be found.

Connie's eye was on one couple in particular – Lisette, one of the singers at the club, who was like an unofficial auntie for Connie and her friends, and Lisette's boyfriend, the mysterious Mr Wyngate. He looked like a matinee idol, with his strong jaw and broad shoulders, always dressed in classy, well-made suits. He always tried to keep the kids on the straight and narrow, but Connie found it hard to believe that his clothing coupons could stretch to such an elegant wardrobe.

Lisette's head was resting on Wyngate's shoulder, then she looked up at him and claimed his lips with a kiss. Connie's stomach turned somersaults; there was someone she wanted to dance with like that. Jack, another of the Blitz Kids and one of her closest friends. He was in the room with them, sheltering in the nightclub. But she didn't dare glance his way. Would he want to dance with her?

Jack was the same age as Connie, but always seemed so grown-up, so brave, even when other lads his age were still boyish. He was almost as tall as a man now, and looked smart with his short, tidy hair, even though his shirt had worn patches and his shoes were scuffed no matter how hard he polished them. Together Jack and Connie looked after the younger kids; honorary parents even though they were still children themselves.

Connie turned her attention to her friend Ned, who was sitting at a table with Mr and Mrs Dupree. Mr Dupree ran Soho's clandestine business, and often visited the club. Ned, his legs swinging because they weren't long enough to reach the floor, had a pencil stub tucked behind his ear and a scrappy bit of paper in front of him. Connie knew what was going on – he ran messages for Mr Dupree, for a price, and it looked like Ned was totting up his bill.

Ned was only just ten, and Connie loved him like the younger brother she'd never had; they looked out for each other. His round face was circled by his halo of golden curls, which made him look like a cherub. And yet, that innocent exterior belonged to a boy who delighted in making money through his wide-boy contacts and their black-market goods. No one would struggle against the shortages if Ned and his contraband network could help it.

Ned turned towards her and beamed as Connie sang. She knew he was proud of his honorary big sister.

Then it happened.

Connie felt the bomb hit before she heard it; a tightening in her head, then an explosion so loud it made everything shake and sounded like the end of the world.

She was flung violently to the stage as a rain of plaster and wood and brick pelted down on her. She couldn't see a thing in the thick, choking dust and smoke, but felt someone's arm wrap tightly round her. They were pulling her away.

'I've got you,' Jack said, his arms tight round Connie as he pulled her towards the doorway. She couldn't see it in the smoke-filled air, but she could feel a breeze that guided them towards safety.

But then, as she blinked against the smoke and the dust, she realised she couldn't see Ned. A section of wall had collapsed, right where he'd been sitting with Mr and Mrs Dupree.

'Ned! Oh, no, not Ned!' Connie wailed for the brother she never had. He was so little. He couldn't die down here.

Connie looked back at the dance floor. The men in uniform who'd been so energetic before were stunned, struggling to their feet.

And then, Connie caught sight of Lisette and Wyngate, lying still on the floor in each other's arms.

ONE

CONNIE

Outside in the street, Connie's head was ringing with the sound of ambulances and fire engines, fighting their way through the blasted buildings. She'd somehow managed to get up the steps from the basement, even though her legs were shaking and she had to fight to make sense of what she was seeing.

It looked like a bomb had dropped immediately behind Jasper's. The force of it had ripped the front off the building above. Its interior stood open to the world, like a doll's house; the café on the ground floor, the chairs neatly stacked on the tables; an office above with a desk and a filing cabinet, a typewriter teetering over the edge; then cheap lodgings up to the attics, the quilts on the beds flapping in the summer night breeze.

The street was unrecognisable to Connie, full of bricks and shattered glass. She battled to hold back a sob; the place she knew so well was unrecognisable. The war had stolen something immeasurably precious from her, again.

A sailor was staggering along the pavement, his skin grey from the dust, his hat lost and his uniform torn. A woman lay sprawled further along the road, bricks lying in a circle around her, as her friend knelt by her side, screaming her name as she tried to pull her up.

Flames licked up from behind the building, shooting sparks into the sky above.

Connie tried to speak, but was convulsed by a fit of coughing. She saw her other friends emerging up the stairs and into the street, and with relief she counted them one by one. Thirteen-year-old Susan, helping her younger brother, Ben, and Jack's sister, Elsie, who was cradling her little dog. That was three.

Then Connie looked up at Jack. That was four. She was trying to seek reassurance from her friend, because her own reserves of courage were dwindling in the face of such destruction to a place she loved so much. The brick dust had given his long face temporary freckles, and his neat hair was speckled with debris. His face was pale and Connie was sure he'd realised it too; Ned wasn't with them.

'We've got to get Ned out!' she shouted, her voice shrill with panic. She was taken over by another cough, which only served to make her feel even more helpless in the face of the direct hit and the knowledge that her friends were still in danger. 'The wall's fell where he was sitting. And Lisette and Wyngate... they're still down there. And they weren't movin'.'

'It's Mr Wyngate. He wouldn't let anything happen to Lisette.' As he spoke, Jack dropped to his knees and embraced Elsie, holding her tight. For a moment he was silent, then he told his little sister, 'I'm going back in to get Ned. You wait out here with Connie, all right? Stay safe.'

'We couldn't find Ned,' Elsie sobbed as Connie put her arm round her shoulders. She let the younger girl cry, because she couldn't bear to sob in front of her. 'We called for him, but he never answered.'

Jack rose to his feet and took a deep breath before telling Connie, 'Look after the others, Con. I'll be back in a minute.'

'Just you be careful, Jack Taylor,' Connie told him, with a tremble of fear in her voice that she struggled to hide. She looked over at the stairs, which were crowded with people escaping.

'Don't worry about me,' Jack replied, a slight tremor in his voice the only thing that belied his efforts to sound brave. As he set off running he called over his shoulder, 'I'll be back with Ned!'

Connie heaved for panicky breaths as she watched him scramble over the debris in the street, passing the people who emerged from the club, dazed, their clothes torn. Bricks and tiles were sliding down from the damaged building, smashing in the street around them.

Suddenly, at the top of the club's stairs, Connie saw Ned, who still looked like a cherub even with soot smudging his cheeks.

At his side were the Duprees, but the sight of them made Connie's blood turn cold. Mr Dupree was carrying his wife in his arms and her face was turned in towards his chest. Mrs Dupree's arm was slung round her husband's neck, and Mr Dupree was cradling her as gently as he would a child.

But this wasn't the usual Mr Dupree in his Savile Row–cut suit and hat. This Mr Dupree looked like a phantom of himself, white from brick dust, his face streaked with blood as he gazed around in bewilderment and murmured his wife's name.

And Mrs Dupree wasn't her usual glamorous self. Her fur stole trailed on the ground, her hat was long gone, her silk blouse was in ribbons, her stockings ripped to pieces. One of her arms was bent at an unnatural angle like a broken doll. And she was painted red by the blood that was pouring from her head, and from wounds all over her body.

Connie barely had time to breathe a sigh of relief that Ned was all right. She'd taken a first aid course and had helped countless people who'd been injured by the bombings. Slipping into her training pushed back her panic and made her feel in control despite the chaos surrounding her.

She made sure the other kids were standing away from the bombed building, then ran towards the group. With Jack and Ned's help, she carefully laid Mrs Dupree in the road. Mr Dupree made a pillow of his wife's expensive fur stole and gently lifted her head so she could rest it against the mink cushion. Then he told her gently, 'You'll be all right, Mo, don't you worry.' He bent his head and kissed her bloodied cheek. 'I love you, you know that.'

Connie felt under Mrs Dupree's jaw for a pulse. She couldn't find one. But she couldn't tell Mr Dupree, not yet. She still might be able to save her. Connie had to believe that was possible, or she knew she would fall apart.

She tipped back Mrs Dupree's head, hoping it might help her breathe, then took a piece of gauze from her first aid bag and set about wiping away the blood, trying to find the biggest wounds so she could staunch them.

Mrs Dupree stared at her from under her half-open eyelids, but the light in them had gone out. Her skin felt cold, and Connie touched her hand to her face. It brought back the memory of kissing her mother's cheek to say goodbye one last time after she had passed away. Cold, lifeless. Her spirit gone.

'We'll have to turn her over to do that artificial respiration – get her breathin' again,' Connie told them, choking back tears. She wouldn't give up, she wouldn't. 'Rub her back. It does work, you know.'

She looked up at Mr Dupree. And then, beside him, she saw the face of a woman ambulance driver. She was wearing a dented tin helmet. Without saying a word, the woman knelt down beside Mrs Dupree, checked her pulse and lifted her eyelids. Then she slowly shook her head.

'I'm so sorry,' she said.

Mr Dupree gazed at the ambulance driver as though he

couldn't understand what she was saying. 'Sorry?' he asked. 'What're you sorry for? She can't— you do something! You bring her back!'

He gathered his wife into his arms and held her, sobs racking his body. Connie had never seen him be anything other than the boss who ran Soho, equal parts granite and show, travelling in a Rolls-Royce through his territory. But now he looked crumpled, like an old man, as he wept over the body of Maureen.

'Oh, bloody hell, Mr Dupree.' Tears bubbled up in Connie's eyes. Maureen was dead. She hadn't been able to save her. Their place of sanctuary in Jasper's club was gone. And as she scanned the street, she realised she couldn't see Wyngate or Lisette either.

'They're still in the club!' Connie said, getting to her feet, terror flooding through her body. 'Lisette and Mr Wyngate, they're still down there! We've got to get them—'

But she didn't get to finish her sentence. She stared in horror as the doorway collapsed in a crash of bricks and heavy wooden beams.

Anyone who was still down there in the wrecked nightclub was trapped.

TWO

LISETTE

Panic coursed through Lisette; her desperate breathing was shallow and urgent. She coughed against the hot, smoky air. It seared her lungs, and she wondered how much air there was until there would be nothing to breathe at all. She could barely see a thing; just shapes in the smoke and dust.

'Adam!' she tried to call. To Lisette he would always be Adam, but he was Mr Wyngate to everyone else. Her voice rasped. She tried to move, but her limbs were heavy.

One moment they'd been dancing to Connie's song, and then, in a split second, there'd been a horrific crash and they'd been thrown to the floor.

As she tried to move again, Lisette could feel the heat of fire, and heard screams tearing the air.

She could still feel Adam Wyngate's strong arms round her, just as when they had been dancing. She tightened her embrace, hoping against hope that he wasn't harmed. And what about the children? Where were they? Were they hurt?

'Adam,' she whispered insistently. She went on in her native French, 'Are you all right? Speak to me, Adam, please!'

A moment passed before she felt Wyngate's arm tense, drawing her close to him. He whispered, 'We're all right.'

Lisette closed her eyes against the stinging smoke and dust. They had to find a way to get out, but her head was spinning. She felt stunned, and knew Wyngate must as well.

'I'm scared,' she murmured. 'I don't want you to die, Adam. And the children – where are they? Are they safe?'

'We're not going to die.' He sounded so certain and that made Lisette feel stronger too. 'Before we move, we need to make sure we *can*. Fingers and toes, all that.'

Lisette couldn't feel any pain, just a sense that she'd be covered with bruises – if they could escape.

'Nothing broken,' she replied. She wondered where she'd left her gas mask, as it wasn't over her shoulder. She worried that her little flat at the top of a tottering old Soho house had been obliterated. Would she still have a home to go to? But that could wait. They had to find the children and they had to get out.

It must've been a direct hit, or as close as it could come. At first, she couldn't understand why the Nazis had suddenly chosen to bomb Soho when it'd largely escaped until now, but then she thought of the bombing raids in the spring, which had targeted historic cities. Exeter Cathedral had been pummelled; the ancient city of York had come under attack. Perhaps it was inevitable that Soho, with its proud theatrical heritage, would be next.

And what about Paris, where her mother had stubbornly remained, determined not to run off to England where Lisette could look after her, but to stay in the city where she'd been born and do her bit to defend it? If anything, Lisette had to stay alive for her, for the chance, however slim it might be, to see her *maman* again one day.

'You're just shaken up,' Wyngate told her firmly. 'Can you stand?'

'I-I think so.' She rushed a kiss to his cheek. 'And you, you're all right, aren't you?'

'I'm fine.' As Wyngate stood, he kept his arm round Lisette, guiding her to her feet. She knew the club as well as her own flat but everything seemed to be topsy-turvy in the darkness, as though the whole place had turned on its head.

In the smoke and dust, she could make out tables that had been thrown sideways, or upside down, as if they were on a ship tossed by a violent storm. Among the sobbing and crying, she could hear voices.

'Must've been a bloody direct hit!' she heard a woman gasp in a thick cockney accent.

'Jeez, you okay? I can't see a thing!' an American man exclaimed.

She heard a man swearing in Canadian French; between groans of pain, he was bringing down curses on Hitler's head.

But she couldn't hear the voices of the children. Did that mean they had got out?

And there was heat. Fire.

Something, somewhere was burning.

She looked across the club towards the door leading to the stairs that went up to the street, but the wall had caved in and there wasn't a door there any more. There was no way to get to the street from there. She could see figures moving towards it in the light from the few candles that hadn't gone out, and the tiny flames of cigarette lighters held aloft like torches. Voices called in panic.

'We can't get out!' one of the American servicemen who'd been in the audience called. 'We're trapped!'

There was another exit at the back of the club, into a yard, but as Lisette turned to look she knew that route was impossible: the wall on that side had bulged inwards. Had the bomb landed behind the club?

The club didn't seem quite so dark now though, thanks to a

faint glow that seemed to be creeping through the shadows. At first, for a wonderful moment, Lisette let herself believe that it was the sunset coming in, that there was a way out after all. But it was too late for sunset. And a woman's voice was screaming, 'Fire!'

Lisette held Wyngate's hand tightly. She swallowed down her panic but it rose up again. They'd been so sure that the club was safe. A basement below street level; it was a natural air-raid shelter.

Someone was frantically shoving aside tables and chairs, making for the back door. Then she saw Jasper, who owned the club. His normally smart suit was torn. His hair was wild. Blood was running down the side of his face from a ragged wound on his forehead.

'If we can't get out the front door, we can get out this way, through the back!' he shouted desperately.

As he reached for the door handle, Lisette saw the glow of the unseen flames illuminate his hand, then Wyngate was moving fast towards him with a barked command of, 'Don't open that door!'

Jasper turned to stare at him, his eyes on stalks. 'But we have to get out!'

'Listen to Mr Wyngate, you know he's right!' Lisette warned him. 'Don't open it, Jasper!'

'We're trapped!' Jasper reached for the door handle again, wincing. The metal must've been red hot from the fire beyond it. This time Wyngate seized Jasper's arm and pulled him roughly away from the door, towards the crowd that was starting to gather there in the hope of escape.

'There's a fire back there,' Wyngate told them. 'If anyone opens that door, we'll all be burned alive. The only way out is the front.' Then he turned to a burly man in the uniform of the USAAF. 'If anyone tries to open this door, knock them out.'

Without waiting for a reply, Wyngate turned on his heel

and picked his way through the smoky club towards the place where the door ought to be. As he passed Lisette, he reached out and took her hand, and drew her along with him.

Her heart was beating fast. She saw a woman in a silk dress lying across the floor. Lisette almost stopped to help, but Lillian the barmaid was there already, kneeling beside her, stroking her face.

There was no way out.

THREE

LISETTE

'I want every able-bodied man in here clearing this doorway!'
Wyngate shouted, his voice commanding authority. 'Everyone
else get down low to the floor under the smoke!' He dashed a
kiss to Lisette's cheek and told her more softly, 'Keep down low
or you'll choke.'

Lisette blinked at him through the stinging smoke. She
couldn't bear the thought of letting go of his hand. What if—? In
her mind, she returned to a memory from nearly two years
before of a sheet drawn over a lifeless figure on a stretcher; her
boyfriend, Tom, her Monsieur Anglais, who she had lost early
in the Blitz to a bomb.

But, no, no, it couldn't happen again. She couldn't lose
Wyngate.

'Be careful, Adam,' she said to him in French, quickly
touching his hand. Then she did as he said and retreated.

'If you're not helping Mr Wyngate, come over here,' she
called through the smoke and the sobs.

She could see figures coming towards her, some limping,
evidently too injured to have run out of the club. There had
clearly been so little time to escape before the door collapsed.

Lisette needed to keep herself busy to stop herself from freezing up with panic. She couldn't help to clear the doorway, and she had no idea if they'd get out.

Instead of lying down on the floor herself, she instructed everyone else to get down low; the women in their best dresses, the locals wearing coats over their nightdresses and pyjamas. She stared at each person she helped through the dark smoke, and each time realised that none of them were the children. They must have all escaped in time, and that one thought kept her going. The children were outside in the street. They would be waiting, worrying, for her and Wyngate.

She cleared away debris so that there was space for everyone who needed it, even though she was beginning to feel light-headed from the lack of air. She helped Lillian with the unconscious woman, making sure their casualty was comfortable. Then she lay down on the floor, huddling low, her arm round a young woman in a satin dress who was shaking and sobbing with fear.

'We'll be all right,' Lisette whispered, trying to keep her own terror from her voice. She thought again of her mother in France. She had always been heroic, raising Lisette on her own, and now she was risking her life by doing her bit for the French resistance. If her own mother could do that, then Lisette could too.

Looking up, Lisette saw figures – men, some in their evening wear, others in their uniforms, standing side by side with Wyngate. With bare hands, they hurled away the rubble that was blocking the front door. Some of them were Americans who were new to Britain and had come as part of the war effort; they were usually so tidily groomed and smiling, so full of enthusiasm. They could never have known that they'd end up here, trapped in a smoke-filled basement.

'I've got the Blitz Kids out here!' It was Tiny's voice, on the other side of the blocked doorway. The enormous doorman who kept the undesirables out of Jasper's was safe then and so, thank God, were the kids. 'We'll soon have you out!'

Relief coursed through Lisette; she could dare to be hopeful now that she knew the children had escaped.

'We've got a fire down here, Tiny!' Wyngate shouted, hefting a large slab of toppled masonry away from the wall of rubble that had entombed them and setting it aside on the growing pile. Lisette heard a woman somewhere in the darkness give a gasp of relief as a breath of fresh air swept through the club, followed by a shaft of moonlight.

'We'll get you out!' Connie called urgently.

Despite her fear, Lisette smiled at the sound of the girl's voice. She saw so much of herself in her, so unsure of herself until she started to sing, and then she was transformed.

It wasn't right for children to have been caught up in the violence and horror of war, for their innocence to be shattered. She wished they'd had a happier time in the countryside and hadn't needed to run away, back to air raids and to bomb-scoured streets. Some children had even been evacuated to Canada and America at the start of the war. They were thousands of miles from danger, but they must miss their home and their families terribly. Lisette knew how that felt; she hadn't spoken to her mother for several years, as she was trapped in occupied France. Connie had been forced to grow up quickly and was like a mother to the rest of the children. All Lisette could hope was that Connie would see the war out, without her voice fading.

More light was beginning to show around the door now, thanks to the combined efforts of the children and Tiny on one side of the door and Wyngate and his team of men on the other. And when Lisette lifted her head, she realised the doorway was clear. Relief washed over her, and it took her a moment to understand that they weren't entirely out of danger. The doorway was listing, the jambs skewed at an angle from the violence of the bomb.

Lisette shakily got to her feet. She squinted through the smoke at Wyngate. 'Shall I lead out the women?' she asked him in French. He was looking at the doorway too, his gaze moving swiftly over the only way out for a moment before he gave a sharp nod.

'And make it fast.'

As Wyngate replied, the whole club seemed to give a lurching shudder and Lisette heard the grinding creak of masonry buckling and shifting. The doorway, through which she could see Tiny and the kids now, moved too and Wyngate sprang forward, bracing his back against the crumbling door jamb. He threw up his arms to catch the splintered frame above him and shouted, 'Out, all of you! Women first!'

'Quick, quick!' Lisette called.

She helped up women who were coughing and struggling, and led the way to the door, then stood aside. She saw the look of strain and might on Wyngate's face as he braced against the falling doorway; she willed every woman to go as fast as they could. No one's heeled shoes were any good on stairs that were scattered with loose debris, and Lillian was half carrying the woman she'd been tending to. But at last, all the women were out.

'The rest of you now!' Wyngate instructed, shifting a little as though that might be enough to somehow lessen the torturous stress his body must be under. 'Come on!'

Lisette hurried up the stairs, glancing back once to see Wyngate still pushing against the collapsing doorway. She couldn't bear to leave him down there, but he was unafraid to face dangers that few others would if it meant he could save lives. And that was why he had taken a piece of her heart. She whispered a prayer, then she was out in the street, gratefully breathing in lungfuls of air, even though it was still tinged with dust and smoke and the fear that Wyngate was not out of danger yet.

Devastation surrounded them. It was as if she had walked out into a completely different street from the one she'd walked down on the way to the club that afternoon. There was nothing but the smashed and shattered remains of what had once been a Victorian street. She had seen so many similar sights over the years of the Blitz, but she shuddered at the sight of a street she knew so well vanishing.

And in the wreckage she saw Mr Dupree, sobbing as he stood over a stretcher. A sheet had been pulled over a shape, and an arm dangled down, a flash of gold bracelet on the wrist. Mrs Dupree was dead. Lisette swallowed hard. She forced back tears as a memory rushed back to her of another bombing raid, another street, another figure on a stretcher. Her boyfriend, Tom, who had been killed on his way to meet her nearly two years before, had been lost to her too soon. Life went on, but she had never forgotten him, or his pale face as he lay on the stretcher as if he was sleeping.

But then, she saw the children standing in the ruined street. They were covered in soot and brick dust, their luminous blackout buttons glowing on their outer clothes, the ID bracelets she'd bought them to keep them safe hanging on their wrists. She tried to sweep all of them into her embrace at once.

'You are so brave!' she told them.

And so was Wyngate. Lisette looked down to see him still holding open the collapsing doorway, every muscle in his body straining.

As the last of the Americans darted through the doorway he gave Wyngate's shoulder a slap and told him, 'That's everyone safe, bud. Now get outta there!'

Tiny seized Wyngate by the elbow and dragged him clear as

what was left of Jasper's club plunged into the spreading flames. The teetering floors above – people's homes and businesses – swayed for a moment, then collapsed backwards with a roar.

To think that Lisette had encouraged the children to stay in the club, and had even had them living down in that basement once, because they'd thought it was safe and there was nowhere else for them to go. There was nothing left now; no stage or curtains, no piano, no bar stocked with bottles and glasses, no dressing room full of costumes.

All Lisette could see was an inferno, and the huge jets of water rising like arcs as the firemen tried to put out the flames.

Lisette flung her arms round Wyngate, kissing the dirt from his cheeks. He was safe. But as she held him, she couldn't help but wonder... what now? She'd worked at Jasper's club for years, and without the club she had no work. Maybe somewhere else would hire her, but she loved singing there. It was like a family.

'I can't believe it's gone,' Lisette whispered to Wyngate. 'It's like I've lost my home. I felt safe there, and so did everyone else.'

'I know.' He held her in his arms and murmured, 'But you're safe.'

Lisette held him tight. 'Mrs Dupree is dead, Adam. And Ned was sitting at the same table, he could've—' She forced down the words. Ned was still alive. He'd been spared. Almost everyone had been.

She looked away as the stretcher-bearers carried Mrs Dupree's lifeless form into an ambulance, Mr Dupree following in tears. Lucien, the club's pianist, had his arm round the man's shoulders, his expression bleak.

Then she noticed a figure, sitting on the edge of a roof beam that had fallen across the road. The man was slumped, in a tattered suit, his head bowed, his face streaked with soot and dust. He was weeping, and another man, just as tattered, sat beside him, his arm round his shoulders. Then she realised that it was Jasper, and the other man was his boyfriend, Edgar, consoling him.

The war had taken so much, and now Jasper had lost his livelihood and a place that had felt like home to countless people who didn't have one anywhere else.

FOUR

CONNIE

'Poor Jasper,' Connie said. 'The man's just lost his club.'

Ned whispered in reply, 'And we nearly lost you an' all.' He gave Connie a nudge. 'Jack got you clear. Proper hero, that one.'

'He's amazing,' Connie said, sounding starstruck. Jack was courageous, and clever, too. The two of them gave the younger kids lessons; he knew so much about maths and history, and how things worked. Connie covered English, helping the children with their spelling and handwriting, and how to hear the music that lay behind a poem.

When she was little, her mum had given her a book of poems that she'd been awarded years before as a school prize. Connie had loved that book and had recited the poems aloud and turned them into songs. She sang them at her mother's bedside as she grew paler and more frail. She'd lost her mother, and had lived with her nan, but she was killed when their home was bombed. The book of poems had sat on a shelf in the front room and had been lost too, but Connie hadn't lost the poems, or the songs. They were the last thread connecting her to the family she no longer had and they remained in her heart.

Mr Wyngate had given Jack an old radio to fix and Connie

loved to watch him with a screwdriver in his hand as he tinkered with the wires and valves. When he wasn't working at this favourite project, he buried his nose in one puzzle book or another, finding solutions to even the most fiendish challenges. He was a genius when it came to things like that and... Connie swallowed. She had to admit it, he was good-looking, too, with his neat, light brown hair, and his warm gaze.

Ned peered up at her through narrowed eyes, then gave a mischievous smile. He said nothing though, sparing her blushes. Instead, he watched the arriving ambulances for a couple of seconds, before picking his way towards Jasper. Connie went with him. She wasn't sure how much comfort she could give, but she was sure Jasper would want to have his friends around him.

'Sorry about your place, Jas,' he said. 'Adolf ain't never been a fan of folks having fun, stands to reason he'd want to drop a big 'un on the bit of London where most of the fun happens.'

Jasper looked up at him, blinking, as if he was tuning in from another world.

Finally, he replied. 'Yes, we all had fun here, didn't we? Do you know how many people meet the love of their lives in my club? The weddings I've been invited to, the christenings as well. People who don't feel welcome anywhere else have always had a place at my club. And the locals, they pop by, it's a home-from-home for them.' He put his hands over his face again for a moment, as if he was trying to hide his tears. Then he dropped them and looked up at the children again. 'But it's all over now. It's gone.'

But Connie already knew that Ned wouldn't countenance that sort of talk. The little boy had grown up in an orphanage, punished and thrashed at every turn by the cruel nuns who had once been his guardians. He had lost his friend to a petrol explosion, his secret stash of money to a German bomb, yet still he kept smiling, still he kept working for the wide boys and the gangsters, running messages and packages and sharing every penny he made with his friends.

'Yeah, it's gone,' he agreed, setting his hands on his hips. 'But it don't have to stay gone, does it? I was sleeping under a railway arch not that long ago, now I've got a bloody house to call my own! You know what that is, don't you? Hard graft. And you ain't scared of a bit of hard graft, even if you do wear fancy suits.'

Connie saw Jasper beginning to smile. 'I worked bloody hard to build that place, you know,' he replied. 'But there wasn't a war on when I started. How on earth can I rebuild it? And Mrs Dupree was killed in my club – it's my fault she's died.'

'It ain't your fault at all, Jasper,' Connie gently told him. 'And besides, Mrs Dupree loved it here, she'd want you to bring the club back.' She had the beginnings of an idea. 'We just need some cash, don't we? And a new place for your club to call home. This is London, mate – there must be loads of places you could turn into a club. All you need's the dosh to do it with!'

Connie felt a surge of hope. What if the club could be rebuilt? Not here, but somewhere else. It was more than bricks and mortar. It was all about the people.

It'd always welcomed everyone, and, once the Americans had joined the war, Jasper's dance floor had filled with men in USAAF uniforms, jiving as though it were a form of acrobatics. Not to be shown up by the Americans, the British servicemen, and the Canadian and the French, had joined in, turning it into an unofficial international jive contest. The regulars who'd been coming to the club for years loved it, and so did the locals who sheltered there whenever the sirens sounded. Everyone who was fighting the evil that emanated from Nazi Germany bonded together at Jasper's and had much-needed fun. Surely they could bring it back?

'Money?' Jasper shook his head, as Edgar consolingly patted his shoulder. 'God knows how long it'll take for the insurance to pay out – and, in the meantime, what will everyone do? Where will they work?' It was just like him to worry about everyone else.

Connie had been surprised at first that Jasper and Edgar were boyfriends, but, once she realised they were a happy couple, it no longer seemed strange to her. Jasper had run away from a loveless home as a teenager and had worked in the theatres of Soho, doing a bit of everything. That was how he'd met Edgar. And one day, Jasper had decided to break out on his own, and he and Edgar had pooled their savings and opened the club. They were both in their fifties now, which meant they were too old to be conscripted into the armed forces. And everyone knew, too, that the club kept up morale and had – until that very evening, when the bomb had hit – been a safe shelter from the air raids.

Connie chuckled, her eyes gleaming with excitement. 'We'll do a fundraiser. You've got me, and all them singers.' She grinned cheekily. 'People'll put their hands in their pockets for your club, Jasper, 'cos you've had all them fundraisers for others — all those whip-rounds to help people what've been bombed out, and for the refugees and all. You helped us once, remember? So it's time we helped you.'

'A few comics, our Lisette on the microphone... chuck some pretty girls at it,' Ned said with a grin, 'and we'll soon have the cash ringing in. Jasper's has helped London, now it's time for London to give some back.'

Jasper, who had looked so devastated only moments before, got to his feet. His face was steely with determination. 'You're right, we can do this — for Mrs Dupree, and for everyone else who ever belonged here. Our nightclub *will* return.'

FIVE

LISETTE

A day had gone by since the bomb had torn Jasper's nightclub apart and killed poor Mrs Dupree. Lisette had kept close to the children, and gone with them to their house in Whitechapel in east London, down by the docks. She told herself she couldn't let them out of her sight for their safety, but that wasn't entirely true; being around them helped her feel safe too. And she couldn't bear the thought of going to her little flat in Soho, not after what had happened to Jasper's, only a couple of streets away.

The children lived in a small two-bedroomed terraced house in a row that had been condemned as unsafe thanks to bomb damage. But that hadn't stopped them. They had electricity for light and coal for heat, clean water and a roof over their heads. Even better, the couple who had once lived here were happy to have their home taken care of as they saw out the war in rural safety. Lisette and Wyngate stayed over with them sometimes, sleeping on the sofa. They didn't want to move in officially; there wasn't much room, and in some ways the children had grown up quickly, and they valued their independence.

Their front room had a sofa and two armchairs, and a set of shelves full of books that Jack was usually reading. The only family photograph that Jack and Elsie still had stood on the mantelpiece, flanked by two china dogs. The kitchen was at the back, with a big ceramic sink and a table. It looked out onto the small garden, which was full of rows of vegetables that Ern and Agnes, who lived nearby, had helped them to cultivate. Upstairs were two bedrooms; a double one at the front where the girls slept, with a bed for Elsie's dog, Pippa, at its foot, and two singles at the rear for the boys, with a camp bed between them for Ben.

For all that a house full of children could've been horrendously untidy, the children delighted in caring for it, as if it was an extra-large version of a Wendy house. They kept it as neat as a pin, putting away any toys before they could be trodden into the carpet and always taking turns to do the washing up and the laundry.

Lisette was sitting in the front room with the children chattering around her. All they'd been able to talk about since she'd walked through the front door that day was their plan to rebuild Jasper's club. She was relieved they had found an idea to latch onto, after facing such a disaster and seeing Mrs Dupree die. It was the painful reality of living in the middle of a war, but something no children should have to witness.

Only Jack was silent, his attention held by the wireless he had been given by Mr Wyngate. The back of the set had been removed and the young man, old beyond his fifteen years, was peering into it intently, looking at the valves and wire with what seemed to be a practised eye. Perhaps, if he could get the radio working, Lisette might hear news from Paris.

Now and then he glanced towards the other children and smiled at their enthusiasm, and Lisette was reminded of a father indulgently watching his youngsters tell tall stories. She hoped this wouldn't be a tall story though, and that they could rebuild Jasper's.

Connie was kneeling beside him, staring at the workings. She was keen to get the radio working so that the house would be full of music, but there was a more serious side to their project as well. Wyngate had told them that it might be possible to pick up stations in Europe, and even hear what was coming out of Germany. The prospect of tuning in to stations that ordinary Germans were listening to added a layer of curiosity that spurred Jack and Connie on.

Ned had decided that they'd put the fundraiser show on in just two weeks' time because he was so keen for the club to be resurrected. When the children had told Jasper how quickly they'd arrange it, his despair had melted enough.

Lisette admired Ned's enthusiasm, yet she couldn't help but worry.

Without her job singing at the club, she had no income at all. She'd always loved having work that meant something to people and lifted their spirits at such a dark time. Tired people would arrive at the club, their faces clouded with worries, and, by the time Lisette had finished her songs they would be smiling. At the club, servicemen and women in uniform could get a precious break from the enormous strain they were under. Everyone could forget about their troubles for those few evening hours they spent laughing and dancing at Jasper's.

And when she sang, she thought of her maman and how they had sung together all the time, like a pair of songbirds, whether they were tidying their little flat in Montmartre or sharing a stage. Sometimes, she sang the old tunes that her maman had softly sung to her as lullabies, and hoped the audience wouldn't notice that her eyes had filled with tears.

Perhaps it was an unconventional way for Lisette to do her bit, but it was still important. What on earth would she do until Jasper's was rebuilt? But even so, she wondered if people would stay away, spooked by the prospect of that awful bombing happening again. And as much as she loved the children's enthusiasm for the fundraiser, she wondered if they could pull it off. There were so many shortages and so many pressures that she wasn't sure if rebuilding a nightclub was high enough in people's priorities.

She could ask around at the other venues, to see if they'd hire her temporarily, but there were no guarantees that anyone would say yes. There were a lot of performers in London, and now all the girls who'd sung at Jasper's would be out looking for work as well.

She had some savings, but not very much. She wasn't sure how long they'd last. And it wasn't just herself she was worried about, or her friends from the club; there were the children to think about.

While Ned brought in money from his wheeling and dealing, there were six children to look after and that money would only go so far. Connie could get pennies from singing on street corners, but it wasn't much. Jack had now lost the odd jobs Jasper used to give him around the club. The kids weren't on their own; Mr Gray and Wyngate both chipped in to make sure they had what they needed and Lisette helped them buy food and clothes, and things for Elsie's dog. But without any income, how could she do her bit to help them?

'Way I see it,' Ned declared, 'all's we need is some high-kicking birds, our Lisette and a couple of blue comics. That'll bring the money rolling in!'

Jack winced and shook his head. He rocked back on his knees and looked up from the radio where he was working. 'You should hear yourself,' he said and chuckled. 'Jasper's was a classy place, not the end of the pier.'

But Ned shrugged. 'Many a fortune's been made on the end of the pier, squire,' he told Jack archly. 'Anyway, Lis is the expert. What do you say, mademoiselle? Girls in glittery bits or a touch of class?'

'A touch of class, always,' Lisette replied. 'But I know lots of girls who've danced at Jasper's, I'm sure they'd do a turn if I asked them. Although it won't be anything saucy!'

'Too right it won't!' Connie planted her hands on her hips. Behind her on the wall was a framed print of a woman in a crinoline and bonnet, underlining Connie's attempt to be grown-up and ladylike. 'And I'll be singing an' all, so it'll be classy all the way. Just like Jack says.' She shone a cheeky grin at Jack.

'And I've taught Pippa to jump through a hoop. People'll love that!' Elsie announced. Then she was suddenly downcast. 'If they come.'

Elsie scooped up her little dog, who had a grey body with the woolly fur of a poodle, black floppy ears, and the questing button nose of a terrier.

Jack beamed at his sister with pride, then his eyes met Connie's, and she flushed and looked away. In that stolen glance, Lisette knew that she had been right in her suspicions. Their feelings went beyond friendship; Jack and Connie were carrying a torch for one another.

On the one hand, it was adorable to see young love in its early stages, but on the other hand Lisette was worried. If they did become sweethearts, she'd have to talk to them about the birds and the bees, and how they needed to wait a few years before all that. She blushed with embarrassment at the thought; it was a conversation she'd never had with her mother.

A memory suddenly came to Lisette from when she was a little girl. She was sitting on the piano stool next to her mother as she played Chopin, watching her lithe fingers dance on the keys. She remembered the scent of roses from her perfume, and the lace trim on her dress. Lisette had never known her father and, although life hadn't been easy, her maman had always made sure Lisette knew how much she was cherished. She recalled the sound in the street outside, the cartwheels on the Paris cobbles, and the voices of the street sellers.

Paris wasn't like that now, not since the Nazis had taken over. And Lisette hadn't heard from her mother since the moment the Nazis crashed the shutters down. All she knew was what Wyngate had told her; that he had met her maman after being sent behind enemy lines, and that she was alive, and working for the French resistance. The thought of her mother's gallantry in the face of tyrants buoyed Lisette up, even as it filled her with foreboding and an anxiety she struggled to fight. She was safe and alive, but for how long? What if she was caught?

There was not a thing Lisette could do, so instead she imagined her mother meeting the children one day. She would be a wonderful grandmother to them, Lisette was sure. She would love the children just as much as Lisette herself did.

'And we'll have to see who replies to Esther's article,' Susan said. 'There must be people in London who want to perform. We just have to hope that someone has a theatre to spare.' She twirled one of her pigtails round her finger. Her smiled faded as she asked, 'They haven't all been bombed, have they?'

Esther Hammond was a reporter for the *Evening News* and had written many stories about the children's exploits. She always moved quickly and had contacts all over London, so she'd managed to get the story into the newspaper's early edition.

Susan held it up, showing Esther's front page story: *FAMOUS SOHO NIGHTCLUB BOMBED!*

Then in a block of text in the middle of the article, it said, *SAVE THE DATE – THE BLITZ KIDS PUT ON A SHOW TO BRING JASPER'S BACK!*

'And me and Ned are goin' to do our double-act, so people *have* to come and see us,' Ben insisted. 'We'll tell our jokes, and – Jack, you'll 'ave to be our straight man!'

Lisette had a feeling that appearing on stage was the last thing Jack would want, but he nodded all the same. 'Go on then,' he said. 'How can I refuse Whitechapel's own Flanagan and Allen?'

'Do you think they'll come?' Ben was wide-eyed.

The comedy duo were both local boys; Bud Flanagan had been born in Whitechapel, and Chesney Allen was from over the river in Battersea. They sang the sort of songs that people wanted to hear during wartime, like 'We're Going to Hang Out the Washing on the Siegfried Line'; songs that belittled the Nazis and relieved everyone's worries through laughter.

Their song 'Underneath the Arches', about a homeless man who slept beneath a railway arch, had a special meaning for the children. They had been forced to sleep just like that themselves when they'd had nowhere else to go.

'My man Toe drinks with Bud Flanagan,' Ned said with authority. 'I'll bet he can get them to come. And if he can't, Ma Mahoney definitely will.'

Toe Mahoney was to the East End of London what Mr Dupree was to Soho. He ran the wide boys who Ned worked with, and no one could move black-market goods in the East End without Toe knowing about it. And for all that he was fearsome, his mother was terrifying – unless you were on the right side of her. She adored the Blitz Kids, especially since they had saved her life.

'Well, that's our stars sorted,' Susan replied with a grin. 'Along with all of you lot, of course.'

Ned glanced over his shoulder at the window that looked out onto the little street of old terraced houses in Whitechapel where they had made their home.

'These ideas are brilliant.' Jack smiled, but Lisette could

see a hint of concern. She knew what he was thinking: for all their dreams, this might not end up being the big success the children were hoping for. 'But we're asking for a lot here and I don't want us all to get our hopes up too much. We'll do all that we can to help Jasper rebuild, but we can't be sure it'll work.'

'Nice one, Jack!' Ned sighed, rolling his eyes. 'Look, we've all had a crap time of it, we know more than anyone that your eels don't always come out jellied. But we've got to try, haven't we?'

Lisette nodded. Ned always tried, and that was how he had managed to survive as long as he had, an orphan abandoned on the streets of east London.

'Yes,' Lisette agreed, as she heard a car engine purring outside. 'We've got to try.'

'Oi oi!' Ned called. 'Look lively, troops, we've got company!'

A sleek red sports car had pulled into the kerb outside, its roof open in the summer sun. In the passenger seat sat Wyngate and at the wheel his boss, Mr Gray. He was wearing a suit made from blue paisley. He was doing his best to make do and mend but, where he found his supply of such extraordinary fabric from, Lisette couldn't guess.

Despite the hours he devoted to his vital role in the War Office, the children knew Mr Gray well, as he dropped by to see them sometimes. He brought them whatever treats he'd been able to lay his hands on and gave them history lessons in his own eccentric style.

Once, Lisette had arrived to discover the front room had become the scene of the Battle of Waterloo, complete with a set of toy soldiers and Mr Gray lapsing into French whenever he talked about Napoleon. He'd taught the kids smatterings of other languages he knew, too. They could now introduce themselves in French, German, Persian and Mandarin.

Pippa had jumped up at the window to bark at their guests,

her tail frantically wagging, and now she ran after Elsie as the little girl went to answer the front door.

Lisette wondered why they had come in the middle of the day, although her heart skipped at the prospect of seeing Wyngate. She got to her feet, ready to make some tea for their guests.

Elsie reappeared with Wyngate and his boss.

'Look who's come to see us!' she announced proudly, and stood aside to let the two men pass as Pippa chased them in.

'And I come bearing news!' declared Mr Gray in his plummy voice as he dropped down to one knee to fuss Pippa. 'For I have been spreading word of the concert for Jasper's far and wide.'

Wyngate greeted Lisette with a kiss on her cheek, then whispered in French, 'And loudly, of course.'

Lisette chuckled and kissed him back.

'We need to talk to you alone,' Wyngate whispered.

Lisette caught his gaze as she drew back from him. Whatever they needed to talk to her about was evidently not for the children's ears.

'You are too kind, Mr Gray,' she replied, smiling at the same time as she wondered what Gray and Wyngate could need to talk to her about on her own. 'We are just deciding on our acts. Ned thinks he can get Flanagan and Allen to appear – but we need a theatre to put our show in.'

'No theatre?' Mr Gray widened his eyes comically, then lifted the monocle he always wore. Today it was on a shimmering ribbon in the same blue as the pattern on his suit. He peered at Elsie through the glass, making the little girl giggle. 'What a bind for an impresario to find themselves in! Flanagan, Allen, Connie and Lisette and no theatre in which to put them!'

'We'll score one, guv'nor,' Ned told him confidently, but Lisette wasn't so sure. It was a lot to ask in a city that was already struggling against bombs and deprivation.

'Would the king and queen let us build a stage outside Buck House?' Susan asked, using the cockney name for Buckingham Palace. 'I know they've got all them vegetables growing on the lawn now, but they might have somewhere we could use.'

Wyngate smiled and glanced towards Mr Gray, who was rising to his considerable height once more. 'They probably would if Gray asked them,' he said dryly.

'Indeed,' said the most unlikely spymaster Lisette could imagine. But a spymaster was what Mr Gray was, commanding the likes of Adam Wyngate from his impressive desk in the War Office.

'But why would one need to, when one has the Theatre Royal Drury Lane, at one's disposal? Children, Mademoiselle, I have spoken with our friends at ENSA and they have agreed that the theatre is all yours, in recognition of all that you and the good people of Jasper's have done for the folk of London.'

'Blimey!' Connie gasped, and Lisette was momentarily lost for words. ENSA arranged shows for British servicemen, and had their base at the famous theatre.

'Mr Gray, thank you so much!' It seemed to Lisette as if the summer sunlight that was streaming through the window had grown brighter. She took a step towards him and clasped his hands. 'Jasper and everyone at the club will be over the moon. I don't know how to thank you!'

But Mr Gray waved away her gratitude breezily. 'I dined last night with Mr Noël Coward and he has agreed to perform a song or two, should you wish him on the bill. Mr Coward, in turn, breakfasted with Miss Gracie Fields and our divine Miss Vera Lynn, who is now *also* on the bill. Miss Lynn then took tea with our beloved pals at *ITMA*. Needless to say, by the time the sherry was poured Mr Handley and his cast were also committed to the Blitz Kids' theatrical bash!'

Lisette was amazed. Gray had managed to get an astonishing set of performers onto the bill – the comedy radio show *It's That Man Again* was hugely popular and its cast well known.

'Oh, heck, that's amazin', Mr Gray! I dunno how you do it!' Ben said, but then he bit his lip. 'D'you think they'll still want my knock-knock jokes?'

'Of course Londoners want to hear your jokes – and listen to Connie sing, and see Elsie's and Pippa's tricks. You're the Blitz Kids.'

Yet what if Londoners didn't? Everyone was exhausted by war and perhaps they wouldn't want to turn out. It would mean venturing further away from the relative safety of homes and familiar bomb shelters, just to raise funds for a nightclub. Londoners loved the orphans who had become such a mascot for them, but that didn't mean they would be willing to fund Jasper's. Every day was a struggle for them, living in a city at war with shortages and gnawing uncertainty.

But Ben smiled at Lisette's words of encouragement. 'I can tell you one now, if you like, Mr Gray? Knock-knock!'

'Who, Master Ben, is there?' asked Mr Gray expectantly.

'Tank,' Ben replied, grinning his gap-toothed smile.

'Tank who?' chorused Mr Gray and Wyngate.

'You're welcome!' Ben bent over with mirth, and the other children laughed too. 'Get it? And there's a lot more where that one come from.'

Wyngate grinned. 'You kids are still the stars of the show. But the more famous faces supporting you, the better.'

Connie had gone pale, and it made the scar on her cheek stand out more than usual. That scar, a pale, puckered line that ran down one side of her face, was a permanent reminder that she had been badly treated when she'd been evacuated to the countryside.

'I can't believe it... blimey...' she breathed. 'Never thought

I'd see the day we'd be on stage in Drury Lane. Thanks, Mr Gray!'

'And they say being a duke's a waste of time,' Wyngate deadpanned, looking to his boss.

'A duke?' Lisette gasped, blinking at the man in the paisley suit. She fumbled a curtsey, not sure how else to react. 'I had no idea!'

The children stared in surprise too.

'Give over, you ain't a duke,' Ned scoffed. 'You're not fusty enough!'

And Mr Gray gave a hoot of laughter, before telling them all, 'The Duke of Rievaulx, to be precise, the sole unfusty duke in these isles.' Then he gave a smart clap. 'Now, matters of housekeeping beckon for we three adults, but we shall come to the matter of our theatricals soon! Ned, you and I shall discuss the date of the performance and the necessaries later, as I believe you *are* the impresario in charge?'

That made sense. At ten years old, Ned had more street smarts than many three times his age. He gave Mr Gray a nod, then told the other children, 'Come on, I reckon he's after us clearing out and he's too posh to say!' With that, Ned scooped up his Home Guard cap and put it on his head. 'We'll leave you three alone to have whatever natter you're after.'

The children were gone in a moment. Ned and Ben rushed out in a whirl of laughter and chatter, with Pippa barking and chasing after them. But the others were more quiet and thoughtful. They knew it would be hard work to pull this off and save Jasper's.

So Wyngate and his boss weren't just here to bring news about the show after all. Lisette thought of her mother, trapped in Paris, working with the resistance, and how danger must've become part of her daily life. She tried to swallow her fear as she pictured whispered meetings in dark alleyways, a gun hidden in the back of a wardrobe, a message with a secret tucked between books on a shelf. She imagined her mother hiding a look of hatred as she walked past the enemy soldiers who had stolen her country.

Had she been unlucky? Had the Nazis come to her door?

SIX

LISETTE

Lisette swallowed and glanced from Wyngate to Gray and back again. She could hear the children in the garden, Ben and Ned laughing and Pippa barking, as if they existed in another world from this grown-up one that she inhabited.

'I wonder, mademoiselle,' Mr Gray said, 'Whether you have been successful in finding new employment now the club is temporarily out of action?'

Lisette shrugged. 'I'll ask around at the other clubs, but I don't know if there's any work for me. I saw in the newspaper an advert for waitresses at the British Restaurant on Charing Cross but... I don't know.'

The British Restaurants had been set up to help people who'd been bombed out of their homes, and ensured everyone could get a cheap, healthy meal. It was essential work but, with all that gravy and cabbage, it was far from the glamour of the London nightclubs.

Wyngate was watching her, his expression tender. He gave the barest hint of a smile and she caught her breath. Whenever he was near Lisette, she could feel the air crackle between them.

'Valuable work; we all love a jaunt to the British Restaurant!' Mr Gray enthused. 'But I wonder – between ourselves, you understand – whether there might be a better outlet for your skills? This is wartime, after all, and fluent French speakers are not necessarily best used to wait tables.'

'Mr Gray knows about your family connection,' Wyngate added. There was no need to elaborate; they all knew her mother was fighting in occupied France to free the country from the grip of the Nazis. 'France is on our doorstep; we need to see her liberated. And that starts here, in England.'

Lisette decided to switch into French, even though there was no one to overhear them. The reminder that her mother, fighting in the French resistance, could well have come to harm, made her feel as if a cloud had crossed the sun. The information she'd had from Wyngate's mission behind enemy lines could only tell her that her mother was safe. But was she still? She knew it was too dangerous to try to get a letter to her or to ask anything more; it could reveal her mother's work to the Nazis. Lisette was being called on to do her duty, something maybe more important but also more dangerous than her essential role as a singer, keeping up morale; perhaps she could help to protect her maman, and all her friends she'd left behind? 'This isn't about singing, is it?'

Wyngate glanced at Mr Gray, then returned his gaze to Lisette. He said nothing, leaving his boss to reply, 'No, mademoiselle, it isn't.'

Last year, Gray had made her an incredible offer: a tour of the country, singing to the servicemen to keep up their morale. But she'd turned it down because she couldn't bear to leave the children.

Mr Gray continued. 'We need fluent French speakers who bring with them impeccable references from our trusted operatives. And Mr Wyngate believes – as do I – that you, like your mother, have much to offer the Allied war effort.'

Lisette clenched her hands for a moment, trying to still the tremble that had come into them. She wouldn't be called on to leave the children and go into France, she knew that. So, what then? In her mind, Lisette saw the stage and its spotlight retreating, and it made her heart ache. But she had a chance now to help the war effort, to liberate the country of her birth, and see her mother and her friends living in freedom and safety once more.

'I would love to use my French to help the Allies,' she said. 'What would I need to do?'

Wyngate gave her the tiniest ghost of a smile, as Mr Gray explained, 'We have a vacancy on one of our translation teams for a fluent speaker of French and English. Alongside our Free French allies.'

'Me? You want me to translate for the Free French?' Lisette gasped with surprise. What an honour. She'd never thought of herself as a translator, or realised that she could do more with her talents than sing French songs in a Soho nightclub. And yet she'd had English lessons in Paris when she was a child. She knew local slang, too, in London and in Paris .

'I have always admired them, but I had never thought for a moment that I might one day work with them! Oh, I would love to,' Lisette said as she took Wyngate's hand in hers. 'Thank you, both of you, for thinking of me. Oh, I could translate in my sleep!'

'Wonderful!' Mr Gray exclaimed. 'Our friend Mr Wyngate has the details and will, I'm sure, apprise you. You will be working with our Free French allies in the War Office. Mademoiselle Souchon, our country and your own thank you.'

Lisette had never worked in an office before. She'd never worn a uniform, either, apart from as a costume on stage. And to work in the War Office, of all places, where the war could be won or lost – she was thrilled and nervous all at once.

'We all have to do what we can,' she replied. She remembered how Wyngate had braced himself in the falling doorway so that the people in Jasper's club could escape the flames and the collapsing building.

'Well, with mission accomplished, I shall take my leave and see how our young performers are faring in the garden,' Gray said decisively. 'Mr Wyngate, perhaps you would be so kind as to give our new recruit her details of employment?'

'Of course,' Wyngate replied. Gray inclined his head and strode from the sitting room.

Wyngate took a white envelope from his jacket. It was unremarkable, no trace that it held anything of any import, but the thickness of the papers within made it bulge. He held it out to Lisette, offering her a gentle smile. 'Welcome to the War Office, Lis.'

Lisette took the envelope, her hand trembling. Then she wrapped her arms round Wyngate.

'You know what this means to me,' she whispered against his ear, before gently kissing his cheek. 'I feel so lost without Jasper's. I know the kids are convinced they can rebuild the club, but I just don't know if it'll succeed or how long it'll take. I don't even know if I could find work in the other clubs... I didn't know what to do.'

Wyngate took her into his arms. 'There's no better candidate for this than you.'

'It will be strange working with the people I've been singing to!' Lisette exclaimed. She had just realised that so many of the people who came to the club to hear her sing French songs were the very people she'd now work with side by side. 'Thank you for putting my name forward – at least, I think it was you.'

He gave a shrug and murmured, 'Maybe,' before pressing a soft kiss to her lips. 'And it shouldn't get in the way of your musical career. We still need those songs.'

Lisette kissed him back, feeling the warmth of him as she caressed his broad shoulders, and stroked the nape of his neck. She was overwhelmed sometimes by the strength of her affection for him, and she held him ever tighter. She knew she'd have to look inside the envelope, and read about her office hours and duties, but all she wanted at that moment was to be alone with the man she adored.

These times with Wyngate were precious. He couldn't always be with her and the children; there had been weeks and months where he was away. She knew he must've gone behind enemy lines, even though he couldn't tell her. When he came back, his face was thinner and he'd be a little distant sometimes, as if he was trying to forget whatever he'd seen.

She held him tighter and kissed him once more. At any second he might get the call again. He might not even get the chance to say goodbye before he went into danger. He never told her what he faced – not that he could, and that made it worse. What was he doing while he was away? Did he quietly observe, or did he put himself in the firing line?

While he was gone, she'd lie awake, because if she slept she was haunted by nightmares. She always knew that he might never come back, just as she knew she might never see her maman again.

SEVEN

CONNIE

Connie stood outside the famous theatre confronted with a massive queue that wound past the columns at the front and around the side of the building.

Connie stared and stared. She'd never seen anything like it, not even when, one year, her much-missed nan had taken her to the West End to see *Peter Pan* at Christmas. Surely they'd raise enough money to bring Jasper's club back.

But what if she forgot the words to her songs, right there on stage under all those lights and in front of such a huge audience? And with all those stars in the wings?

Jasper was welcoming people, shaking hands as they entered the building. He was delighted at the turnout. He'd worked day and night on the preparations, with the help of the children. It had given him something to focus on now that he didn't have a club of his own, and he had put his all into it as it was perhaps his only chance to bring his club back.

Connie stared in amazement. A small film crew was setting up, and *Pathé News* was written down the side of their camera.

She turned back to her friends, who were enthusiastically greeting the waiting crowd, walking up and down the queue.

Connie was so stunned that she couldn't do more than grin broadly and wave. Ben was practising his knock-knock jokes, and Elsie and Susan were letting people fuss Pippa. Jack was staying close to Elsie, protective as ever, but Ned was lapping up the attention, treating the crowd to the full force of his cheeky cockney humour.

Her stomach was now tied in knots and she tried to distract herself from her nerves by pulling out details from the crowd and thinking about where everyone had come from, what their own wartime stories might be.

The columned arcade that ran down the side of the theatre offered shade to the people in the queue, who were a mixture of ordinary Londoners. There were women in their cotton summer frocks, and men with their suit jackets draped over their arms, their ties loose. Lots of servicemen and women had turned up in their uniforms. And everyone was carrying a gas mask.

Some of the women had even brought folding fans with them, to keep the summer heat at bay. They'd all travelled through London and some of them from the suburbs and maybe further still; on trains diverted to avoid tracks smashed by bombs, through dusty streets where the smell of burning never entirely disappeared.

No one seemed to pay any attention to the government information posters on the wall behind them; the warnings that *Careless talk costs lives*, or the gleeful woman, arms aloft, standing outside a factory as aeroplanes took to the sky behind her. There was laughing and joking; a holiday spirit.

And not even the protest that was being mounted outside the theatre could dent the atmosphere.

When they'd arrived a couple of hours earlier, Connie's excitement had been dampened for a moment at the unwelcome sight of Sister Benedict in her austere black and white habit. The nun had run the cold, uncaring orphanage where Connie and her friends had once had to live.

The orphanage had been obliterated by a bomb, thankfully, but Sister Benedict wouldn't give up and wanted the children back with her – specifically their ration books. The other children from the orphanage had been taken back to the countryside – they'd written to Connie and the other Blitz Kids after seeing them in the newspapers. They were far away from bombs and nuns out there, but Connie didn't envy them; her own evacuee experience had been awful, and she loved London too much to leave.

The scowling nun hadn't come on her own, but had brought some sisters with her. One of them knelt on the cracked pavement in a display of piety, loudly saying her rosary with her eyes fixed on heaven. The others carried a sign, daubed in red paint with the words, *THE IMMORAL PATH LEADS TO HELL!* But it didn't seem to have any effect on the crowds, some of whom were laughing at the nuns as if they thought they were part of the entertainment.

Just then, a figure in the crowd caught Connie's eye. She recognised her; it was a woman she had seen around Whitechapel. She was tall and willowy, with long fingernails and carefully applied make-up. Her hair had a tint that came out of a bottle.

There were many women in Whitechapel who looked like her, but she always unnerved Connie and she couldn't really say why. The make-up seemed too much, the lipstick was too red. Like blood. It put Connie on her guard.

She'd sometimes offered Connie and her friends apples or sweets, and it'd made Connie tremble to accept them, as if they weren't gifts but poisoned lures from a fairy tale. She looked away from the woman, wishing she didn't feel so uncomfortable. Connie told herself she would be just one person among hundreds and couldn't do anything. And yet, Connie felt on edge.

Among the crowd she saw familiar faces, the Blitz Kids' friends, everyone from the club's regulars to Toe Mahoney and his fearsome, beloved Ma, the two of them plumper than ever despite the ration, and wrapped in their fur coats regardless of the warmth of the summer evening. There were their neighbours in Whitechapel and the market stallholders and shopkeepers who supplied the children with their rations, rubbing shoulders with the famous as they waited to take their seats.

Mr Gray had been true to his word, supplying not only the glittering theatre on Drury Lane but a coterie of rich patrons who were keen to make their own donations to the fund. In the end, Toe Mahoney hadn't signed up Flanagan and Allen as Ned had hoped, but had gone one better. Connie watched open-mouthed as not only the popular duo but every member of comedy troupe the Crazy Gang strolled through the stage door, large as life.

Suddenly people she had only ever seen in films at the pictures were greeting her like an old friend, running through their lines together backstage and exchanging jokes with the stagehands who were so familiar to them because they'd worked together so often. All of these people had taken to the stage or propped up the bar at Jasper's and now, it seemed, they were returning his hospitality.

It was time for the children to go back inside to their own small dressing room, which they were sharing with Lisette. Pippa climbed onto her cushion in one corner and wagged her tail as she watched everyone get ready.

In the corridor outside, a large white arrow had been painted onto the wall, pointing towards an air-raid shelter. Connie couldn't bear to think about bombs and explosions tonight; she was already a bag of nerves. They had a show to put on.

Susan was looking after costumes. She neatened the hem on Connie's dress – the best one she could find in her wardrobe – as Connie was trembling and couldn't do it herself. Then Susan rearranged the folds of Lisette's gown, even though she was very experienced at dressing for the stage and didn't need Susan's help, before tying a ribbon in Elsie's hair. She'd tried to brush Ned's unruly blond curls, and Connie had laughed at her failed attempt.

'No one can brush that haystack!' Connie teased.

'And they better not try!' Ned laughed, setting his Home Guard officer's cap at its usual jaunty angle. 'My crowning glory's part of my charm. That and my big, blue eyes! Folks can't resist.'

Ned was a consummate actor, capable of turning on the waterworks whenever it might give him the edge. When the kids had been reduced to begging for pennies on the streets, he had transformed from a miniature wheeler dealer into a helpless cherub, sobbing with hunger and helplessly offering around his cap to receive the generous donations of the passers-by whose hearts broke at the very sight of him.

Ned much preferred to be the wily lad who knew the streets better than anyone, but they had been desperate back then and that cherubic little face melted Londoners' hearts. Not that long ago, it had been the only way they could afford even the most meagre scraps of food.

Elsie had gone into the corridor for a last-minute rehearsal with Pippa, and Connie, who couldn't rest, decided to go and watch. She wasn't alone; Jack was already there, watching his sister take Pippa through her paces.

'C'mon, Pip, jump!' Elsie urged, holding out a hoop. The little dog wagged her tail, before running at speed and jumping through it. She looked very pleased with herself once she'd landed.

Connie nudged Jack as she came to stand beside him. 'Ain't they cute?' she whispered.

He nodded. 'I never thought she'd smile again after Mum—' Jack shook his head. 'But just look at her. Dad'll be so proud, she's turning into the image of our mum.'

Connie smiled at him. He seemed older than his years sometimes, a boy who'd been forced to grow up so quickly.

His mum had been killed in an air raid nearly two years ago, just before Connie had lost her nan to a bomb as well, and their dad had disappeared when his plane went down. Jack and his sister had thought they were orphans until the moment a letter arrived from their dad. He was safe, but in a prisoner of war camp in Germany. One day, with luck, they'd see him again and be a family once more.

'And he'll be proud of you, too,' Connie told him warmly. 'I wish I'd had a big brother like you when I was growin' up. Someone lookin' out for me.'

'Well, you've got me now.' Jack turned to look at her. 'I'll look out for you, Connie. We're all family.'

Connie's heart flipped, and she felt herself blushing. She wished her body didn't react like it did. Jack viewed her as a sister, nothing more. But he was getting more and more hand-some as he grew older, and he was so kind and brave. What could she do?

'We're like the mum and dad of the group, ain't we?' She chuckled, then wished she hadn't said so, because wouldn't that give away her feelings? 'I mean... 'cos we're the oldest an' that.'

Jack's smile grew. 'We are,' he agreed. 'Not that Ned seems to think so! We're doing all right, though, you and me.'

'Ned's in charge!' Connie laughed, and tapped the side of her nose, as he joined them in the corridor. 'I wish I was more like you, Ned. You're never scared of anything, are you? My stomach's full of butterflies – and moths as well, I'm that nervous! All them people who've come to watch the show...'

'Why would you be scared?' Ned asked Connie cheerfully. 'You're our very own Deanna Durbin, you are. Pretty as a picture and voice like an angel. A proper cockney sparrow!'

Jack nodded enthusiastically. 'And when you're a big star, we'll all be able to say we knew you when you were just getting started. And you were super then too!'

Connie smiled as she imagined herself posing on the front of a magazine, like Vera Lynn. Then she touched the scar that ran down one side of her face. Vera Lynn had perfect skin, and Connie looked like she'd come off worse in a pub brawl. People stared, and yet, once she started to sing, they didn't see her scar any more. But still, it was a lot of people to have staring at her all at once.

To Connie's surprise, Jack reached out and took the hand that had lingered against her scar. He gave it a gentle squeeze and said, 'Your nan will be looking down on you with so much pride.' Then he smiled. 'And I'll be in the wings, watching my amazing, beautiful friend as she knocks her audience sideways with that voice of hers.'

Connie's face was suddenly very warm, and she knew she was blushing furiously. Jack thought she was beautiful. She'd thought no one ever would.

If she lived inside a film, right now she'd hear a sweeping orchestra, and everything would go soft, and then – right there – she'd kiss him. Her Jack, her lovely boy who didn't see her scar, and made her feel a hundred times more confident than she was. Her heart was thumping madly as she gazed back at Jack, and she leaned just a tiny bit closer to him, and—

'Scuse me, coming through!' said Jasper, striding along the corridor in a shiny suit. He was smiling broadly, despite the bandage that he still wore on his forehead. 'I'm about to give my big speech. It's showtime, kids!'

And with that, the orchestra in Connie's mind fell silent.

The thought of that missed kiss hung about her thoughts as

she and the other kids stood in the wings at the edge of the stage. They could hear the audience, laughing and chatting as they settled in their seats, but were warned by the stage manager – a woman with immaculate nails and perfect hair – that, if they could see the audience around the edge of the curtain, the audience could see them. Connie bit her lip, trying to hold back her nerves. All those people, just on the other side of the curtain, waiting for the show to begin.

Jasper gave his speech. He sounded overwhelmed as he welcomed everyone to the show, and Connie could hear a tremble in his voice. After losing the club he'd spent so many years building, seeing all those people packing out such a huge, legendary theatre to support him clearly meant more than he could say.

And so, the show began. It went by Connie in a whirl of song and sounds, jokes and colour. The Crazy Gang had everyone rolling in the aisles with laughter, and Mr Fluke, the legendary magician, wearing a vivid purple suit, sent everyone gasping in astonishment. Lisette's songs got an ear-splitting round of applause, while Ben and Ned's joke routine with Jack made the theatre ring with mirth. The audience loved Elsie's act with Pippa and her tricks.

And then, as if time was running too fast, it was suddenly Connie's turn to sing.

'And now, another of our Blitz Kids,' Jasper said, holding his hand out towards the wings. 'A star in the making? Well, we all think so. Ladies and gentleman, please put your hands together for... Connie!'

As the audience burst into applause, Jasper bounded back into the wings, and gave Connie an encouraging wink. Her heart hammered in her chest and she had suddenly forgotten how to speak, let alone sing.

She walked out onto the stage, and once she reached her

spot – in the middle, near the edge, but not too close because she didn't want to fall off – she stopped and turned.

She'd never seen so many people in one place in her whole life. And they were all staring at her – she could feel their gazes from the dark auditorium, and could see the expressions of the people sitting in the first few rows, where the stage lights bled. Despite the spotlight, she felt a shadow pass across her; she thought of the songs she made up to sing for her mum and her nan. If only they had been spared so that they could've sat in the audience to watch her. They would've been bursting with pride.

But then her gaze fell onto the front row, where Wyngate, and Esther the journalist, and Mr Gray, who was in fact a duke, were sitting. And suddenly she didn't feel quite so nervous, because she could tell herself she was singing just for them, and for her friends who were watching from the wings.

Lucien was behind a grand piano in the orchestra pit. He nodded to her – he was still managing to play even with two fingers in a splint – and Connie launched into her set.

She started with 'My Old Man (Said Follow the Van)', an old music hall number that got the children's cockney friends tapping their feet. She moved onto 'Everything Stops for Tea', a song that the Ministry of Food had adopted for the rationing effort, and she sang it with knowing humour.

Then Connie started to sing her big number, one that she'd practised at home only when she could convince herself that none of the other kids could hear her. She'd chosen it because she was sure the Americans in the audience would love it. But they wouldn't know her main reason for wanting to sing it.

As she started to sing 'Dream a Little Dream', she knew that Jack was in the wings, listening and watching. Would he know that she was thinking of him? She could feel her voice filling the theatre, up to the gods and to the very back of the auditorium.

All those people were hearing her voice, yet only she knew what was in her heart.

Then, once the song ended and the last note from Lucien's piano had faded into silence, she took two steps forward and bowed. Her heart was racing and everything was a confusion of applause and cheers. She felt as if her legs were going to give way beneath her, but she smiled and waved, then headed back to the wings.

And almost tripped over Noël Coward.

He was one of the most famous people in England, after Churchill and the royal family, an actor and singer, and he wrote his own plays and songs. In fact, she'd almost included one of his songs in her set. She cringed; she couldn't believe how clumsy she was.

'Miss Connie, you're a talent!' The man known to theatre-land as 'the Master' beamed. '*Who* is your agent?'

Connie stared up at the famous man, with his signature bowtie and neatly oiled hair. She was astonished. So he wasn't annoyed that she had blundered into him? 'Th-Thank you, sir! Erm... an agent? Blimey, I don't have one of them!'

'That'd be me, guv'nor!' Ned was suddenly at Connie's elbow, looking up at Noël Coward with a shrewd air. 'I look after Con's business; you wantin' to talk turkey?'

Connie couldn't think of a better person to manage her singing career. There was no way Ned would let anyone rip her off. But she'd never thought of singing anywhere other than at Jasper's, or on street corners around Whitechapel – singing in this huge theatre on Drury Lane was just a one-off, surely.

'You have to go through Ned,' Connie told Noël. In the background, she heard Jasper introducing Gracie Fields to the stage. 'And he's as sharp as they come!'

'I believe you may be perfect for my spring revue next year,' Coward told Connie as he took a silver box from his dinner jacket. He opened it with an elegant tap of one thumb and removed a neat calling card, which he handed to Ned. 'We shall keep in touch.'

Ned tucked the card into his pocket. 'We'll do that, pal,' he said. 'And you tell all your mates, Connie's the next big thing!'

Connie could feel her cheeks heating with embarrassment. The next big thing? She wasn't sure about that. And yet here was Noël Coward himself saying he wanted her for his spring revue.

'Thank you, sir,' Connie mumbled.

Coward inclined his head politely. 'You have something special,' he assured her with a kind smile. 'Very special indeed.'

Connie was lost for words as she stood in the shadow at the edge of the stage with her friends. Side by side with Ned and Jack, she watched the rest of the show, then it was time for the bows at the end. She was never sure whose idea it was, but after all the celebrities had taken their bows all six of the Blitz Kids, with Pippa the dog, were brought on, and stood right in front of them as the audience whooped and cheered.

Connie couldn't believe it. Her feet barely touched the ground as she and her friends made their way back to their dressing room, and she stood there, stunned, not quite knowing what to do next.

Then there was a knock at the door. Lisette went over to answer it.

Behind it, there stood a woman in a skirt suit that looked like it was made from expensive thick silk, and she filled the air with a heavy perfume. Her blonde hair was streaked with silver and piled on top of her head in curls, and a hat with a spangly net balanced on top. She wore a vast chiffon scarf that trailed behind her, and she kept swishing it back across her shoulder, her long, scarlet nails catching the light each time. Her eyelids were heavy with blue eyeshadow, and every time she blinked her long, mascaraed lashes seemed to wink like spiders.

'I hope I'm not interrupting,' she said, with the confident air of someone who knew very well they were. Her voice claimed the room like an actor's. 'My name is Miss Delamotte, from the Piccadilly Agency. You may have heard of me? I've represented the best! There's stars who've walked this stage this evening who wouldn't have got their break without me. My books are positively heaving with big names – And Connie...' She gave a theatrical pause as she swished her scarf back again. 'I'd like to have a word.'

The Piccadilly Agency? Their offices occupied a plush-looking building in Soho, and, whenever Connie had peered through the criss-crossed tape on the windows, she'd seen staff at typewriters and talking on phones – every one of them busy. What a dream, to be represented by them.

Ned leapt to his feet from the chair he was settled on. He approached the new arrival and told her, 'I'm Ned, I'm Connie's manager.'

Miss Delamotte chuckled indulgently and reached out to rumple Ned's hair. 'I'm sure you are, sweetheart. But I'm a real theatrical agent, and with me, Connie – you'll make it to the big time.'

EIGHT

CONNIE

Connie's heart was still racing from taking her bow on stage. She stared at Miss Delamotte, not quite able to take it in. Hadn't Noël Coward asked her who her agent was? What if she could tell him it was Miss Delamotte from the Piccadilly Agency?

'Well, Mr Coward says he wants me for his revue next year,' she said, trying to sound professional, even though she felt as if she was dreaming. Every song she'd ever sung had brought her to this moment; ones she'd learned from the radio, ones she'd made up on the spot. She was aware of her friends, standing back and staring. Lisette had rushed her hand to her mouth, and her eyes sparkled with excitement.

'Does he... does he?' Miss Delamotte thought aloud as she swished her scarf again. 'But I have an idea... it came to me before you'd even finished your set! A touring production, up and down the country, bringing in the crowds, and we call it *The Secret Singer!*'

Ned narrowed his eyes. 'What's that when it's at home?'

Miss Delamotte reached into her handbag and produced a cigarette already mounted at the end of a long ebony holder. She lit up, then spoke as she exhaled like a dragon. 'You would be wearing a mask, my dear – a mystery! It's essential, I'm afraid. That scar...' She tutted. 'Even with a lot of thick stage make-up and good lighting, it'd be hard to hide.'

Connie blinked at Miss Delamotte until she turned into a blur. She felt sick and unsteady on her feet, as if the floorboards were rotted through and about to give way beneath her, hurling her down into unseen depths.

Her scar? It was something her friends never mentioned; they never even saw it any more. But she knew other people did. When she stepped out on the stage at Jasper's, she'd always hear at least one pitying sigh from the audience. Some people stared at her when she walked down the street. She could feel their eyes on her skin, a heat that was almost as bad as the burn that had made its permanent mark on her cheek.

Sometimes, when she went to sleep, she'd dream of the day she got the scar. And it wasn't just her face that had been marked, but her heart too.

Because on the day she'd received the heartbreaking news that her nan had died – the last thread of her family – she'd cried and cried. Until the woman who'd meant to be looking after her in the countryside, where she'd been sent to be safe from the bombs, had slapped her so hard that Connie had fallen against the cast-iron range. The red-hot metal had seared her skin, branding her.

Every stare that Connie's scar received reminded her of her loss, and took her back to a time when there had been no one to look after her, and when she had been punished for her grief.

The scar was a permanent reminder of what she had been through. Of all the things that Miss Delamotte could've picked on, she had gone for the worst thing Connie could imagine.

And yet, she couldn't say no. Her singing career, her future, depended on her saying yes to Miss Delamotte.

"You bloody what?" Ned spat furiously.

'I-I dunno, Miss D-Delamotte,' Connie stammered in reply. She felt Lisette's hand on her shoulder.

'She has a beautiful voice,' Lisette told Miss Delamotte. 'No one will notice the scar.'

'You can't hide Connie's face,' Jack said, coming to stand beside Connie. 'People will want to see her, and they *should* see her. Connie's as lovely as her voice!'

'She is, she is!' Miss Delamotte said, smiling. 'But can you think of a singer who has a scar?' She ran her gaze around the room, and Connie felt as if she was at school again, and that Miss Delamotte was a teacher trying to identify who was talking in her class. 'No, Connie would have to wear a mask, and we'd play on that – she never reveals her face! We can come up with a wonderfully exotic biography, too. A shipwrecked princess from the East! Or the whole cockney angle... no, I'm not sure about that...'

Connie couldn't help it. She let out a sob and hot tears began to fall down her face. Miss Delamotte was expecting her to abandon her background and even her own face for fame. Except what sort of fame was it? No one would know who she was. And surely it wouldn't last; it sounded like a gimmick.

'I'm not ugly!' she exclaimed through her tears. 'I'm not!'

Jack put his arm round her shoulders and opened his mouth to speak. However, before he could say a word, Ned's voice rang around the dressing room.

'Right, missus, 'ere's how it is,' he said fiercely. 'You come in here all fur coat no knickers, giving it a lot of yap about what you reckon you can do for our Con, and the way I see it, it's all a load of old cobblers.'

'Ned!' Jack admonished, but the little boy wasn't to be silenced.

'Connie's a Blitz Kid, get it? She's somebody. She's already famous and who're you? Nobody, that's who you are. No. Body. Fact is, love, you need us more than we need you, 'cos she's

Connie the bloody Blitz Kid.' And Ned's voice was getting louder, his anger only growing as the volume did likewise. 'She's already got Noël Coward on the hook. Noël bleeding Coward! And Noël bleeding Coward don't have no problem with Connie showing her face. If I was you I'd get out of 'ere before folks hear the balls you're spouting!'

Miss Delamotte pursed her lips. Then she narrowed her eyes and said, 'You, little boy, have just cost your friend here an amazing opportunity – one that won't come along again! Word spreads in showbiz! Oh, yes it does!'

'And I fart lavender blossoms, love!' Ned bellowed. 'Now clear off!'

With one last swish of her scarf, Miss Delamotte stormed out of the room, and slammed the door behind her.

Connie glared at Ned. 'What the heck are you doin', Ned? You've blinkin' well ruined my chance!'

'No, Connie,' Jack replied. 'Mr Coward wants to work with you. Mr *Coward*!'

'I know! But imagine if I could've told Mr Coward —' she adopted a well-spoken voice – '*Well, as it so happens, I've got an agent with a fancy office down the West End!*'

It hurt; it hurt inside her as badly as the searing agony when her face had been burned. Why did people have to stare at her? Why did she have to bear such an obvious scar, which only reminded her of how cruel the world was?

She knew it wasn't Ned's fault, and yet she couldn't stop the words coming out, pain and fury in every word. 'Only I can't now, can I? Because Ned's stuck his oar in and told that woman to clear off! It wasn't your decision to make, Ned! It was *mine*. That could've been my big chance, but I've lost it now! You're just a silly little boy pretendin' to be grown-up, and messin' it all up for everyone else! I hate you!'

'I ain't never been a little boy, 'ave I? I never had the chance!'

Connie had never seen Ned so angry, but she couldn't take back her words now. Her heart sank as she thought of the grim, loveless orphanage where he'd spent most of his childhood until now. 'Sod it all!'

And Ned dashed across the room and through the door, dodging Jack as he reached out to catch the younger boy's elbow.

As the door closed with a bang that made the mirrors shake and their reflections shudder, the air-raid siren began to wail, heralding enemy planes with their lethal cargos.

'Ned, come back!' Connie called, even though Ned couldn't have heard her. He'd run off without his light summer jacket, and it hung over the back of a chair.

Lisette rushed to the door and opened it, calling Ned's name. Before she could leave the room, Connie ran past her into the corridor. It was full of performers who hadn't gone home, and the stage manager was directing them all to the theatre's basement to take shelter. But there was no sign of Ned.

'Ned!' Connie called again, helplessly. Jack put his hand on her arm to comfort her, but nothing would salve Connie's upset until Ned was back with them, safe where he belonged. 'I'm sorry!'

'Ned, come back!' Lisette shouted. But their voices were barely audible over the sound of the siren and the chatter and footsteps of everyone leaving their dressing rooms for the basement.

Connie hated herself for what she'd said. What if the last thing she ever said to the boy who was like her little brother were those cruel, angry words?

'I'll go after him,' Jack said, pulling on his jacket. 'The rest of you get to the shelter. I'll be back with Ned!'

She spotted Mr Wyngate coming towards them, pushing through the crowd. She and Lisette stepped back to let him into the room, then Connie turned to Jack.

'I'm coming too, Jack,' she said, before looking across the dressing room for her coat.

'Wyngate, thank goodness you're here,' Lisette said. Her face was already pale with worry. 'There's been a falling-out, and Ned's run off. Just as the siren started. And he left this…'

She held out her hand, and lying on the palm Connie saw a silvery metal chain. It was Ned's ID bracelet.

NINE
CONNIE

'Right.' Wyngate gave a tight nod, then reached out and took Ned's bracelet. All the kids had received one from him and Lisette, and had been told never to remove them. Ned, of course, never listened, and Connie had lost count of the number of times she'd reminded him to put on his bracelet before they went out into the streets. Tonight, true to form, he had left it behind. 'I'll go with you. Everyone else get down to the basement; it looks like Adolf's going to give us hell tonight.'

'Stay here,' Jack implored Connie, reaching out to take her hand. 'Please, Con, let us go.'

Connie wanted to tell Jack and Mr Wyngate not to go, to stay down in the basement with them. And yet, even if Wyngate and Lisette had told Jack not to go after Ned, he would anyway. Connie pictured Ned, all on his own, running on his short legs through streets where fires blazed and buildings collapsed. And it was her fault that he'd run away, and that now Mr Wyngate and Jack were having to put themselves at risk to go after him.

'No, no, I'm coming with you!' Connie insisted, her voice

high with panic. She squeezed Jack's hand. 'It's my fault he's gone!'

'*Non*, Connie, Jack's right – you must stay here,' Lisette told her.

Lisette gave Mr Wyngate a kiss on his cheek, and Connie looked quickly at Jack. Maybe they were right. She was panicking and couldn't think clearly. She'd be a liability out there.

After Elsie had hugged Jack, Connie patted his arm.

'Good luck, mate,' she whispered, as they were swept from the room towards the basement, Pippa at Elsie's side.

They hurried along the corridor and down the stairs, with its far from glamorous brick walls. Once they reached the ground floor, Mr Wyngate and Jack headed outside. The stage manager had her hand on Connie's shoulder, steering her along, so she couldn't turn to take one last glance at them.

They went down another set of steps, even more functional than the last. This was the basement under the stage, where props, scenery and costumes were kept. It'd be odd to shelter down here with a rail of Tudor costumes fit for a Shakespeare play on one side, and a huge papier mâché head of Churchill on the other.

Connie put her arm round Elsie's shoulder. She could feel the little girl's fear. Connie was terrified too, and she couldn't throw off her guilt, which plummeted inside her like a lead weight. Why had she lost her temper with Ned?

'On we go!' A familiar voice rang out, as plummy as it was commanding, and Connie saw Mr Gray up ahead, clapping his hands as he directed the group. 'Quick as you can, if you please!' As the group passed him, Mr Gray joined them. He stooped and swept Pippa up from where she was trotting along beside Elsie, and carried the little dog safely as the crowd surged onwards. Elsie smiled up at him.

They carried on, past the scenery for an Edwardian

drawing room, past an Egyptian mummy's coffin, past a mountainous pile of hatboxes, past a stack of metal-edged tea chests with LIGHTS stencilled on the side.

At what must've been the centre of the space, chairs that had once been props in plays were being drawn up by the performers.

'What a place!' Ben breathed in astonishment, as the stage manager guided the children to their seats. He nodded over towards Mr Fluke the magician and whispered, 'Do you think they've got one of his sawing-the-woman-in-half boxes down here?'

'Mr Fluke sawed my own mother in half in 1925,' Gray told Ben, who listened wide-eyed. 'To this very day, she will not disclose how on earth the deed was done! But I saw it as I see you, young sir. Two halves of one mother!'

Suddenly there came a shuddering crack from somewhere across the city and the whole building seemed to shake on its very foundations. The Luftwaffe were overhead already then, and one of their bombs had just hit London.

Everyone in the basement fell silent as one as the lights dimmed, a buzzing of electricity filling the air for a second before the illumination sprang back into life. It felt as though they all let out a breath as one and, as they did, Mr Fluke stepped forward and asked Ben, 'I think the time is right for a little magic, don't you? Heaven knows, we all need some.'

Connie smiled. An impromptu performance from Mr Fluke was definitely what they needed to take their minds off what was going on. If only he could wave a magic wand and bring Ned back in one piece.

Ben nodded, gazing at the magician in amazement. 'The time's always right for magic, Mr Fluke!'

Connie sat on a pink chaise longue between Elsie and Susan, watching Mr Fluke's card tricks. They laughed as Ben looked ever more surprised. His amazed asides of, 'How the heck did he do that?' and, 'That's only my blinkin' card!' made even the Crazy Gang laugh.

But as Connie watched Mr Fluke's impromptu show, she kept thinking of Ned. Another bomb fell, and a huge roll of fabric, which she supposed was a backdrop, fell sideways with a crash and sent the stage manager jumping out of the way.

Where was Ned? Would he try to get from the West End back to Whitechapel in an air raid? And what about Jack and Mr Wyngate? She hoped they'd found Ned on Drury Lane and that all three of them had gone to the nearest shelter.

But she knew what they were like. They wouldn't want to sit in a shelter, not when they could go out and help. Connie often went out to help, too, along with the other Blitz Kids. But they were already in a shelter, and she didn't know the streets around the theatre very well. Besides, it felt too dangerous tonight. And that made it worse. If anything happened, it'd be all her fault.

It felt as if the raid would never end, and Connie felt help-less, waiting it out in the basement. But finally the all-clear sounded.

A huge sigh of relief ran through everyone who had been sheltering with them, from stagehands to celebrities.

Everyone said their goodbyes, and they all left the theatre. It was late, but the fierce orange of the fires burning across the city in the wake of the raid lit up the sky. The air tasted of smoke and in the distance, the urgent bells of hurrying fire engines and ambulances rang.

Thank goodness the theatre hadn't been hit, and yet else-where in the city homes and shops and businesses had been lost. Lives, too, Connie knew.

She and her by-now sleepy friends were helped onto an Underground train by Lisette. She admired her big-hearted friend, who was always watching over Connie and the other children like their very own guardian angel; she wasn't sure if Lisette knew how much they all loved her.

They had to carefully step over the people who were determined to spend the night on the platforms, not trusting that another wave of bombers wouldn't follow the last. Connie knew how they felt. It seemed never-ending.

She blinked back sleep as they travelled through the tired city. Each time her eyelids descended, she saw Ned again, running away. She longed to make him come back but she couldn't.

Once they made it back home, Connie got the three younger children to bed, with Pippa curled up on the foot of the girls' bed.

But she didn't sleep. She didn't feel as if she deserved a soft, warm bed after Ned had gone out into the air raid. Anything could've happened to him, and it was her fault.

Connie came back downstairs and sat on the sofa next to Lisette. She didn't have to say anything; Lisette put her arm round her and they waited in silence for their men to come home.

The pale fingers of dawn were beginning to creep over the city by the time the front door finally opened. There was an exaggerated care to it, as though the new arrivals were doing their best to be quiet and not wake the sleeping house. Even Pippa had wandered downstairs to join them, leaving Elsie safely asleep in bed so she could settle on the rug, close to Lisette and Connie in their vigil.

Connie looked up, blinking. 'Lisette, they're here.' She strained her ears, trying to count the footsteps. That was Jack, his step light and quick. And then Mr Wyngate's step, heavier, more determined. And then – and then...

Connie got up off the sofa and ran into the hallway. 'Ned! Did you find 'im? Did you find Ned?'

But even before he said anything, she knew they hadn't found him. Through the patches of soot and dirt on Jack's face, which he'd picked up from hours combing the bombed city for their friend, she could see fear and worry.

Jack shook his head even as he told her, 'But you know little Ned. He's probably conned his way into a suite at the Ritz! He'll be back later, bright as a button.'

Connie reached across to Jack's face and wiped a smear of soot away from his cheek. Goodness knows what he'd seen and done last night. 'Yes, that's it,' she said, as if saying the words out loud would make them come true. 'He's in the Ritz, that's where he is, and he'll come home in a Rolls-Royce!'

Jack smiled his gentle smile. 'And the king will probably be driving,' he joked as Mr Wyngate closed the front door, shutting out the still-smoking city.

Yet despite his attempt at humour, Connie knew that he shared her anxiety. Ned knew the city better than anyone but, even if he'd escaped the air raid unscathed even he couldn't avoid all its dangers.

Lisette had followed Connie into the hallway, and took Mr Wyngate in her arms. 'You are both so brave, going out to look. Thank heavens you came home.'

But Ned was somewhere out in the vast city. Just one little boy in the bombed-out wilderness.

TEN

LISETTE

The next day, her eyes gritty with tiredness and her nerves stretched taut for any news about Ned, Lisette was behind her desk at the War Office. Her flat in Soho wasn't too far away, so she'd been able to go home to pick up some of her things. She'd stay close to the children until Ned was found. Subdued light filtered through the taped crosses on the windows that would stop glass flying if a bomb dropped nearby, and illuminated the rows of desks where everyone wore khaki. And that included Lisette, ever since she'd started working here a week before.

They all had badges on their shoulders proudly saying FRANCE and displaying the Cross of Lorraine. The room buzzed as ever with low, hurried conversations in French, and rang with the clatter of typewriters and the jangle of telephones.

Men and women worked side by side. Some, like Lisette, had been born in France; others were French Canadian, or the British-born children of French parents. They had come from all manner of backgrounds; secretaries, waiters, accountants. There was even a Battle of Britain hero on their team who'd been shot down during a dogfight, and had been burned so badly that surgeons had needed to recraft his face. It astonished Lisette what medicine could achieve, as the horrors of war drove pioneering innovations that gave people back their lives. And it meant that their hero could still do his bit, albeit from behind a desk now rather than from behind the controls of a plane.

Just as Lisette's sense of self was split in two, between being Parisian by birth and Londoner by choice, her focus and concentration was split in two between the importance of her work in the fight to liberate France and protect her mother and everyone there, and her concern for a lost boy she loved so dearly. The busy office faded away as she mentally walked the city streets, past bombed-out buildings and through shattered debris, trying to find Ned.

But she couldn't go out and look for him; she needed to be here, to do her crucial war work. She'd been hired for a reason. She knew that the streets would already be teeming with the many people who knew Ned and loved him, but she'd go out searching later, once she'd clocked off. She wouldn't sleep until he was found.

At every sound of footsteps echoing along the corridor, she looked across at the office door, wondering if someone was bringing news. She stared at the silhouettes that passed the frosted glass panel, hoping she would see Wyngate and the distinctive shape of the fedora that he was never without. When the telephones rang, she turned her head sharply, wondering if the call was for her.

And yet each time she realised that the shadow at the door wasn't Wyngate's, and the caller on the phone had no news for her, she forced herself to focus.

She didn't know who was writing the messages she translated or where they were going, but she took pains with everything, checking and checking again. And when she wasn't sure of something – obscure slang or regional dialect – she wrote a quick note in the margin. But then there were footsteps in the corridor again; a telephone rang. And she was pulled out of her Parisian self and back to worrying about Ned.

Lisette glanced up as Capitaine Ardouin, the tall, stately, grey-haired woman who ran their team, hurried across the room. The capitaine's sensible, highly polished shoes tapped against the floor.

Lisette's heart leapt, and she started to get to her feet. Ardouin must have a message for her about Ned – surely, by now, there was news. But Capitaine Ardouin, in her immaculate khaki uniform, passed Lisette's desk without stopping and went into her office in the corner of the room where a telephone was ringing.

Lisette held her pencil so tightly, it nearly snapped. She knew that phone was the hotline to Charles de Gaulle, leader of the Free French in exile, at his offices in Carlton Gardens.

Lisette finished a translation into English of a message from someone in the French resistance. She often wondered if one day a message sent by her mother would cross her desk, but how would she know?

The message this morning reported their latest guerilla action – *Tanks on the road from Rouen to Caen. The bridges fell!*

She wished she could tell the children about these exploits. Ned especially would love to hear about the guerillas blowing up bridges. But it was all top secret, and besides... where was Ned for her to tell him?

At the neighbouring desk Lisette's colleague, Marie, looked up from her typewriter as she transcribed the messages. She blinked rapidly and said, 'I was born in Rouen... they won't beat us.'

'You're right, they won't,' Lisette replied, clinging to the hope in Marie's voice. 'They didn't reckon with the French, did they? We don't like being walked all over.'

Lisette knew France and Germany had a long history of conflict, to the point that, seventy years before, Paris had been under siege for months. Back then, the post had to be sent by hot-air balloon. But nowadays they had radios, which were hidden in attics, barns and cellars across France, sending messages back to the Free French command in London.

And in the War Office, in a room clouded by cigarette smoke and heavy with the scent of coffee, Lisette, Marie and their colleagues decoded the messages coming out of the occupied country. The country where most of the people in this section still had loved ones living under the shadow of the Nazis.

Lisette was grateful that there were at least some positive stories coming out of France. Otherwise, she would just be translating messages that left her in tears. Especially today, with no news about Ned.

There were messages that came through reporting retaliations, where villagers would be rounded up and shot as payback for the resistance blowing up another bridge or an SS staff car with an officer inside it. There was always a price to pay for what the resistance did, a price that had to be paid in innocent blood. And who in that room didn't wonder every time if the dead were people they knew? A shiver ran through Lisette; she tried to fight the image of her own mother being dragged out of her front door to the nearest square and forced, blindfolded, in front of a firing squad.

Just then the office door opened, and Lisette looked around to see Gray walk in with a man who looked familiar, but whom she couldn't place.

'Morning, Monsieur Gray!' she called in French. He'd probably come to see Capitaine Ardouin.

'Good morning, Mademoiselle Souchon, Mademoiselle Bescond!' Gray replied in his fluent French. Then he and his companion strode across the office towards the capitaine's desk. There, they conducted a conversation in low voices, before Capitaine Ardouin rose to her feet. She and the unnamed man made their way to the closed door of the section's private office and disappeared inside, leaving Mr Gray alone once more.

'How goes the fight for fair France?' he asked, speaking French with all the fluency of a native speaker once more. He perched on the edge of Lisette's desk. 'And what of our little Ned? Home after a night on the tiles and none the worse for it, I'll wager!'

Lisette knew he'd be pleased about the news of the bridges being attacked, halting the Nazi tanks heading across Normandy. As for Ned... there was a war on and he was just one lost boy in a city of many lost boys. And yet, he was a boy who she knew, and cared for.

'I'm so worried, Monsieur Gray,' she replied as, around her, typewriters clacked and telephones rang. 'Wyngate and Jack came back just as the sun was coming up, but not with Ned. They couldn't find him. Nobody knows where he is.'

Gray furrowed his brow and shook his head. 'I was a wayward lad,' he admitted. 'I spent a good few nights that left my mother's nerves in tatters. But I always came home. Has he done this before?'

'Not overnight, no.' Lisette sighed. If Gray always came home, then surely Ned would too. 'But then he makes his own rules. He disappears during the day, and the other kids have no idea where he is. Off to see the wide boys, I expect.' She shrugged. 'Perhaps he took shelter with them?'

'Perhaps,' he agreed. 'If there is anything I can do, please tell me. Any calls one can make, tendrils one can unloose. You need but make the request.'

Lisette nodded gratefully. 'Anything you can think of, please, Monsieur Gray. Can we put up missing posters? I was worried about going to the police, because of all those black marketeers and wide boys he hangs about with, but I reported him missing on the way to work anyway – I don't care if it stirs up trouble; his safety is what matters. I've left a message at

Esther's office – she'll print it in her newspaper. And he took off his ID bracelet, you see.' She held up her wrist and the light caught the metal chain of her own. 'The hospitals will be so busy, and I wouldn't know how to start contacting them.'

'Leave it to me.' Gray smiled. 'My own sons are away fighting and my girl is nursing our brave boys. One worries so, doesn't one? Mark me, we will find the lad.'

Lisette smiled for the first time that day. Gray cared about the children and she knew he'd do whatever he could to help track Ned down.

'Ned has many friends. That means search parties will be easy to assemble,' Gray said gently. 'Not many lads of his age have managed to wrap gangsters, Vera Lynn and one devilishly handsome duke round their little finger. And Mr Wyngate is a unique sort of gentleman. If he is looking for Master Ned, then Master Ned will be found.'

ELEVEN
CONNIE

Connie and her friends had gone out searching for Ned as soon as they'd finished their hurried bowls of porridge that morning. He'd only been gone a few hours, but they wouldn't waste a second.

Jack had suggested that they stay close to home to start with, because they knew the area as well as their own freckles, and maybe something had happened to Ned on his way home. They strode along the dusty streets, Pippa trotting alongside, dodging past fallen masonry and past craters, the scent of old fires always lingering in the air from all the bombs that had fallen on this part of the city. Whole streets had vanished, and yet life still went on. There was still shopping to do, even though the shops were never full these days, and there were still jobs to go to.

They went to see the ARP wardens and the firemen too. Ned had been at their side during countless raids, and had vanished.

Only a couple of hours into their scouring of Whitechapel, Connie nearly tripped over her own feet. Ned's face was staring back at her.

Only it wasn't really Ned – just a poster on the wall with her friend's face printed on it.

MISSING! HAVE YOU SEEN THIS BOY?

'Look at that!' she exclaimed, pointing it out to her friends. But they'd already seen it. In it Ned was grinning, hands on his hips, his cap at a jaunty angle, standing among the wreckage of a bombsite. Underneath the photograph, it said NED MITCHELL, ONE OF THE BLITZ KIDS, IS MISSING. PLEASE FORWARD ALL INFORMATION TO YOUR LOCAL POLICE STATION, OR ROOM 181, THE WAR OFFICE.

'The War Office? I bet that's Mr Wyngate or Mr Gray!' Susan breathed in amazement. Her brother, Ben, nodded in agreement. 'It ain't bad having blokes like them looking out for us, is it?'

'They'd do anything for us,' Elsie said, smiling broadly.

A little further along the street, Connie heard the bellow of the old man who sold the newspapers. And as she tuned in to what he was shouting, she heard the same message.

'Read all about it! Blitz Kid goes missin'!' he called.

A tingle went through her, and she almost sobbed. People cared, and were trying to find him.

As they went past Whitechapel tube station, they bumped into Jasper and Lillian from the club. Jasper stood out in Whitechapel in his pale cream linen suit. He looked tired and gaunt, a haunted look in his expression, as he insisted that he would help to find Ned.

The fundraiser had made plenty of money to help him get his club back on its feet, but Ned's disappearance had clearly deeply upset him. Jasper wiped his hand down his haggard face, and told them that there wouldn't be any rebuilding while Ned was missing. And if he couldn't be found, Jasper wouldn't rebuild the club at all. He didn't have the heart for it after what'd happened there. All that money from the fundraiser would go to the war effort instead.

Connie swallowed. No more stage, no more audience, no more club that welcomed everyone. And it was all her fault that Ned had run away.

They agreed to split up, and Jasper and Lillian took the road that led down towards the docks while the children headed towards Aldgate Underground station. They'd cover more ground that way and find Ned in no time, Connie was sure.

Soon they bumped into some of Ned's associates, wide boys who were unloading a van down an alleyway behind one of Toe Mahoney's pubs near Aldgate. Once Jack and Connie had explained that Ned had vanished, the men – big, broad-shouldered bruisers to a man – looked heartbroken with concern, and declared at once that they'd join the search to find the missing boy as well.

Toe Mahoney and his mum appeared from the back of the pub and, when Ma Mahoney heard what'd happened, she told Toe he had to help. And Toe said he'd phone up Dupree as well – he'd spoken to his opposite number only the night before. Dupree wouldn't stop talking about how much he loved little Ned for trying to save his wife in Soho. There was no stone they wouldn't leave unturned.

Connie had struggled to hold back her tears at the mention of poor Mrs Dupree. Her funeral had been lavish, with two fine black horses with feather plumes on their heads pulling a Victorian glass-sided hearse.

Mrs Dupree's coffin had barely been visible beneath the bouquets of roses and lilies, and the wildflowers that grew everywhere on the bombsites. All of Mr Dupree's family had been there, and even his relatives who were serving had been given leave to attend, wearing black armbands on their uniformed sleeves. The bosses who ran the other parts of

London had turned up to pay their respects as well, men Ned had talked about because he'd run errands for all of them.

Mr Dupree was a criminal kingpin, that was true, and yet there wasn't anyone who didn't pity him for losing his wife. He had been a picture of dignity, straight-backed self-composed, but his eyes were red and looked sore from crying. He was holding the hands of two of his grandchildren, a boy and a girl, one on either side. All the mourners were finely dressed in black; there wasn't any sign of make-do-and-mend for the people who ran London's black market.

Connie couldn't accept that Ned would be next, his small body carried slowly through the battered streets to the cemetery. He had to still be alive somewhere. And yet as every minute passed, the thought of laying a wreath of bomb-site wildflowers on her honorary brother's grave became increasingly real to her. She knew full well how dangerous it was to stay in London; she'd lost her nan to the bombs, and she'd seen more than enough when the sirens called them to duty. She had to suppress a shiver each time the image of a cold, unmoving Ned came into her mind, and she pressed her hand to her heart, which ached at the thought that he was lost for ever.

But she couldn't give up hope, and she was humbled that so many people were mobilising to hunt for her friend. They had to find him soon.

So much could happen to a boy on his own in the city. Just as the thought went through Connie's mind, she noticed a woman walking down the street towards them. It was the one they'd often seen around Whitechapel and who had appeared in the queue outside the fundraiser show.

It was as if she'd materialised out of nowhere, with her face that was caked in powder and her blood-red lipstick. What if she'd found Ned on his way home, alone? What if she'd offered him sweets, and then snatched him? And it'd be all Connie's fault, because she'd shouted at him.

Connie tensed and instinctively grabbed Jack's hand. He started, his gaze fixed on the woman as she gave them a smile and said, 'I hope you find him, poor love. London's a dangerous place for kiddies.' She dropped her voice to a confidential whisper. 'I live over the river, down by the row that got flattened last Christmas, and I'm always having to chase kiddies off. Poor lambs, they don't know no different, do they?' Then she walked on, her heels clicking as she went.

Susan shivered, her arm round Ben's shoulders. She whispered, 'She gives me the creeps.'

'I reckon she lives in a gingerbread cottage,' Ben murmured, then he looked along the street and smiled.

Connie followed his gaze and spotted two figures in khaki uniforms strolling along the street. They were Americans – she could spot them a mile off, with their broad smiles and easygoing air. Not many people looked like that in London nowadays, not after all the bombing raids and shortages.

'Say, old-timer,' one of the servicemen said, as they paused to address the old newspaper seller. 'What the heck's a *Blitz Kid*?'

The newspaper seller jerked his thumb towards Connie and her friends. 'Well, that's some of them up there, for starters,' he said. He spent so much of his day shouting that he couldn't speak quietly, and Connie heard every word. 'They're the kids what come back after they'd been evacuated. They want to look after their city. And this little lad's disappeared! Must've been tryin' to rescue someone and...' He swallowed, before going on, 'We'll find him, don't you worry! The whole of London's lookin' for him. Even that Vera Lynn was on the radio this morning, making an appeal to find him.' Then he reached out one stubby finger and tapped it to the newspaper. 'Noël Coward an' all, look. We're all keeping our fingers crossed for the little 'un.'

Connie gasped, her heart swelling with hope. The famous Vera Lynn herself, who'd appeared at the fundraising show, had taken the time to go on the radio and plead for people to find her friend. If only she and Jack had got their radio working, they would've heard Vera's appeal too. And Mr Coward was in the newspaper, using his celebrity to help. Surely Ned would be found soon.

The young man frowned, then furrowed his brow as he peered more closely at the newspaper. He handed a coin to the old man and told him as he unfolded the paper and read the front page, 'Oh, I heard of these kids. They're the gang you guys have looking after the whole city, right?'

'That's right!' the newspaper seller said. He offered Connie a smile. 'We're blessed to have them.'

But the American was still studying the grainy photograph of Ned, his attention entirely taken by the little boy who beamed out of the image. A moment passed and then he stabbed his finger into the paper and asked his companion, 'Isn't this the kid who was giving that bunch of nuns a whole lot of backchat in the subway last night?'

His friend stroked his chin before replying, 'Sure is! You gotta hand it to the kid, he really let rip.'

Connie thought she might burst with excitement. They'd seen him – they'd seen Ned, after he'd left the theatre. She waved to the others to follow and hurried over to the Americans.

'Where? Where'd you see him?' she demanded. 'He ran off from the theatre up West, and then never come home.'

'Was it during the raid?' Jack urged. 'Was he sheltering?'

'Y'know, he was like a little subway rat or something,' the soldier replied. 'He came right outta the tunnels at Whitechapel while the raid was going on. Sees the nuns and starts giving them a whole bunch of yap. Then he goes right back into the tunnel fast as he came out, heading off towards the Tower.'

Jack seized Connie's hand. 'What time was it?' he asked the men urgently.

Connie had always told Ned to be careful in the tunnels. What if he hadn't been paying attention as the trains came rushing through, or slipped on an oily rail and lost his footing? He could've been hit by a train down there, and no one had found him. And yet, he was too wily for that, surely. She realised she should've been more worried about where he was headed – if he was going south, in the direction of the Tower of London, then he'd be running off towards the docks. And nowhere in London was bombed more heavily than those wharfs and warehouses along the river.

'Musta been about two hours into the raid,' the other American replied.

Connie's mind was whirring. Ned could've got to Whitechapel through the tunnels from the West End in less time than that.

What had he been doing?

'Thank you, sir,' Jack said. 'That's the first clue we've had.'

'We'll talk to our buddies,' the American told them. 'Ask them to keep their eyes open for this little guy.'

Jack gave him a nod of thanks, then turned to address the kids and Pippa. 'We need to go down to London Bridge and talk to the stationmaster.'

Connie squeezed Jack's hand, and the six of them, including Pippa, strode along the uneven pavement. But as they walked, Connie's vision began to blur. The street became indistinct, and she shook with fear.

'Oh, heck...' She stopped walking and ran her arm across her face, trying to catch her tears before they fell. 'He's my little mate! I was horrible to him, and it's all my fault he ran off. What are we goin' to do if we can't find him?'

'We will,' Ben said, but there was a wobble in his voice. He wasn't entirely sure, Connie could tell, but no one wanted to say it.

Just then, Pippa started barking again, and Elsie announced, 'Look, it's Mr Wyngate!'

There he was, striding along the street, his fedora angled just so to keep the bright sunlight out of his eyes. Connie's heart leapt. She'd hoped they'd bump into Wyngate, seeing as Whitechapel was the obvious place to search for Ned. Had he found him? Was he coming to tell them where he was?

'Mr Wyngate!' Elsie shouted. 'We're over here!'

Wyngate looked towards the children, then stepped out into the traffic with barely a glance left or right. As the cars and vans screeched to a stop and Wyngate strode across the road towards them, Connie immediately recalled the illustrated Bible that the nuns at the orphanage had insisted they read, with the painting of Moses parting the Red Sea.

'We've just met some Americans who saw Ned,' Jack said as soon as Mr Wyngate reached them. 'He was at Whitechapel station last night, then went through the tunnel towards London Bridge.'

'I bet he was goin' down the docks!' Connie added. She wiped her eyes again and asked hopefully, 'You ain't found him already, have you?'

Because if anyone had, it would be Mr Wyngate, surely. But there was something in his guarded expression that made Connie's heart lurch.

Wyngate reached into his pocket and took out a folded white handkerchief. He handed it to Connie as he said, 'I'm afraid not. But I've roped in a lot of people who are looking.' Then he reached out and, to Connie's surprise, gave her shoulder a squeeze. 'A lot of people in London owe me favours. I've called them in.'

With that he checked his watch, then nodded. 'I need to be at the War Office in an hour or so. That's plenty of time for London Bridge.' And with that he set off walking again, with the kids in tow. As they went Wyngate called over his shoulder, 'You can keep that handkerchief, Connie. It's royal.'

Connie, who had just wiped it across her eyes, held it out and stared at the corner. An elaborate monogram was embroidered into the corner, topped with a crown. 'Bleedin' Nora, it is an' all!'

They followed Wyngate south, down to the river, and past the Tower of London, with its moat full of rows of vegetables while a barrage balloon floated silently above. The castle had stood for nearly a thousand years and Connie was convinced that even the Luftwaffe couldn't destroy it. A tug chugged along the river and, once it'd gone by, the two halves of Tower Bridge lowered to let Connie and her friends over the river. How Tower Bridge was still standing despite the bombing, she didn't know.

Once they were on the other side, they picked their way past roped-off craters where bombs had fallen. But there were still warehouses operating, even ones with holes in the roof.

Finally, they reached London Bridge station. It was teeming with people heading for the overground platforms, and there was a long queue for tickets for the Underground.

Along with the usual bustling crowds of servicemen in uniform, there were the Americans now as well, and the ordinary Londoners dotted among the military travellers were eyeing their transatlantic arrivals with interest.

Connie sighed. 'How are we ever going to speak to the blooming stationmaster when it's so busy?' she said to Jack.

'We'll just have to join the que—' But before Jack had finished speaking, Mr Wyngate strode past the snaking queue that led to the information desk and cut in at the front, as though there was nobody else waiting at all. He addressed the woman who was on duty. 'Wyngate, Ministry. Call the stationmaster.'

The woman blinked at him in surprise, then pressed a

button on her desk. Suddenly, a metallic voice echoed around the ticket hall. 'Mr Driscoll to the ticket hall. Mr Driscoll to the ticket hall, please.'

Connie could feel the eyes of everyone in the queue on Wyngate, and then a short man in his stationmaster's uniform of waistcoat and jacket, looking red-faced, came hurrying over. He wiped his white moustache as he looked at Wyngate.

'Sir?' Mr Driscoll said.

To allow the queue to move again, Wyngate stepped away from the desk as he produced a newspaper clipping from his pocket. It was the photograph of Ned.

'We're looking for this boy. He's one of the Blitz Kids,' he explained, though there would be no need. Ned regularly travelled on the tube all over London, either through the closed tunnels or by taking the train itself. He didn't believe in buying tickets of course, so was well known to the stationmasters across the network. 'He's been missing since the raid last night. Did he come through here?'

'Young Master Mitchell,' the stationmaster said, with warmth in his voice. He evidently ignored the fact that Ned travelled without tickets. Then he turned to Connie and her friends and nodded. 'Gone missin', has he? That's a worry. Now... last night, you say?'

Wyngate gave a brisk nod. 'Last night. During the raid.'

'Ah, now, I did, as a matter of fact,' Mr Driscoll replied. 'He turned up just at the end of it, popping out of a tunnel. I had a word, told him how risky that kind of caper is – though I expect he won't take any notice. Then we heard the all-clear. So I thought he'd scurry off home.'

Connie breathed a sigh of relief. All the fear that had pulled her insides tight began to dissolve and she sagged like a puppet with cut strings. So Ned had been safe, all the way through the raid, until the all-clear. But where was he now?

'Anyway, so the folk what wanted to go home set off, and

there was an old dear trying to get up the steps. A handle on her bag broke, and her knitting went for a burton – there was balls of wool rolling about, and Ned's darting about in the crowd to collect 'em up and help her. Then once he'd done that, he took her arm in his, and... well, I expect he got her safely home, don't you?'

'Name?' Wyngate asked. Connie prayed that Mr Driscoll would know, but surely he couldn't know everyone who passed through his station, especially in an air raid.

'That'd be Mabel,' Mr Driscoll said. Connie was amazed that he knew her name. 'She was goin' to knit me some socks, she said, but only once she's finished knitting them for the airmen and the fellas in the submarines, you see. But I can't say as I know where she lives, and I doubt any of our staff would neither. We get hundreds in here every time that siren goes off. Can't be far away, though.'

'He must be around here somewhere, then!' Ben said excitedly. Connie suppressed a shiver; wasn't this the area where the strange, witchy woman said she lived? Next door to a bombsite where children ran about?

'Start knocking on doors and searching everywhere you can think of. And be careful,' Wyngate instructed. 'You know how dangerous bombsites can be. I'll see you back here in two hours. Understood?'

He directed that question at Jack and Connie.

'Understood,' Jack replied. Then he turned to the others. 'He's out there somewhere.'

Connie nodded. 'We'll find him. We will.'

TWELVE

CONNIE

They went from street to dusty street, past houses that had lost most of their tiles, along pavements pitted with holes, knocking on every front door they could find. They didn't really know the area south of the river, but Ned did. He knew every street and alleyway of London as if he'd written the famous A–Z map himself. He would've had to come this way to get back to Whitechapel from London Bridge station.

The south had suffered just as much as the places they knew in the East End. They'd turn a corner and find a wasteland of shattered homes and ruined warehouses, with soot blackening what was left. The stench of smoke stayed here too, lingering like a pall. Even in streets where the Victorian terraces seemed unharmed, some of the houses had CONDEMNED painted across their walls and no one home.

At least the people who answered their doors, or who they stopped in the street, knew who Connie and her friends were, from their exploits appearing in the newspapers. And the news was spreading that Ned was missing. Men would take off their flat caps and scratch their heads, wondering if they'd seen him. Women would tap their chins in thought as a baby balanced on their hip. Then they'd shake their heads and say they'd look out for him.

The sun was beating down on them as they walked along a street that had been smashed to bits. Only stubs remained of most of the walls, and front doors, scorched by incendiary bombs, opened onto voids where houses had once been. Broken glass crunched underfoot and a black cat with a bent tail perched on a snapped rafter and hissed at them. Elsie picked up Pippa and hugged her.

'I don't like this at all,' Connie sighed. 'It's like Ned's vanished into thin air.'

'Not our Ned,' Jack assured her. He paused and blew out a long, tired breath as he surveyed the bomb-shattered street. 'I don't think there's anybody around here at all. Nobody's living in these houses.'

There wasn't much left of them. A warehouse had run along part of the street, and only the wall that faced the street remained. A narrow house stood beside it, and, as they got nearer, Connie realised that it had somehow survived.

'Do you think anyone's living there?' Susan asked, pointing towards it. There were grubby net curtains in the window and a plant pot on the sill.

'Well spotted!' Jack said. He approached the door as, behind him, Pippa gave a warning bark at the twitch of the net curtain that concealed the room within from the street. Behind the panes of glass, each with its taped cross to protect it from bomb damage, someone was watching.

Jack approached the door and lifted the knocker. Before it could fall, however, the door opened and a powdered face peered out into the sunshine.

It was her, the woman they'd seen in Whitechapel and who'd been at the fundraiser show. The woman who made Connie's skin crawl. Ben had said she lived in a gingerbread cottage, like a witch, but she didn't: she lived in the one house still standing in a street reduced to a bombsite.

Connie swallowed, her mouth dry. She could feel her friends tense around her. Ben grabbed Susan's hand. Elsie tightened her grip on Pippa's lead and stood closer to her brother.

Connie tried to shake off her fear. They couldn't run off. They had to ask her, because what if this woman knew something?

''Scuse us,' Connie began, trying to rattle off the same question she'd asked over and over again since they'd started knocking on doors. 'Only we're lookin' for our mate, Ned. You might've heard about him. He's gone missing, you see, and he was seen not far away last night at the Tube station. He was leavin' with an old dear called Mabel. Don't suppose you've seen him?'

The woman tapped one red-nailed finger to her pale cheek, then shook her head. 'Well, I see all sorts around here.' She raised one insinuating eyebrow. 'All sorts. It's not a safe place for a kiddie alone. You never know who's skulking about after the blackout.'

Jack nodded, then asked politely, 'Do you know of a lady called Mabel, maybe?'

She narrowed her eyes thoughtfully, then shook her head again. 'I don't, lovey,' she admitted. 'But I wonder... there's all kinds of little nooks and crannies round here, what with the bombs falling. Now, if your little friend's tried to cut through and had a tumble...' The woman shrugged her narrow shoulders. 'I mean, he could be lying at the bottom of one of the bomb craters even now, couldn't he? And a wall came down while I was having my cuppa this morning. Would've squashed anybody under it like a bug. Happens all the time round these parts. And that's before you get to the odd sorts of folk creeping about, stealing and doing who knows what at all hours.'

Ben turned pale as he mouthed the words, *like a bug*. Connie shivered despite the heat of the day.

'But it's the people who worries me, not the bombs,' the woman went on, with a theatrical shudder. 'There's funny folk all over London. I wouldn't want any kiddie of mine running about these streets on their own. It's not safe for little 'uns.' Then she lifted one thin hand and pointed towards the wasteland where once there had been shops and homes. 'All bombed out. If he's come a cropper in that wreckage, you'll never find him.'

Connie planted her hands on her hips, as if she'd been set a challenge. Her fear of the woman had transformed into defiance. 'Oh, you think so? Me and my mates aren't afraid of bombsites. If that's where Ned's got stuck, then we'll find him!'

'So long as you don't come a cropper yourselves.' The woman gave a blood-red smile, serene as she closed the door.

'Right, you heard her – Ned might be on that bombsite,' Connie declared as if she was rallying the troops. She had raised her hand to her eyes to shield them from the sun as she peered across at acres of rubble. 'And if he is, *we'll* be the ones to find him!'

THIRTEEN

LISETTE

Lisette hadn't realised she'd doodled a picture of Ned's cheeky face until it was grinning up at her from her notepad. She touched her fingertip to the drawing, wondering once again where in the city he could've gone. Maybe he wasn't even in London any more, and had found his way into a lorry, or onto a train, and was somewhere out in the countryside. At least he'd be safe there.

'Lisette, Marie.' Capitaine Ardouin stood in the doorway of the room in which she held her private meetings. 'If anything comes up in the translations regarding a Kriegsmarine ship named the *Amfortas*, let me know straight away.'

Lisette nodded. She mentally filed away the ship's name. 'Of course, Capitaine. As soon as we know, you'll know too.'

Something was going on, Lisette knew. All day, she'd seen people coming in and out of the office, speaking with Capitaine Ardouin in the private room. Even Wyngate had come in at more than one point, but as ever when he was working his face was unreadable, and he didn't stop to talk. He paused at the door to the room and glanced back at Lisette, catching her gaze with his own. Only when he was sure he had her full attention did he offer her a tender smile and a gentle nod of acknowledgement. It would go unnoticed by everyone else, Lisette was sure, but in that moment it felt like an embrace.

Wyngate was in the private office now, and he wasn't alone. There were people in uniform, some with chests bristling with medals, and Gray came back several times as well, looking serious and determined. He didn't perch on her desk for a chat.

It made Lisette cold with worry. What was happening in her homeland? But she was doing what she could, translating the messages that came in quickly and accurately, making sure the latest updates were swiftly passed on.

And the telephone on her desk had remained stubbornly silent. Every time she looked at it, she'd hoped it might spring into life, with news from the children that Ned had been found alive and well. They must still be out, going from street to street, hunting for their friend; no news came.

GESTAPO ACTIVITY INCREASING IN RENNES, read one message. WIDESPREAD DETENTIONS AND REPRISALS. PUBLIC EXECUTIONS TO BEGIN AT DAWN.

A cold finger of fear ran down Lisette's back. She didn't know what messages her colleagues were translating, but, if they were all as bad as that one, no wonder panic was rushing through the War Office.

REGULAR REPORTING AGENT FAUCON HAS BEEN EXECUTED. THIS IS PERROQUET REPORTING.

Executed? Lisette was stunned; she had translated several messages from the resistance fighter who used the codename Faucon. And Perroquet had courageously stepped into Faucon's shoes, even with the risk that they, too, could be found and dragged off to be shot.

Lisette wiped away a tear as she put the message and its translation into its buff folder.

'Mademoiselle Souchon?'

She looked up at the sound of Wyngate's voice. He was standing beside her desk. She closed her fingers round her handkerchief. Was there news about Ned? 'Monsieur Wyngate?' She couldn't call him *Adam* when she was at work, surrounded by their colleagues. 'I didn't realise you were there. I was...'

'Drifting?' he asked as the door opened to admit the uniformed members of the Free French who would take over the seats and desks of Lisette, Marie and their colleagues, continuing the translations throughout the night. The War Office never slept, as Lisette was already aware, because the enemy never rested.

'I am sorry, there's so much...' She gestured to the buff folder. 'These messages... and I haven't heard anything about Ned.'

She got up from her desk. What a day it had been. But there was no going home, not with Ned still to be found.

'This work...' Wyngate swallowed. He reached out and touched his hand to Lisette's. 'I know it isn't easy sometimes.'

'Do you have any news about the children?' she asked.

'Positive sighting at London Bridge Underground,' he replied. 'Ned escorted a woman home after the raid. They're scoping the area; I'm going over there now to meet them.'

'I'll come with you,' Lisette told him. Her heart was rushing. That was what she needed to hear. Ned had survived last night's air raid. 'Thank heavens he's alive! Maybe he left a message for someone in the street and it didn't get through? If only the children had a telephone...'

Wyngate nodded, but he seemed distracted. He was a man of few words, as Lisette had learned, but usually he would speak to her of his concerns if he could. Yet, in his job, she knew that he often couldn't. Perhaps that might change a little, now they were both covered by the acts they had signed, which bound them together to keep the nation's secrets.

As they headed for the door, Lisette touched his arm and looked into his dark gaze. 'We've lost one of our agents,' she said gently. 'They've executed Faucon.'

Was this careless talk? Lisette doubted it; he was privy to the messages she translated, after all.

Wyngate gave a tight nod, his jaw set. 'I know,' he said, pausing with his hand on the door handle. Once they went into the corridor, the conversation would have to be over. It was a discussion they could only have in rooms where everyone had signed the same agreements, where everyone had promised that there would be no careless talk. 'He was a good man. A friend.'

'Oh, Adam, I'm so sorry,' Lisette said. She hadn't meant to say his name out loud in the office, but was trying to hold back the sob that wanted to escape her and had forgotten for a moment. And when she looked into Wyngate's eyes again, she realised that, one day, he'd go back into France, and would bear a codename that might come up in a message that arrived on her desk. 'Please... When you're out there again... please be careful.'

He pressed his hand to his chest and whispered one word. 'Corbeau.'

Lisette absorbed the word. That was his codename. Corbeau: raven. She hoped she'd never see it in a message, unless it was to say that he was alive and well.

'I'll remember,' she murmured in reply.

They headed out of the War Office together, and, once they were away from the building, Lisette linked his arm in hers. While he was with her, she would hold him tight.

They travelled on the Underground from Westminster. It was only a short journey to London Bridge, but it couldn't have been fast enough for Lisette.

The train was busy with people heading home from work in

offices that were still standing, along with sailors with their big kitbags, and children with suitcases, either heading out to the countryside, or on their way back.

They stood close together, Lisette feeling the draw of Wyngate's body. She rested her head on his shoulder and breathed in the scent of his cologne, and it made the rest of the world fall away; the other passengers, and the smell of oil and people that filled the Underground, disappeared for that moment.

He put his arm round Lisette's waist, holding her close to him in the press of the passengers, then lowered his head and whispered, 'It'll be all right.'

Lisette trembled as she lifted her head to look at him. 'I hope so, Adam. I hope so, with all my heart.'

'I don't like to see you like this. All this worry,' Wyngate admitted softly. Then he leaned down and kissed her.

She kissed him back, losing herself in the softness of his lips and the reassuring strength of his body. Her heart skipped, as it always did when he kissed her.

They arrived at London Bridge and squeezed along the platform to get out. Every advert pasted on the walls referred to the war somehow. Along with the ubiquitous government information posters – LOOK OUT IN THE BLACKOUT! – there were adverts from favourite brands trying to remind their customers that they still could buy their goods, if they were lucky enough to find them.

Lisette and Wyngate ran down the steps at the front of the station and suddenly Ben and Elsie barrelled into them. The children's eyes were wide, and they were dusty from the streets. They must've been clambering over bombsites in their search. Lisette drew in an anxious breath.

'What's happened?' Wyngate asked. Because something *had*, Lisette could tell.

Elsie was cuddling Pippa to her; she had been crying, and

Ben, who was usually crackling with energy, looked pale and distraught.

'We've come to get help! It's Connie,' Elsie said. Her voice broke and she couldn't go on.

'She fell into a bomb crater!' Ben said urgently, grabbing Wyngate's sleeve. 'It's full of water and she can't get out!'

Lisette saw Wyngate's jaw tighten and the flash of fear cross his dark gaze. Then they were running through the crowded summer street, as she prayed desperately that they would reach Connie before it was too late.

FOURTEEN

CONNIE

Connie kicked and kicked beneath the water, desperately trying to keep her head above the surface. Her breaths were shallow and quick as she fought with every fibre to keep herself alive. She was tiring and she wished she could put her feet on the bottom, but the dark expanse of water underneath her seemed to go on for ever. Something was down there in the unknowable depths, something sharp that caught against her leg each time she moved.

She racked her brains trying to remember what her nan had told her – the golden rule if she ever fell into the river. But she couldn't find the memory. And thinking of her nan, she wondered if she would go to heaven and meet her and her mum again there; but they wouldn't want her to die yet, surely? She had to survive.

'Help!' she shouted, waving her arms. The filthy water rushed into her mouth and made her cough.

Above her she could hear the sound of fabric being torn, and then Jack shouted down, 'We've got a sheet, Con, we're going to tear it up and I'll lower it down to you. Just you hold on!'

Connie sank beneath the water for a moment, and it made her eyes sting. She urged herself back to the surface. She had to hold on. They had to find Ned. She'd been so busy staring across the bombsite looking for any sign of him, after fruitlessly searching, having been misled by that creepy, witchy old woman, that she'd missed the edge of the crater. She'd lost her footing on the loose soil and plunged straight into the pit of dirty water.

She couldn't see Jack or Susan over the lip of the crater, but she heard the fabric tear again. They were going to get her out. She'd be all right. She'd be on dry land again any moment.

She went on kicking, and her shoe was suddenly caught by something under the water. She couldn't move her leg, and her fear transformed into panic.

'Help me! Help!' she yelled.

Was she going to die like this, drowning in a bomb crater full of filthy water? This couldn't be how her life ended; she still had so many things to do. She'd never had a boyfriend before, and maybe one day she'd get married. If this was it for her, she'd never get to push a big pram along Whitechapel High Street, full of her rosy-cheeked babies. And she'd never get to sing at Noël Coward's show. And what about Ned? If she drowned here, she'd never know what had happened to her friend. She'd never be able to tell him how sorry she was, for what she'd said last night.

'I'm just tying it round a roof beam,' Jack shouted. 'Then I'll lower it down! You grab on and Susan and me will pull you up!'

From within the deep pit, Connie could hear Jack and Susan urgently working, their voices clipped as they tore the sheet and secured it. Then they appeared at the lip of the crater, looking down at her. Jack carefully lowered what Connie could see now was the remains of the bedsheet, torn into strips and knotted to make a rope.

'Tie it round your waist and hold on,' Jack told Connie. 'Don't be frightened!'

Connie was tiring now and, with what little energy she had left after trying to keep herself afloat, she made a grab for the end of the rope. But it was just out of reach, and she couldn't get any closer.

'My foot, it's—' Connie sank below the water again, then came back up spluttering, releasing a spout of dirty water before saying, 'It's caught on something under the water! I can't reach!'

'Watch for the others,' Jack instructed Susan. Then, without a second thought, he took hold of the knotted sheet and swung his long legs over the edge of the crater. Carefully, he began to descend the rescue rope he and Susan had made, slithering lower and lower until he dropped into the water with a gentle splash.

Connie could feel the water dragging her down. It was hard fighting against it, trying and failing to keep herself floating. She was trapped and would vanish into the depths.

But she couldn't give up. Jack was risking his life to rescue her.

'Can you feel what's caught you?' Jack asked. He put his arms round Connie's waist, holding her above the water as her strength threatened to desert her. 'You've not broken a bone?'

'Dunno...' Connie said with a struggle. She wanted to put her arms round Jack, but she was scared she'd pull him down with her. 'It's sharp, it's like a broken beam...'

Jack nodded. He looked up at the yawning opening of the pit, then back at Connie. She thought he was going to say something, but instead he drew in a deep breath and held it, then plunged into the water.

Connie was stunned. Jack was risking his life to rescue her. She felt him grip her trapped foot, then with a firm yank he freed her.

Relief washed through Connie. She'd be able to get out

now, wouldn't she? Any minute, they'd all be back on dry land, and they could carry on searching for Ned. Jack burst through the dirty water and took in a deep breath of air. It was anything but fresh, but it was oxygen, and he gulped it down even as he put his arms round Connie's waist to hold her steady again.

'Put your arms round my neck,' he instructed breathlessly. 'I'll get you to the side. Then we can tie the rope round your waist and I'll climb up and haul you after me. Can't risk you climbing until we know you haven't injured that foot.' He swallowed hard, his gaze searching Connie's. 'You had me worried sick, Con.'

Connie gazed back at him and started to cry. 'I'm sorry I scared you,' she replied.

Jack touched his forehead to Connie's and told her, 'Don't you ever say sorry.' Then, his arm still nestled round her waist, he swam them both to where the knotted sheets waited. Jack didn't let go of Connie until he had to, and released her only so he could wrap the sheet round her waist and tie it tight.

'You'll be out of here in no time, Con,' he promised gently. 'You just give me a minute to climb up, all right?'

Connie nodded. She hadn't the energy to speak. She watched Jack as he started to climb up the knotted sheets towards the lip of the crater, the soil sliding under his hands and feet as he hauled himself up.

She heard something creaking. It sounded like a huge wooden rafter. Hadn't Jack said he'd tied the other end of the makeshift rope to a roof beam?

Suddenly, Susan's voice tore the air.

'The beam's splitting! The rope's coming free! Jack – watch out!'

As Connie looked up into the distant sunlight at the edge of the bomb crater she heard a sound like splintering wood, then Jack tumbled back towards the darkness.

FIFTEEN

Connie's heart was racing as she helplessly watched Jack fall. She gasped in alarm and the filthy water rushed into her mouth, but she didn't notice as she braced herself for the splash that would follow as Jack hit the water. What if he went deep and was caught on the splintered wood under the surface? What if he couldn't come back up for air? He couldn't die here. She couldn't lose him.

But suddenly, before Jack could hit the surface, the rope of knotted sheets went taut. He swung to one side, only an inch above the filthy water. With one end tied round Connie's waist, she was pulled forward, closer to the edge of the crater with its jagged wall of broken bricks and torn rafters.

Connie looked up and saw concerned faces crowding around the lip of the crater beside Susan; Ben and Elsie, Pippa – and Lisette.

'Jack!' That was Mr Wyngate's voice, strained with exertion. 'How far are you from the water? Can you safely let go so I can tie this off again? You're a hell of a weight to shoulder!'

Jack let go of the rope and splashed down beside Connie. Then he cupped his hands to his mouth and called, 'We're both safely in the water!' Now rescue was here he allowed himself a moment of mischief and whispered in Connie's ear, 'Is he calling me tubby? A lanky lad like me?'

Despite being soaked through, despite being tired and afraid, Connie giggled at Jack's joke. 'You're not tubby!' He certainly wasn't; with his shirt stuck to him she could see he was a slip of a lad. And yet he had such strength in him, and Connie felt it like a wave of warmth through her.

His humour gave a boost to her flagging energy, and so did the fact that Mr Wyngate and Lisette had arrived. She was aware of movement just out of sight. Their friends had retreated from the crater's dangerous edge, which had been disintegrating into dust and sludge under their feet.

'Should've looked where I was goin',' she whispered to Jack. But he shook his head and reached to take her hand.

From above, Connie could hear Lisette's voice, organising the kids in their rescue effort. She blinked up through the swirling dust that sparkled in the daylight as Mr Wyngate looked down over the edge of the crater and said, 'The rope's secure now. We'll haul you up one at a time. Just hold on to the rope and let us do the work.'

'Connie goes first!' Jack shouted, earning a sharp nod from Wyngate.

'Of course she does,' he replied. Then he retreated from the edge with the last instruction. 'Hold on tight! Ready?'

'Ready,' Connie called, as loudly as she could, but the effort made her splutter. She gripped the rope of grey, knotted sheets with both hands, and turned her face to Jack. 'You'll be out soon too,' she whispered. She hoped with all her heart that he would; she couldn't bear it if Jack was hurt because of her.

He nodded and said, 'Before you know it.' Then, to Connie's surprise, he darted a kiss to her cheek. 'Good luck!'

Connie blinked at him in surprise, the water dripping from her eyelashes. 'Jack, you—'

He'd kissed her cheek. She could feel a heated patch on her face where his lips had touched her, and she wanted to remember it for ever. Her heart rushed at the thought that maybe he liked her too. Maybe he'd want to be her boyfriend?

But before she could reply, she began to rise from the water. She could hear Mr Wyngate shouting for everyone to pull, and Pippa was barking as if she was giving them encouragement. Bit by bit, Connie rose higher and higher, until she could grab the edge of the crater and find purchase with her feet against the side to push herself up. Mud slipped beneath her feet and splattered into the water below.

She felt strong arms grasp her by her shoulders and pull her up and over the edge. She lay on solid ground, stunned at the bright sunlight of the summer evening. She felt the sharp edges of broken bricks and was prodded by twisted nails. Lisette was gently rubbing her back, and she coughed and coughed, the filthy water she'd swallowed spilling out from her lungs.

'Jack! You've got to save Jack!' she pleaded, so vehemently that she made herself cough again.

Wyngate was at her side too, already unknotting the rope from her waist as he asked her, 'Any injuries?' Then he called to Jack, 'Rope incoming!' and hauled the knotted sheets back into the bomb crater.

Connie couldn't find the strength to stand. She was shaking from head to foot, and her legs felt like blancmange.

'I caught my foot,' she replied, glancing down and realising she'd lost her shoe. She told herself not to worry; even though clothing was rationed and hard to find, losing a shoe was nothing compared to what could've happened to her in the water-filled crater. 'And cut my leg on something. But it don't matter!'

Wyngate glanced down at Connie's leg, then gave a nod. 'Rest. We'll get Jack out.' And he headed back towards the knotted sheet, which she could see was securely knotted to a twisted piece of metal that had once been part of someone's home.

'Everyone back to position!' Wyngate instructed the others. 'Jack, hold on and we'll have you out!'

She watched in utter amazement as she saw all her friends pull together to lift Jack out of the crater. Wyngate was at the front, his jacket off, straining with the effort of lifting Jack's weight. The cotton of his shirt was pulled taut across his broad shoulders as he heaved and heaved on the makeshift rope.

What did Wyngate do at the War Office? He was so strong, and yet he wore those smart suits as if he worked behind a desk all day. But Connie was sure that couldn't be all he did. And after all, he kept disappearing, and he flung himself into danger at home without a second thought, whenever he was needed.

Lisette was behind him in her uniform with FRANCE stitched on the shoulder, her lace-up heeled shoes scrabbling against the debris as she pulled with all her might. Susan was behind her, gripping the rope tight, her face pink with effort, and Ben and Elsie, despite being the youngest of the children, were pulling too.

Pippa ran up and down the line, her ears cocked, her tail wagging, barking for all she was worth.

Finally, Jack appeared over the edge of the crater, his face gritty from the dirty water. He pushed himself up over the lip and stood on solid ground once more, catching his breath. Elsie rushed towards him and flung her arms round her brother, holding him tight, and Pippa pawed against his leg.

Connie hugged her legs, shivering as she gazed up at Jack, so relieved that he was on dry ground again.

And that kiss. She could still feel it on her cheek.

'That's enough searching for today,' Wyngate said firmly. He dusted off his hands. 'Connie, you need to go home and get that leg cleaned up. You've both been lucky, let's not push it today.'

Lisette had put her arm round Connie and was helping her to her feet.

Even though she was unsteady on her legs, Connie shook her head, water spraying out from her plaits. 'We can't go home. We've got to find Ned!'

'Mr Wyngate's right,' Jack soothed, still hugging Elsie. 'We won't be any good to Ned if we're injured. Let's get some rest and start again tomorrow. Please, Connie.'

Connie nodded reluctantly, and then she started to cry. 'It's all my fault. He would never have run off if I hadn't shouted at him. And then I fell in that crater, and now we can't go and look for him!'

'You mustn't blame yourself,' Lisette said. She wiped Connie's face with a handkerchief, which was soon dirty, and Connie was worried that she'd washed Jack's kiss off her cheek as well. 'You've had a fright and you're hurt. Let's get you all back home, yes?'

An army truck drove by on the nearby road, its huge wheels bouncing easily over the debris strewn across the street. As soon as Wyngate saw it he was dashing across the bombsite so he could cut off the vehicle as it slowed to navigate the rubble that still covered the road. There was a short exchange with the driver, then Wyngate turned and hurried back towards the group.

'We've got a lift home,' he said. 'I'll carry Connie to the truck.' Then he looked over the little group and said, 'You're doing your best for Ned. But you need some rest too.'

Connie couldn't remember the last time anyone had carried her anywhere. She felt safe in Wyngate's strong arms, and it wasn't long before she was wrapped up in a grey army blanket in the back of the truck. Everyone else climbed in too, and Jack was given a blanket as well. They sat side by side, shivering, as the vehicle took them back over the river and through the streets home. Connie wished she could hold Jack's hand, but she didn't dare.

After a bath, which left the water filthier than any Connie had ever seen, she went up to bed early. She lay under the blankets, exhausted from her ordeal, and hoped the Luftwaffe wouldn't bother London tonight, so she could get a good sleep. She could hear the others' voices downstairs, but not distinctly, and as she dozed she thought about Ned.

She'd met him for the first time when she'd arrived at the farm that was her billet. He'd been evacuated there too, along with Robbie, another boy from the orphanage. They'd kept each other smiling, even though the farmer and his wife had forced them to work hard.

Ned, the eternally chipper younger boy, had come to feel like the brother Connie had never had. He was cheeky and naughty, and when they'd gone back to London, with no choice but to return to the orphanage, she'd seen him turn that cheekiness on the nuns. It was only when Robbie had been killed that Connie had seen his smile waver.

He'd lived in that orphanage all his life, right from when he was only a few hours old and the nuns had found him abandoned in a basket on the convent steps. Connie wondered how desperate his poor mum must've been to leave him there, but she couldn't have known how badly the nuns treated the children in their care. Although *care* was hardly the right word. Connie hadn't been there for long before she'd seen children whipped with the nuns' heavy rosary beads that they wore tied to their belts.

And yet, despite living with nuns who seemed to punish Ned for the circumstances of his birth, he'd never lost the sunny soul or the iron will he'd been born with. No number of beatings could knock that out of him, and Connie loved him deeply.

She had no idea who her father was, and sometimes – she'd never told the other children this, and especially not Ned – she daydreamed that maybe they shared the same dad. Maybe they really were brother and sister, in blood as well as spirit.

Connie shakily drew her handkerchief out from under her pillow and wiped her eyes as she started to cry.

'Oh, Ned, I'm so sorry I yelled at you,' she cried, her voice thick with tears and heavy with desperation. She couldn't hold back her despair and sobs racked her body. She felt so hollow, and shivered with fear for all the horrors that could've claimed her friend. 'Where have you gone?'

After all the children had gone up to bed, Lisette went into the front room with Wyngate. The lamp cast a gentle glow across the room and softened Wyngate's face. He had stayed close by since they got home, leaving only to walk to the phone box at the end of the road. There he rang Mr Gray to let him know where he and Lisette could be found, should there be news of Ned.

Jack's dismantled radio was waiting tidily in the corner for him, and Ben's joke book had been left open on the armchair. The family photo that belonged to Jack and Elsie watched them from the mantelpiece. Pippa's rubber bone lay beside the fireplace, and Susan's sewing box was in its place by the window. Schoolbooks populated the old wooden bookshelves. Some had been rescued from a bombed library, others had been donated by well-wishers. They were used by Connie and Jack to teach the other children.

Lisette took off her jacket and hung it over the back of an armchair, before picking up a magazine that had been left on the sofa. It was a copy of *Picture Show*. The Americans had given it to Ned on one of his tours of the city, and Gabriel Cooper, the muscled movie star with the perfect white smile, was beaming from the cover. Lisette felt a pang. She remembered how proud Ned had been of the magazine, a boy who'd had so little in life, but where was he?

'I'll stay with them,' Lisette told Wyngate in French, a tremble in her voice as she carefully put Ned's magazine in the rack by the armchair.

Wyngate looked shattered, and he must've been sore from all the effort to lift Connie and Jack out of the crater. 'You don't have to go home, you know,' she said. 'Why don't you stay too?'

Wyngate dropped onto the sofa with a long sigh of fatigue. He had already surrendered his jacket and tie, and looked as though he wasn't planning to go anywhere. For a moment he settled his gaze on Lisette, then he gave the hint of a smile and teased, 'Are you inviting me to spend the night with you, Mademoiselle Souchon?'

'Would I do that?' Lisette teased in reply, batting her eyelashes at him. Wyngate's gentle humour was soothing and it made her playful in return. 'Well, yes, I am, Monsieur Wyngate.'

'I'd be a fool to say no to that.' He looked up at her and smiled, then reached out and took her hand. Holding Lisette's gaze, he brought her hand to his lips and kissed it.

The back of Lisette's hand tingled at his kiss, and she dropped down onto the sofa beside him and rested her cheek against his shoulder.

They were growing closer and closer, Lisette knew. Although they weren't going to be intimate while they were at the children's house, they would still kiss and cuddle, and it felt as if their hearts were cleaving together through their touch. Lisette found herself closing her eyes so that when he was sent away again she could bring their closeness back to mind, and it shrank the distance between them, even though she never knew when he'd return.

She thought of him in Paris, dropped behind enemy lines by parachute on a mission and blending into the tired crowds. The city wasn't how she remembered it, now that Nazi flags lined the boulevards and the people went hungry; her own mother, her friends she'd left behind. Wyngate had told her that the stylish women in the city sometimes spent their money on hat trimmings rather than food to try to buoy up their spirits, and she wondered if her mother sometimes did the same; she had always been so chic. She closed her eyes for a moment, trying to bring back the Paris she had known.

'In Paris, when the weather was warm, I used to walk along the boulevards, and have an aperitif on a café terrace,' she said, her voice soft with reminiscence. What a world that was to remember, where children didn't go missing in air raids. 'I would watch the people go by – the elegant ladies in their summer dresses walking their tiny dogs, and the men in their overalls going from job to job sparing a moment to look up and smile at the sunshine. You could hear the flower-sellers calling and it sounded as though they were singing. And I would go and stand on a bridge over the river and watch the boats full of tourists and the tugs going by, and see the booksellers at their stands on the shore. The city was always full of life.'

Wyngate rested his head against her shoulder. 'Would you live there again?' he asked. But Lisette wasn't thinking of just herself strolling along the boulevards of Paris any more, but of a day when she would be there with Wyngate at her side. 'When the country's free?'

Lisette closed her eyes for a moment as she thought of the awful news about Faucon, executed for fighting in the resistance. 'I would love to – us, together. We could live in an apartment in Montmartre and look down at Paris as if it was ours, as far as we could see. But so many awful things have happened there. Would I think of those monsters marching down the Champs Élysées? Would you want to live there too?'

Wyngate drew in a breath, his expression thoughtful and his brow furrowed. Then he nodded. 'Yes. Because if we let their memory dictate what we do, then they win. They don't keep me away now and they won't keep me away when we've kicked them back to Berlin.' He kissed her cheek tenderly. 'I want us to see it together one day.'

Warmth rushed through Lisette. Through all her visions of bombsites and fear and despair, there was hope. There was Paris, with her and Wyngate, sitting together on that terrace, their chairs drawn up close to each other, drinking aperitifs as the flower-sellers called and the tugs went by on the river. It glowed in a golden light in her mind, but then she felt guilty. How could she be dreaming about their future together when Ned was missing? When they didn't know if he had a future at all?

'I want that so much,' she whispered, stroking her fingertips against the stubble on Wyngate's jaw. 'I think of peace – I dream of it. We have to win this war, Adam. I think of the people across Europe fighting – not just soldiers in uniform, but men like Faucon, who are caught and killed. And then...' Her breath caught as the memory came to her of a newspaper article a few weeks before. Her hand dropped from Wyngate's jaw and she clutched his arm, as if being close to him would somehow diminish the horror. 'That village in Czechoslovakia... Lidice. Hundreds of people, slaughtered in revenge because the resistance fighters had killed an SS officer. And my mother, and all those other resistance fighters— every time they blow up a bridge or shoot an officer, those Nazi reprisals are so cruel, so vicious...'

In Lidice, children had been massacred among the adults. How evil did a regime need to be to mow down such young, innocent lives? She thought of Ned, wherever he had gone; no children were safe in a war.

'If Hitler thinks slaughtering a village will terrify the rest of Europe into giving up the fight, he's wrong. It just puts more fire in our bellies.' Wyngate lifted his head, his jaw set. Then he said quietly, 'I've been there in the middle of it, Lis, seen a resistance hero shot in cold blood in the town square. I watched ten more people step up to take his place in the fight. They might have taken Tobruk, but they won't win.'

Lisette hadn't known that he'd seen a resistance fighter shot. She went cold at the thought. He couldn't really tell her what he'd witnessed; there was too much risk. He shouldn't even tell her anything about her own mother. And yet, how much danger had he been in? What if the guns had turned on him?

Then there was Tobruk; the news had been shattering. The Nazis had taken the Libyan harbour town, and with it several tank regiments and their troops, and battalions of Indian and Gurkha soldiers. And yet, Wyngate was right. They had to keep pushing, they had to keep fighting, because the deaths of gallant men and women, and children too, couldn't be for nothing.

Lisette ran her hand across his back. She could feel the tension in his muscles. 'You took all the strain, pulling the children up.'

Wyngate circled his right shoulder. 'I thought I'd pull my arm out of its socket catching that rope. Jack's heavier than he looks.'

Lisette rubbed his right shoulder, circling her thumb against the muscle through his shirt. 'The children are growing up fast. Jack and Connie... well, perhaps you have noticed?'

He turned to look at her, his gaze soft with affection. She never saw him look at anyone else like that, as though he cherished her. Perhaps he lacked the words to say it, but he didn't have to.

'Aren't they a bit young for all that?'

Lisette chuckled and went on rubbing his shoulder. She could feel all the power and strength in him, which had so many times made her feel safe. And even though she was carefully stroking away the knots in his muscles, she still felt that building closeness between them, as if the heat of her desire for him was reaching through her touch and into his tired body.

'The way they keep looking at each other – I can tell,' Lisette said. She paused to brush a kiss to Wyngate's neck, breathing in the warm spiciness of his cologne, before going on. 'There's a special smile that I only see them give to each other. And when Connie's looking away, I see Jack gazing at her. Then Connie does the same when Jack's not looking. He turns back and she's suddenly very busy. And blushing. They're sweet on each other, Adam!'

'Well, I'm sweet on you,' he teased, leaning back to kiss her. His kiss was soft and deep and Lisette responded, warmth filling her body. It was as if a magnet was drawing them closer and closer. Then their kiss gently broke. 'Do we need to say something? I'd rather go toe to toe with a tank.'

Lisette laughed. It was hard to picture how Wyngate would approach the matter, and she wasn't sure how she would either.

'We're not their parents, but we're the closest they have,' she replied, but her voice trailed into a sob as Ned's cherub-like face came to mind again. She and Wyngate had become responsible for the six children, and she couldn't bear to let them down. Her mother had always been there to look out for her, and she now had to do the same for these motherless children. All six of them had their different needs, and even while Ned was out there, lost in the city, Lisette needed to think about the growing attraction between Jack and Connie.

For all that she'd just talked about Connie blushing, now Lisette could feel her face heating with embarrassment. She stroked Wyngate's shoulder again, and could feel the muscle loosening. 'I've had to talk to Connie and Susan about... women's things. But I didn't talk *de la rose et du chou* with them,' Lisette said. She added the English near-equivalent, 'The birds and the bees. I just worry – we don't want things to go too far between them. Jack is a sensible young man, and I don't think he would. But even so...'

'The birds and the bees?' Wyngate chuckled. 'Even you and I haven't had that conversation yet.'

Lisette bit her lip, blushing even more. It was true, they hadn't. She could feel the air thicken around them, thrumming with longing. 'I know, Adam, but...'

'I've got a feeling that I don't have a choice,' Wyngate said good-naturedly. He snuggled closer to Lisette and kicked his feet up to rest on the coffee table. 'I'll talk to Jack once this Ned thing settles down, okay? And I'll give Ned a talking-to about taking off while I'm at it.'

'Thank you,' Lisette replied, and kissed him softly again. She drew her lips away as her thoughts returned again to Ned. 'Perhaps we could get a telephone installed here? I know it's not cheap, but it would mean that if Ned goes off to wherever he's gone – and if it's to Margate on a jolly with the wide boys I will *not* be pleased – he could at least telephone the others to let them know where he is.'

She hoped Ned was just being naughty and thoughtless, because the thought that anything else had happened to him was too much to bear. Seeing Connie and Jack soaked through and caked with dirt from the bomb crater had reminded her of just how dangerous the city was, even when the bombs weren't falling.

Wyngate nodded. 'I'll get a phone installed,' he agreed. Then he kissed Lisette tenderly. 'I've been like Ned. Too grown up, too young,' he reminded her. Wyngate had been an orphan too, forced to care for himself on the streets when he was nothing but a little boy. 'He'll come home, Lis.'

They snuggled down on the sofa together, fitting together as if they were two parts of a whole, and shared a pillow and a light summer blanket. Lisette listened to Wyngate's soft breathing, and soon they were asleep in each other's arms, his lips still resting against her hair.

But she never seemed to sleep deeply these days; she was always half listening out for the wail of the air-raid siren. Wyngate slept deeply though, holding her in his embrace. Lisette wondered what he dreamed of, what he'd seen, but she took comfort in the fact that, tonight at least, he was peaceful.

She was dreaming about being in the office, with the tapping sound of typewriters all around her, when the noise pulled her out of the dream: someone was knocking on the front door.

'Adam, Adam, wake up,' she urged him as she fought away the last of her sleep. Wyngate was suddenly wide awake at the sound of the very gentle knock, sitting bolt upright as he listened.

When the soft knock came again, he slipped from the sofa and told Lisette in a whisper, 'I'll see who it is.'

Ned had a key. He wouldn't need to knock. So who was at the door?

Lisette couldn't stay sitting. She got to her feet and anxiously clasped her hands. 'I'll come with you,' she said. Together they padded into the hallway on bare feet, and Wyngate turned on the light before opening the front door.

To Lisette's surprise she found herself looking at Mr Gray. His face was white, his eyes heavy with tiredness as he nodded his head in an uncharacteristically silent greeting.

Lisette knew at once that something was very, very wrong. It felt as if a lead weight was plummeting inside her.

'Oh, no, it's Ned, isn't it?' she whispered urgently. 'What's happened?'

'I have received a telephone call,' Mr Gray said sombrely. She saw his throat bob as he swallowed. 'A boy's body has been found on a bombsite near the Tower. He has been taken to the Tower Bridge Mortuary.'

Wyngate shook his head wordlessly as Gray went on. 'The poor lad matches young Ned's description. I'm so sorry.'

Lisette's legs buckled and she desperately grabbed Wyngate's arm.

SEVENTEEN
LISETTE

Dark specks danced in front of Lisette's eyes and she struggled to breathe. She clung to Wyngate, who was pale, haunted.

'Ned...' she gasped. How could that bright spark of life have been put out so tragically? 'We will have to see him. Oh, poor Ned.'

'Yes, I'm afraid there's a need to identify the poor lad,' Gray said gently. 'Someone who knows him well.'

Wyngate put his arm round Lisette's waist and held her as she clung to him. She saw his jaw tighten a moment before he told Gray, 'I'll do it.'

'And me too,' Lisette added. The fact that there was something practical for them to do gave her strength despite the grief that was swelling up inside her. She stood firm, even as she wiped away her tears. 'We'll go together.'

Lisette wasn't surprised when Wyngate shook his head. 'No, Lis, you don't want to see this. Stay here.'

Gray reached out and touched Lisette's arm lightly. 'I'll sit with you while Mr Wyngate goes,' he said kindly. 'I wouldn't advise you to go.'

But she wanted to go. She wanted to be there for Ned, even

if he could no longer know. And besides, she wanted to be there for Wyngate. He'd identified so strongly with the orphaned boy, and she couldn't bear for him to be there alone with the lifeless little body.

Back when the Blitz had first started, Lisette had seen her boyfriend, Tom, lying dead on a stretcher. The memory kept coming back to her, and yet she'd needed to see him. And she needed to see Ned now.

'You are both so considerate of me, but if I stay here I'll keep thinking of him, all alone at the mortuary,' she replied. She wiped away more tears before she looked up at Wyngate and added, 'And I don't want you to go there by yourself.'

Wyngate studied her face, then nodded. Seeing their agreement made, Mr Gray said, 'Take my car. I shall stay here with the children; if they wake, the two of you have been called into the Ministry on an urgent matter.' Then he bowed his head for a moment before lifting it again. 'I'm so sorry for the little mite.'

Elsie had put some flowers from the garden in a jam jar on the hall table. Lisette took one of them, a peach-coloured rose, with her trembling hand. She would give it to Ned.

Lisette and Wyngate went out to Gray's car, which was drawn up to the kerb outside. It was a bright blue Bugatti, its soft-top roof folded down. On another day in another life, how Lisette would've loved to take a spin in the fancy car through the country lanes in the sunshine, her hair billowing out behind her. But not tonight. And she wasn't sure she could ever be frivolous again.

She sat in the passenger seat, holding the rose, not noticing that she'd pricked her thumb on one of the thorns until she spotted the blood. She glanced at Wyngate as he drove. How on earth would they break the news to the other children? And how would Connie react, when she still blamed herself for Ned running away?

The streetlights were heavily shaded for the blackout, their beam focused down so much that it was like passing between spotlights on a stage. It added to the sense of unreality, and part of Lisette wondered if perhaps this was all a dream. But she knew that of course it wasn't.

The car's headlamps were hooded to minimise the light they would spill, and had been covered in black film. The letters *WO*, for *War Office*, had been cut through the film, to show that the car was on official business. With so little light to illuminate their way, Wyngate drove with painstaking care to avoid the debris that was scattered everywhere.

Wyngate was silent as they drove, but Lisette could sense the tension seeping from him. She could see it in the set of his mouth, hear it even in the breaths he was taking. As they crossed a silent junction where every corner seemed to be nothing but devastation, he suddenly slammed his hand against the wheel and spat, 'This bloody war!'

Lisette touched his arm. Anger and despair radiated from him, and there was nothing she could do to take it away from him. Neither of them could stop the war; all they could do was give their all to the war effort.

'No child should have to die in a war,' Lisette whispered. 'Not one. Oh, Ned.'

'I hope to God he isn't Ned. But even if he isn't, he's somebody's son,' Wyngate said. 'He matters to somebody. Somebody's missing him.'

Lisette drew in a breath, trying to hold back a sob. Then she glanced at Wyngate again. He'd never known his father, and after his mother had died he'd been lost on the London streets.

Would anyone have missed him? Lisette wanted to believe that every lost child was missed by someone; it was too bleak to think otherwise. And yet sometimes there was no one to stand by the little grave and weep.

Eventually, they arrived at Tower Bridge, with its turrets reaching for the sky. The Luftwaffe hadn't bombed the iconic structure, but then Lisette had heard someone at Jasper's say that they must've been using it as a landmark so they'd know where to locate the docks that were their target. She shivered. The brutality of such deliberate, mechanised death made her cold. And this was the result: a dead little boy in a morgue.

It hadn't occurred to Lisette until Wyngate drove down beneath the bridge that he knew exactly where he was going. He had had cause to visit this unhappy place before, then. The masked headlamps cut through the darkness in the shadow of the bridge and she saw two large stone archways in their low beam. Then he pulled the car in to the kerb and turned off the engine.

'I don't want you to come.' He turned in his seat. 'Please, Lis.'

'You can't do this on your own,' Lisette told him. She tried to ignore the looming archways under the bridge, where the mortuary waited for them. 'I know you've had to go through your life alone, but you don't have to any more. You've got me, Adam. I want to come – for you, and for Ned.'

Wyngate studied her face for a few moments, then nodded. 'You're bloody strong, Lisette.' Then he opened his car door and climbed out.

Lisette got out too, and linked her arm through Wyngate's as they went to the archway, the rose still clasped in her other hand. Tears were rising in her eyes, blurring her vision. Wyngate pressed a button, and the heavy door opened.

The mortuary attendant – a grey-haired man in a long white apron – stood back to let them into the small vestibule, his expression grave. The walls were whitewashed, and the small space smelt of the river.

'Evening,' he said. His voice was kind even though he must've welcomed people to this grim place many times. 'Have you come to see the little lad?'

Lisette nodded. Now they were here, she felt too oppressed

by sadness to speak. All the lives cut off; accidents on the river, or people too full of despair to carry on, their bodies left here to be claimed. And how many people had been brought here since the bombings had begun? How many children?

'We have,' Wyngate confirmed, his face betraying nothing once more. He had put on the mask of the man from the Ministry again.

'Would you mind coming this way, please?' the attendant said. He opened another door that led off from the vestibule, and took them into a small room.

A small figure lay under a pure white sheet as if it had snowed over a sleeping child. Lisette tightened her arm round Wyngate's. She could feel her tears rising again, tightening her throat and prickling her eyes.

Wordlessly, Wyngate tensed the muscles in his arm. He was here beside her. They would face this together.

Somewhere Lisette could hear a clock ticking in the heavy silence, but beyond that there was nothing. Wyngate looked down at the sheet, then nodded to the attendant.

'Go on.'

The attendant swallowed. 'The ambulance driver who found him said he wouldn't have felt a thing,' he said. 'He fell and broke his neck. He looks like he's asleep. He... he looks like a little angel.'

Lisette thought fondly of all the times she'd seen that halo of curls and thought the same thing. Ned, the little angel, who was anything but.

The attendant drew back the sheet, as gently as if he was trying not to wake up the boy who lay underneath.

Lisette saw the curls, she saw the lifeless face. She saw the scratches and the dirt. Poor boy. Her tears rushed up all at once, overwhelming her.

This bloody war.

She was choked by so much sadness, so much despair. The dark spots danced before her eyes again and she clung on to Wyngate as her legs gave way beneath her.

EIGHTEEN

CONNIE

Something was dragging Connie down into the dark, filthy water, a claw tight round her ankle, cutting into her skin. She windmilled her arms, trying to keep above the surface, but she couldn't fight against the monster that had caught her. Ned was down there too, down in the murk, trapped and afraid. She tried to breathe but swallowed water. She tried to scream, but no sound came out. The last sight she saw was her friends, high above her on a platform, staring down as she vanished from view. And behind them, that creepy old woman, laughing as Connie fell. She—

Connie forced open her eyes and lay back on the pillow, her hair stuck to her face with sweat as she stared into the dark of the bedroom. It was a nightmare, just a nightmare. She was all right. She wasn't in that crater any more. Jack had rescued her, Jack and her friends.

Even so, her heart was hammering, and she wrestled with the blankets that had tangled around her. She needed a glass of water to calm down.

She softly placed her feet on the bedroom floor, to avoid waking Elsie and Susan; Connie could hear their steady, contented breaths. But Pippa stirred. As Connie's eyes grew accustomed to the dark, she saw the little dog lift her head. She gave a soft bark.

'It's all right, Pip, don't worry about me,' Connie whispered. She stroked Pippa's head, before pulling a dressing gown over her pyjamas and picking up the shaded blackout torch that she kept beside the bed. Barefoot, she padded out of the bedroom, following the weak light thrown by her torch.

She heard a footstep somewhere in the house. Someone else was awake, too.

She paused at the top of the stairs. 'Jack?' she whispered into the darkness. 'Is that you?'

'Did I wake you?' Jack stepped into the shaft of moonlight that illuminated the foot of the stairs. With the windows open to let in a breeze, the blackout curtains must have been disturbed somewhere in the sleeping house, Connie supposed. 'I was just working on some radio bits. I couldn't sleep and Mr W and Lisette are in the living room.'

Connie came down the stairs towards him. He was thinking about Ned, wasn't he? That was why he couldn't sleep.

'Nah, you didn't wake me. You're quiet as a mouse when you're working on that radio. Wonder when we'll be able to hear what the Germans do?'

'Shouldn't be long now,' Jack whispered. 'Me and Dad used to tinker all the time with engines and bikes and everything really. He'd love having a wireless to fiddle about with in the POW camp.' He took a couple of steps towards the stairs. 'You couldn't sleep either?'

'I had a nightmare,' Connie told him with an embarrassed shrug. But Jack wouldn't judge her, would he? He'd kissed her, and, as she looked into his tired eyes, she touched her fingertips to the spot where his lips had met her cheek. 'Dreamed I was in the crater again, and that Ned was down there and all... Were you thinkin' about him too?'

Jack nodded. He looked suddenly young in his striped pyjamas, his hair disordered from a sleepless night as he sank down to sit on the stairs. 'I think about him all the time,' he admitted.

Connie came down the last few steps and sat down beside him. She turned off her torch and set it down at her feet, then took Jack's hand in her own. It felt larger than hers, and strong, and yet he was still vulnerable.

'Me too,' she said, squeezing Jack's hand. *And this is all my fault.* She was quiet for a moment, before a starburst of panic broke inside her and her words rushed out, 'What'll we do if we can't find him?'

Jack swallowed, then said, 'We will.' Yet Connie caught the sigh that followed and he must have known, because he admitted, 'I don't know, Con. I can't let myself think about that. We can't lose our Ned.'

Connie bit her lip for a moment, then said, a sob in her voice, 'We've already lost Robbie, and that was awful.' She thought back to the smiling boy with the cow's-lick hair, who had been Ned's guiding light at the orphanage, and who had been evacuated with them to the farm. One dreadful day, Robbie had been killed, all because they lived in a dangerous city. 'I still think about him sometimes, when Ned's bein' cheeky, I think, *Robbie would be laughing his head off right now.* Maybe he is, if he's looking down at us from heaven. And maybe that means he's keeping an eye on Ned, too.'

She wiped a tear away on her sleeve and rested her head on Jack's shoulder, wondering if the thought of Robbie watching over them gave him even the tiniest crumb of comfort. Jack put his arm round Connie's shoulder and held her gently. She wished she could sing to cheer them both up, but her throat was too tight with worry for her to get a note out.

They sat there for a little while before the door to the sitting-room opened and, to Connie's surprise, she found herself looking into the shadows at the towering figure of Mr Gray.

She lifted her head from Jack's shoulder and blinked, wondering if she was still dreaming. He was wearing a tailcoat, polished shoes and a spotless white shirt and tie, as if he'd been dancing at the Ritz. What on earth was Mr Gray doing in their sitting room in the middle of the night?

'A sleepless night?' he whispered.

'Yeah,' Connie replied, staring up at him. 'I had a nightmare. We're worryin' about Ned. We *will* find him, won't we?'

'We will!' Jack said firmly. 'We will, Con.' Then he looked at Mr Gray and asked, 'I don't want to sound rude, but... what're you doing here?'

Mr Gray took his monocle from within his tailcoat and lifted it to his mouth. He breathed on the lens then shook it, before screwing it into place on its length of dark silk ribbon.

'Mr Wyngate and Mademoiselle Souchon were called into the War Office on an urgent matter,' he explained. 'And yours truly was enlisted to mind the fort. Think yourselves lucky the youngsters are all asleep, or I would be presiding over organised mayhem!' And he gave them a beaming smile, then added with a more gentle tone, 'I'm so sorry about little Ned. How quiet the house is without him.'

Connie thought of Mr Wyngate and Lisette, heading off into the night together. It must've been serious, whatever it was that had called them back to the office after dark. She wondered what they did, especially Lisette, who had swapped evening gowns for a khaki uniform. It had something to do with the fact that Lisette could speak French, and Connie thought about that not-so-distant country on the other side of the Channel, held hostage by Nazis.

But her mind travelled back to Ned. Nazis were one thing, but she'd let her friend down, and she wasn't sure she could ever forgive herself for losing her temper and pushing him away.

'He's like my little brother,' Connie said, her voice cracking, 'and...' *It's my fault he's gone.* She took a deep breath, chasing the thought away, then she gently released Jack's hand and got to her feet. 'How's about I make us some nice cocoa, then we can try to get back to sleep? We won't be no good searchin' for Ned tomorrow if we're tired.'

But Mr Gray held up his hand. 'How about *I* make the cocoa?' he offered. 'You all do enough.'

Jack gave a soft laugh. 'I've never had cocoa made by a duke before.'

'Thanks, Mr Gray,' Connie said, and sank back onto the step beside Jack. 'It's nice bein' looked after.'

And when Ned came home, Connie would look after him. She'd spoil her little brother and look after him always. He'd never want to run away again.

NINETEEN
LISETTE

'This isn't our Ned.'

Lisette wiped her hand across her face, chasing away the spots in front of her eyes. It wasn't Ned, but it was someone's son, a child who shouldn't have died.

The attendant nodded. 'Thank you. We'll keep an eye out for your boy, although I hope we don't see him here, of course... And hopefully this little chap's folk will come to find him.' He drew the sheet back over the nameless boy's body.

Lisette, feeling stronger now, took a step forward and laid the rose from the garden on top of the sheet.

'If nobody claims him, will you let me know via the War Office?' Wyngate handed the attendant a small visiting card. 'I want to make sure he's properly laid to rest.'

The attendant took the card. 'Of course, sir. It's the youngsters like this one that make my job the hardest. I should like to see him have a nice funeral.'

Wyngate was still looking down at the small figure, shrouded in white. He reached out one hand and, very briefly, touched the rose that Lisette had left there. Then he took in a deep breath and looked at the attendant.

'If anyone does come for him, give them my card,' Wyngate instructed. 'In case they need help with the funeral.' Then he turned to Lisette and took her hand.

There was nothing more that could be said; nothing more that they could do. They headed back to the children's house in Whitechapel. They gave Gray the news; it wasn't Ned; there was hope he was still alive. And yet, another little boy had died.

Lisette kept picturing a poster she'd seen from the time of the Spanish Civil War. The Nazis had helped the Spanish fascists, perfecting their skills of murder from the sky, and had bombed civilians in towns and cities across Spain. The poster was stark with its imagery and its warning. Above the photograph of a dead girl, killed in a fascist bombing raid, it read: IF YOU TOLERATE THIS YOUR CHILDREN WILL BE NEXT.

Wordlessly, Lisette curled up around Wyngate on the sofa. He wrapped his arms round her, cradling her in the darkness. Somehow, she managed to sleep, although her dreams were restless and frightening; dark shadows crawling across bombsites, flowing like spilled oil.

The next morning, the children were fretful and worried. They picked at their breakfasts, wanting instead to be outside hunting for Ned, and Lisette had to encourage them to eat up, telling them that it would give them strength to find Ned. They had no idea about the dead boy, and Lisette didn't want to tell them about him.

Lisette and Wyngate headed off to the War Office together. They stood near the doors to their carriage, Wyngate's arm round her waist, as the train rattled through the tunnels underneath London. At each station on the Underground, evidence of people sleeping there the night before could still be seen:

sheets of cardboard to keep away the chill, forgotten blankets, lost handkerchiefs. But the owners would be back that evening, sheltering again, under the gaze of the figures in the government information posters. They'd sleep as a Land Girl in a field beamed at the sun, and a pig lifted the lid of a rubbish bin, pleading for kitchen scraps.

The train was busy with travellers: smartly dressed men and women heading to offices, and people in uniform. Some carried huge kitbags, off to be deployed or heading for training, while others were travelling home for a short spell of leave. Lisette watched the people travelling to work, and she wondered if among them were the parents of the unknown boy.

They arrived at the War Office. Just as they went past the reception desk, a woman hurried over with a folded piece of paper. She was in the dark blue uniform of the Wrens, the women's branch of the Royal Navy, who, along with women from the Army and Air Force, helped to keep the administration side of the War Office running.

'Mr Wyngate, we received a call for you,' she said. Wyngate took the note with a nod of acknowledgement and unfolded it. Lisette watched as his eyes scanned the paper before he slipped it into his pocket.

'They've found the lad's parents.'

Lisette released a breath she hadn't realised she'd been holding. 'Oh... thank goodness. Thank goodness. That poor boy, and his poor parents. But at least he has a name now. I couldn't bear the thought of him lying there in that grim place without a name.'

They went off to their separate offices, or wherever it was that Wyngate went. Lisette's thoughts wouldn't settle. Where on earth was Ned? He'd been missing for over thirty hours by now. He'd spent two nights on his own, and nobody knew where he was.

How could a boy just disappear?

As she sat down at her desk and pulled towards her the buff envelope containing her first translation of the day, a thought occurred to her. The nuns had been protesting outside the theatre before the show had started. What if Ned had run straight into them and they'd carried him away?

But she shook her head, dismissing the idea. There would've been people in the street who would've seen if the nuns had grabbed Ned, and he wasn't the sort of boy to go quietly, either. He would've turned into a ball of rage, whirling out of their grasps like a dervish.

No, she couldn't blame the nuns for this.

Lisette had been working for an hour or more when a new message arrived on her desk to translate.

BATTLESHIPS HAVE BEEN ARRIVING AT LE HAVRE. QUITE A FLEET THEY'VE GOT HERE. THE GERHILDE, INGOLSTADT, VON SCHONERER, SIEGRUNE, AMFORTAS. SOMEONE OVERHEARD THE CREW: THEY'VE BEEN SENT FROM HAMBURG.

There were all sorts of ways that the origin of the Nazi battleships could've been discovered. Lisette pictured a bar, where sailors who'd had a bit too much to drink had said more than they should've done, in earshot of a barmaid who just happened to be in the resistance. And there it was, the *Amfortas*, the ship that Capitaine Ardouin had told Lisette to look out for.

Lisette wrote up her translation and dropped it straight onto Capitaine Ardouin's desk. 'The *Amfortas*,' she told Ardouin, who snapped up the folder right away.

'Thank you, Lisette,' the capitaine said, and Lisette went back to work.

As she picked up her pen she thought of Hamburg, where the ships had travelled from. A drop of ink pooled on the nib, threatening to splash across her blotting pad.

Hamburg. She'd had a friend from there, before the war. Sidonie Valentin had been a singer, just like Lisette. They'd met in Paris when Sidonie had got a residency at a club there. They'd got on so well, and Sidonie had begged Lisette to visit her back in Hamburg. She'd always intended to go, but life got in the way, and Lisette moved to London. The idea of visiting Hamburg had seemed to get more and more remote as Lisette heard more about the Nazis taking over German life, but she worried about Sidonie, and felt guilty that she'd broken her promise to her.

Sidonie had been an enthusiastic letter-writer, never without a book of stamps in her purse; Lisette still had a shoebox under her bed full of her letters.

She had written to tell Lisette that the club she worked at was being targeted for letting 'degenerate' acts on the stage – and that included Sidonie, for the simple fact that she was Jewish. Lisette told her to come to London – that Jasper would give her a slot at his club. But Sidonie was unbowed; she wasn't going to let the bullies win.

Then, one day, Sidonie wrote to tell Lisette that she was being sent away from Hamburg. 'But not for long,' she'd insisted. Another letter came, about a week later, sent from a railway station somewhere in Germany. It wasn't luxurious, Sidonie had said, but never mind.

Another letter followed. Lisette's heart had skipped a beat when she read it. This place wasn't as nice as the last. And the train was filling up. But Sidonie was still cheerful – or appeared to be in her letter.

Another came. It was obvious that Sidonie was unhappy,

and that the letter was written in a hurry. They were nearly at their destination. Sidonie was hungry and cold. She wanted to go home. She signed off with a smudged letter S.

Lisette didn't hear from Sidonie again. A few months after her last letter arrived, war broke out and there was no chance of any more letters arriving from Germany anyway.

Lisette had never known what had happened to Sidonie. Was her friend still alive? She had asked Wyngate, hoping he'd know something, just like he'd told her about her mother in Paris. But a closed look had come over his face; he'd told her there was no way for them to know.

She got up from her desk and dropped her translation into the wire basket with all the other buff folders. But she didn't see the basket or the folders; her mind was taken over by a carousel of faces. Ned's, Sidonie's, Tom's, Mrs Dupree's, the dead boy from the morgue. Round and round the faces went, the faces of the dead and the disappeared.

She did her best to carry on, and picked up another translation. But as she worked her way through it, she shivered. The Gestapo had rounded up more members of the French resistance and had coldly executed them in a village square. She thought, as she did every day, of her mother. And she thought of Wyngate going off into occupied territory. If the Nazis ever caught him on his missions, she'd lose him for ever, wouldn't she? He'd be another face added to the roll-call of the dead.

Lunchtime came, and Lisette went down to reception to meet Wyngate. They were planning to eat at the nearby British Restaurant, but she wasn't sure how much she could eat. All she could think about was Ned. Was he hungry, was he hurt?

She saw Wyngate there, already waiting for her. He was smoking a cigarette.

'Have you heard anything?' she asked him in French. She was sure that if there was any news about Ned, he would've come to tell her as soon as he had heard it, but she still had to ask.

Wyngate shook his head. 'But we will,' he said. 'I see a lot of myself in Ned. He'll turn up none the worse for wear.'

'But he hasn't,' Lisette reminded him as they headed for the front door. 'He could be hungry and frightened, and we don't know where he is.'

It was so hard to picture Ned without his smile, but he'd be afraid, wherever he was. And as she thought of him, another image crowded its way before her mind's eye. The square of a French village; there were no loaves in the bakery's window, and the butcher's shop was nearly empty. Nazi flags hung on the front of the town hall, and six valiant resistance fighters were dragged across the cobbles.

The report of the bullets echoed in Lisette's mind, and blood stained the cobbles, as red as the flowers cascading from the window boxes around the square.

She glanced at Wyngate. No, she couldn't bear the thought that she could lose him like that. She couldn't.

'We should have kept him safe,' she said. 'I just want to keep everyone safe. Even you. I can't lose more people I love, Adam.'

'It's been a hell of a day,' Wyngate murmured. He seemed to be spitting out the words, as though it was an effort to find them.

He knew about the executions, didn't he, of course. He wouldn't need a translation to have understood the message.

'Don't go back over there, Adam,' Lisette said to him. 'You can't. It's too dangerous.'

'We can't have this conversation here, you know that,' Wyngate reminded her. 'It's my job, Lisette. I don't have a choice.'

'But you do!' Lisette insisted, in a hissed whisper. 'It doesn't have to be your job.' Even as the words came out she knew it was a ridiculous thing to say. He couldn't give it up; it was part of him. He wanted to serve the country of his birth in its darkest days. And yet she couldn't bear the thought of grieving for another loved one, especially not the man whose arms she had slept in last night. The man she—

'Don't you know I think about you all the time?' Wyngate asked. 'You and the children and all that we've got here?'

Lisette knew that he did, of course she knew. 'Then stay. For me. For the children. And think of Ned. He needs a firm voice to guide him. He's so young, he's just a boy.'

Wyngate flicked his cigarette into the ashtray beside the door, then pinched the bridge of his nose wearily. 'Ned isn't like a child,' he explained. 'I don't know how to explain it to you, Lisette. You have to understand—'

'There is nothing to understand!' Lisette snapped, as if a dam had burst inside her, setting loose all her fear and anxiety. 'He's a little boy, and he's alone. There is danger everywhere in this city. You saw what happened to Connie yesterday – what if we're not there to pull him out?'

'We can't *be* everywhere!' he told her firmly. 'Nor can the kids. She could've been killed because Ned took off!'

'You are blaming Ned!' Lisette shook her head. 'He and Connie are like brother and sister. That girl dotes on him – she is beside herself with worry and she blames herself too.'

They were walking down the steps in front of the War Office now, out into the sunshine where Blitz-worn Londoners were enjoying the summer heat. Ties were loosened, and people fanned themselves with newspapers. But Lisette didn't notice. She felt as if her blood was boiling as it rushed through her veins, all the tension and fear of the last few days reaching a fever pitch.

'She cares, the other kids care, and *I* care.' Lisette angrily hurled out the words. 'But right now I don't think you do!'

Wyngate stopped walking abruptly, earning a loud tut from

a fast-moving lady in a Wren uniform who nearly barrelled straight into his back. He stared at Lisette, then said, 'I'm not hungry any more.'

With that he turned on his heel and stalked away into the crowd.

TWENTY
LISETTE

Lisette spent the whole afternoon regretting what she'd said in that moment of desperate fear and frustration. But there was no way to unsay her words. After she'd finished her shift, she travelled to Whitechapel to see the children. She didn't see Wyngate in the War Office's reception or on the stairs.

Why had she told him that he didn't care? It was one of the most hurtful things she could've said to the man who'd taken on the group of children with her. Of course he viewed Ned's disappearance differently from her. Although Lisette hadn't had a father around when she was a child, her mother had doted on her, and there were 'aunties' in their neighbourhood who looked out for her – local women who would drop round to mind her if her mother was at work. There had been nothing like that for Wyngate and, like Ned, he'd suffered in the orphanage at the hands of the nuns.

Wyngate and Ned had both had to grow up too early. And yet, Ned was still a child in many ways, and he needed to be looked after.

When she arrived at the children's house, she glanced at the window, hoping she'd see Ned's cheeky face peering out from behind the curtain. But he wasn't there.

She let herself in and went to the kitchen, where the children had just eaten. Plates and glasses stood on the draining board by the sink, along with valves and lights from the radio Jack was working on. She could see from the children's downcast expressions that Ned still hadn't come home.

'We was just having our tea,' Connie explained as she untied her apron. She had a large plaster on her leg, where it'd been scratched under the water in the crater, but it seemed to be just one more battle scar for her. 'We're just about to go out searchin' again.'

Ben and Susan were putting away the freshly washed crockery and pans, while Jack was stitching a button back onto one of Ben's shirts. He looked up as Lisette came into the room and said, 'I think I've cracked the radio. When Ned comes home, it'll be all working good as new. We can listen in to Europe!'

Lisette knelt to fuss Pippa. 'He'll be very impressed,' she told him. 'In fact, all of us will.'

She'd be able to hear what was happening in France, perhaps, for good or bad.

Wyngate especially, she thought, seeing as he'd given the radio to Jack as a project, because he was a bright lad and needed the chance. How could she have said he didn't care?

'We're heading out for a couple of hours,' Jack explained. 'Until night falls. I asked Connie to stay here and rest that leg, but she's not the sort of girl you can tell what to do.' And he glanced towards his friend with a smile, then put the shirt down on the chair beside him. 'Ready, troops?'

Connie took her first aid bag from the hook on the back of the door and slung it over her shoulder. Elsie clipped Pippa's lead to her collar, and Ben and Susan held hands. At a gentle command from Jack, all of the children held up one hand to show him that they were wearing their identity bracelets. On Connie's wrist, Ned's bracelet jangled against her own, ready to be returned to her lost friend. Finally, each of the children took down their gas-mask boxes and slung them over their arms.

'Ready!' Connie replied. 'I really hope we find him this time. I dunno what we'll do if we can't.'

They filed out of the house, Lisette following behind. They were dejected and worried, without a smile between them. But they were still driven to keep looking for their friend, even if it meant going over old ground. They wanted to go back and look – a bombsite where a warehouse had come down, some railway arches, an abandoned factory, alleyways that ran down the backs of people's gardens – because what if Ned was there and they'd somehow missed him the first time?

The fine summer evening brought Londoners out of their houses; men slouched against pubs with cigarettes, and women chatted on street corners in groups. Everyone they met had already heard about Ned going missing – news travelled fast in Whitechapel – but everyone they asked shook their heads.

No one had seen Ned.

As time went on, the children's pace slackened. Ben and Elsie were starting to look tired, even though Pippa still ran her nose along the pavement and kept pausing to lift her head and scent the air. It wasn't just the distance they were covering that was wearing them out, either. It was the complete lack of news, and it dented their enthusiasm. After they'd found out about Ned helping Mabel at London Bridge station, the trail had gone cold.

The shadows were lengthening and there was a chill in the evening air. Connie sighed.

'We better get back home,' she said reluctantly. 'It's late.'

Jack patted her shoulder gently, then addressed the others. 'Tomorrow, let's put the radio back together,' he suggested brightly. He was trying to keep their spirits up, Lisette knew, but she could see the strain on his young face. 'We'll have a listen and see what we can pick up. It should be a good, long range.'

'That's my clever Jack,' Connie replied with a smile. She was trying her best as well.

'And we'll still come out and look for Ned, won't we?' Ben said. It sounded as though the threat of tears was trembling in his voice. He said sadly, 'I've got a new knock-knock joke for him. What if I never get to tell it to him?'

'It's a good one, too,' Elsie added. She picked up Pippa and hugged her. 'I hope we'll find him, because Ned'll laugh and laugh when he hears it.'

They turned and headed for home. As she followed them, Lisette thought of the boy she and Wyngate had seen last night, and she wanted to tell the children how precious they all were. But she wasn't sure she could say it without bursting into tears. If only she'd been able to tell Ned, before he'd disappeared.

And if only she'd said it to Wyngate, too. She'd tried not to think about her angry words while she was searching for Ned with the children, but, as they turned the corner into the children's street, she felt the lack of him like a physical blow. Why had she been so unkind to him?

Then she noticed a smart blue sports car parked outside the house. It was Wyngate. She could see him in the evening shadows, smoking a cigarette.

Lisette paused. She swallowed and an uncomfortable wave of heat went through her. But the children had no idea about her falling-out with Wyngate.

The unexpected sight of him telegraphed to the children that there might be news about their friend. Connie glanced at Lisette and she saw apprehension in her haunted gaze.

'It might be good news,' Lisette said, trying to smile. She patted the girl's shoulder.

Connie nodded, but there was such sadness in her voice as she replied, 'We have to hope so, don't we?'

When Lisette reached Wyngate, she realised he wasn't his usual tidy, groomed self. There were patches of grey and orange dust on him, as if he'd been on a bombsite, and his usually well-polished shoes were scuffed. There was a scratch on the back of his hand as he smoked. And his expression was closed.

'Mr Wyngate, have you come to help us look for Ned?' Elsie asked him. Pippa, still in Elsie's arms, twitched her nose, her ears cocked. 'We was just coming home, but now you're here we could go out and look some more!'

Wyngate took a couple of steps forward to meet Elsie. He allowed himself the barest hint of a smile as he told her, 'I've found him. He's safe.'

There was a moment – just a moment, which Lisette was sure the children didn't notice – when she caught Wyngate's gaze and she felt as if a portcullis had come crashing down. She was locked out.

But she forced herself not to worry. Ned had been found safe. That was what mattered. The spectre of the lost boy, wandering through the blasted city, began to dissolve in her mind, and she thought of the doodle she'd drawn on her notepad. She'd see that smiling face again soon, after worrying so much that she never would again.

The tension in her shoulders disappeared and she could breathe properly again. Ned was safe.

The children had erupted into merry chaos at Wyngate's news, cheering and jumping up and down. Connie pulled Jack into an enthusiastic embrace, holding him tight. Lisette told herself that now wasn't the time to intervene. Everyone needed this moment of joy that at last their missing friend had been found.

Elsie reached for Wyngate for a hug. He dropped to his

knees to hug her and Lisette saw then that, whatever he had been through to find and rescue Ned, it had exhausted him.

He'd once had a little sister, who had died years before. If she had lived, then Wyngate wouldn't have been so utterly alone in the world. But Elsie had taken his sister's place in Wyngate's heart and there was an unbreakable bond between them.

'I found him,' Wyngate whispered to the little girl. Then he drew back a little, looking up at the others. 'He's going to need every one of you. He isn't very well.'

Elsie gazed back at Wyngate, her eyes wide with concern, and Connie jolted as if she'd touched a hot pan.

'What's wrong?' Lisette asked. She put her arm round Connie's shoulder, as the girl had let go of Jack and was staring at Wyngate, shivering, her happiness at his good news now gone.

'What's happened to him?' Connie asked, a sob in her voice. 'What's wrong with our friend, Mr Wyngate?'

TWENTY-ONE
CONNIE

They couldn't all fit in Mr Wyngate's car, so Mr Curtis, the grocer, lent them his van so they could go to the hospital and see Ned.

Lisette sat in the front with Wyngate, while Connie and her friends piled into the back, sitting on old tea chests and piles of rough blankets. It smelt of flour and wood shavings.

Connie leaned her elbow against the back of Wyngate's seat as he drove. He seemed unfazed by the cracks in the tarmac and the rubble in the streets. He only gritted his teeth with annoyance when they came across a route that was closed due to bomb damage.

'You're a right proper hero, Mr Wyngate,' Connie declared. 'Finding Ned like that, and gettin' him out! How did you know where to find him?'

'I pulled a few strings and tracked down Mabel,' Wyngate explained. 'And she told me that Ned was heading home after he saw her safe. She gave him a bottle of ginger beer as a thank-you and off he went.' He glanced into the rear-view mirror. 'Then I put myself in Ned's shoes and thought about which route I would've taken to Whitechapel when *I* was a boy who ran the streets. And Ned had taken that route too.'

Lisette glanced at Wyngate. She didn't say anything, though, and her smile looked sad.

'That's so clever, Mr Wyngate,' Connie said, full of admiration for him. She just wished they'd been able to find Ned sooner. He must've been so afraid, and in so much pain, and it'd taken them days to find him. 'But where the heck was he? We looked *everywhere* for him.'

'He'd cut through the docks where the bomb hit last week,' said Wyngate. 'And half a warehouse had come down on top of him. He had the sense to find some cover before it landed, or he wouldn't have made it. It's only by chance that I heard him calling out; there was so much rubble that—' And Wyngate swallowed, then shook his head. 'I could hardly hear him, he was buried so deep. Mabel's ginger beer likely saved his life.'

Jack nodded, then explained for the younger children, 'No food or water.' He sat forward a little. 'But he's going to be all right?'

Connie thought of all the bombsites they'd been on, and could imagine only too well the dangers. If it wasn't a pit full of water, it was a collapsing wall that might get you. And Ned had been trapped there, calling for help for days on end, alone and scared, his stomach twisting with hunger. He must've felt as if no one would ever come to his rescue. And when the air-raid sirens went, she imagined him just having to wait in the dark with the racket of the planes, hoping another bomb wouldn't land where one had already fallen.

'No wonder we couldn't find him.' Connie sighed. She turned Ned's ID bracelet round on her wrist, and pictured his arm and his little hand, clotted with dust from being trapped in a bombsite. 'And it's just as well that Mabel gave him that ginger beer. And just as well you found him, Mr Wyngate.'

'And you dug him out, on your own?' Lisette asked. She looked worried and sad. 'With your bare hands? Oh, Ned... has he broken anything?'

Wyngate shook his head. 'I don't know,' he said. 'He was in and out of consciousness, but they've got him stable.' He glanced over his shoulder to the kids who were riding in the back of the van. 'Then I came straight to Whitechapel.'

Connie shivered. At least Mr Wyngate had found Ned alive, but what a state he was in. And it was her fault too. If she hadn't lost her temper and behaved like a brat, he wouldn't have run away. She wished she'd managed to keep it in, but the hurt that Miss Delamotte had stoked had risen up in Connie like a volcano. And every other loss she had suffered only served to make her anger boil even more. Her rage hadn't been caused by Ned, but he'd ended up the innocent target.

'I don't hate Ned, you all know that, don't you?' she said, as the hospital loomed up ahead out of the darkening evening. 'I love him like mad, and I'm so sorry this has happened to him.'

'Ned knows it too.' As Jack spoke, he patted Connie's hand. 'We all say things we regret, Ned included. We're a family. And families fall out sometimes, but they always make it up.'

Connie smiled down at the sight of Jack's hand on hers. 'I'll give him a great big hug when we see him,' she said. But was it really enough to show him she was sorry?

They climbed out of the van and Connie looked up warily at the huge Victorian building. They went inside, and it seemed to be nothing but a warren of corridors. There were men in pyjamas hobbling along on crutches, and nurses hurrying by with piles of blankets. A woman in an ARP uniform struggled by, with her arm in a sling and a patch over her eye; a nurse was helping her along. In some corridors, patients waited on wheeled beds, their families anxiously crowded around them.

Every bit of wall seemed to be covered with posters.

DRINK MILK

MAKE DO AND MEND

GROW YOUR OWN FOOD

WATCH OUT IN THE BLACKOUT

BONES FOR GLUE AND FERTILISER

LOOSE LIPS SINK SHIPS!

Mr Wyngate seemed to know exactly where to go, and everyone followed him, with Lisette last. Connie sniffed the scent of disinfectant and something else; it was as if fear and sadness lingered in the air here.

A nurse tried to stop Elsie as she went by with Pippa. 'No dogs in the hospital!' But Mr Wyngate kept going, pushing through door after door.

Eventually, they arrived at a ward, and a nurse in a particularly starched cap came forward and blocked their way through the doors.

'And where do you think you're going?' she asked, sounding like the headmistress Connie had hated at school. 'Visiting time is over.'

'We're going to see Ned Mitchell,' Wyngate told her. She began to shake her head, ready to say no, but then he barked, 'Move!'

The nurse was so taken aback that she bolted out of the way.

'You can't just go in there!' she called after them as they passed, but Connie and her friends ignored her.

The double doors of the ward swung back and Connie

paused to stare. All she could see was bed after bed, going on into infinity, it seemed, and the whiteness of the room made her squint. Usually, the beds would've been drawn up to the walls, with an aisle running down the middle, but not in wartime. The beds had been pulled into the middle of the room instead, back to back, away from the windows in case a bomb dropped and the glass shattered.

Every patient in the room turned to see them, and Connie couldn't believe it. Who were all these children, tucked up in bed? Some had bandages round their heads, others had legs bound in plaster suspended on wires. Some of them just looked pale, with dark circles around their eyes as if they'd been too worn out by the war.

She glanced from face to face, desperately trying to spot her friend, and there he was: Ned! She saw his round face, and his mop of blond curls – although they were partly covered by a bandage. And his face looked thinner. He was wearing striped hospital pyjamas, and his cap was sitting on the table by his bed.

Connie ran down the well-polished aisle to his side. She was about to pull him into a hug when she stopped herself. She didn't want to hurt him.

'Oh, Ned, mate, we were so worried!' she cried, as the other children gathered around the bed.

Ned sat up against his pillows, then managed to smile, but Connie was sure she saw his lip wobble. He opened his arms to her. Connie realised, then, that it was safe to hug him; she put her arms round him to embrace him.

'I'm so sorry,' she whispered against the bandage over his ear. 'I was horrible to you. I don't hate you at all, Ned. I love you so much!'

Ned didn't say anything in reply, but held her tight. When he did speak again, his voice was surprisingly loud and somehow he seemed to be speaking a little slower, as though he was addressing a crowd; and there, under the bravado, Connie heard another wobble.

'Might as well tell you before the doc does,' he said. His voice sounded rasping and he was speaking more slowly than he used to. 'I can't hear much of anythin' at all. Bloody Nazis have done for my hearing, ain't they? I'm deaf as a post.'

TWENTY-TWO

CONNIE

Connie's sense of relief drained away. She held Ned even tighter, as if the sheer force of her love for him could fix him.

No, this wasn't right. It wasn't fair. He'd been found alive, and he should've been all right. A bit bruised maybe, a bit scuffed. But not deaf. Had he really been thrown into a silent world, where he wouldn't hear his friends talk or laugh, just from sheer bad luck? Just because he'd run away from her anger?

She didn't want to believe it, but as she lifted her head from Ned's shoulder she spotted a faint trail of red on his neck. It was as if he'd bled from his ears and it'd dried. One of the nurses must've cleaned him up, but there was still a hint of what'd happened.

'Oh, Ned!' she gasped. 'I'm so sorry. That's awful!' But then she realised he wouldn't have heard what she'd said. And could he hear his own voice? It'd changed.

Instinctively, Connie glanced at the others. She could feel the change in the air; the smiles they'd worn at the news that Ned had been found were faltering. Elsie was still beaming, but it seemed to be an effort, just as much as it looked hard for

Lisette to keep smiling. Ben clutched Susan's hand, and she held his, her knuckles white. When Connie looked at Jack he met her gaze and she saw in it concern for their friend, the same concern that showed in Wyngate's expression. No one knew what to say, or how to say it, and the air was tense with unspoken words.

Lisette's smile broke. She turned away, dabbing at her eyes with a handkerchief. Connie realised she was crying and didn't want anyone to know. Then she turned back and pulled Ned into a hug, the sort that the streetwise boy didn't get very often.

'It's all right,' he said kindly, putting his arms round Lisette's shoulders. It struck Connie that it was just like Ned, to be reassuring everyone else when he was the one who needed help.

Then, after a moment, Lisette slowly released Ned from her embrace and fondly stroked his blond curls, before placing a kiss on top of his head.

Ned sat back a little against the pillows, narrowing his eyes as he peered at Connie. After a moment, he shook his head.

'Still can't hear nothin' much,' he teased. He seemed like his usual cheery self, but Connie knew better. She had seen Ned mask his tears enough times after the nuns had beaten him for some little transgression, never letting anyone see anything other than the front he had learned so early to put on. 'But it's bloody nice to see you all.' Then he looked at Mr Wyngate and added, 'Even you!'

Wyngate gave the small smile that he seemed to reserve for the most special moments and nodded an acknowledgement. Then he frowned and turned to Elsie to ask, 'Do you have your notebook and pen, Elsie? Might come in useful?'

'Of course I do, Mr Wyngate.' Elsie nodded. She always carried them with her, and noted down her day so she could write it up later in her journal, or in the letters she and Jack sent to their father. 'We'll write down what we want to say to Ned.'

Elsie reached into the pocket of her dress and took out her

pencil and her latest notebook, a small, simple pad with a green cover. 'Who wants to go first?'

'Do you mind if I do?' Wyngate asked, and gave Elsie a smile when she handed him the notebook and pencil. He took them from her and wrote a simple explanation for Ned, who nodded his understanding.

We'll write down what we need to say. But we'll say it too.

'Right-o!' Ned acknowledged. He seemed to be sounding out the words he couldn't hear in his head, speaking with obvious care. 'So what a plonker do I feel, eh? Sittin' here, deaf as a doorknob!' Then he beamed a smile and looked around at his visitors. 'I got a fair few quid out of the Yanks before I dropped down that bloody hole, though. Went round with the cap out, giving it the full Oliver Twist!'

Connie gestured to Wyngate for the notepad, and wrote the words as she said, 'What are you like, Ned Mitchell?' Then she drew a heart next to it, to show him that she thought he was adorable and wasn't scolding him.

He gave her a wink and said, 'One of the Yanks said Gabriel Cooper was talking about putting on a benefit show for the war orphans and wanted to meet some local talent.' He widened his eyes, like a magician looking forward to pulling a rabbit out of a hat. 'So I thought, if I could find 'im, he'd want to hear our Connie sing so he could get her booked. Trouble is, he's already on his way back to bloody America!' Ned gave a theatrical sigh. 'So I thought, since I ain't got nothing better to do, I'd do some of the stuff I'm good at. And old Mabel needed a knight in armour, didn't she?'

Connie rushed her hand to her mouth. Gabriel Cooper? He'd been a child star in Hollywood and as he'd got older he'd matured into a handsome leading man. He'd starred in epics and romances, and he'd swashbuckled his way through pirate films. And yet, for all his fame and riches, when America joined the war he'd set all of that aside to do his bit, and now he was stationed in Britain.

She'd shouted at Ned. She'd been awful to him. And yet, he'd tried to find Gabriel Cooper to get Connie her break. He'd tried to help her, and the universe had repaid him like this.

'Thanks, Ned,' Connie said as she wrote the same words in the notepad. 'You're the best mate anyone could ever have. Would've loved singing for Gabriel Cooper! But you're alive – that's the main thing. We was so worried!'

He shrugged. 'I messed up your chance with that old cow back at the theatre. So I'm going to put that right.'

Connie shook her head, then she wrote again. '*You don't have anything to put right – that's for me to do. I'm really sorry I shouted at you. It wasn't your fault.*'

But Ned shook his head. 'It wasn't the first time we've been like cat and dog and it won't be the last neither.' He smiled. 'That's just a family thing!'

Connie smiled back at him. And yet she couldn't shake her guilt.

Just then, she heard Pippa bark. She looked up and saw a tall man in a white jacket with a stethoscope round his neck. He had an enamel badge of a teddy bear on his lapel, which Connie supposed he wore to make himself look less intimidating to his young patients.

'You're Ned's friends, I take it?' he asked as he came to stand by the bed. 'I'm Dr Salter, I'm looking after Ned.'

Wyngate stepped forward. 'What's the verdict?' he asked. 'I'm the man who brought him in.'

'It was an incredibly brave rescue. And I'm glad you did bring him in; he was in a bad way,' Dr Salter said.

Connie noticed that, even though he was talking to Mr Wyngate, he was looking at Ned as he spoke. Was it so that Ned could somehow understand him? She wondered about

Ned's rescue. Mr Wyngate must've had to clear away a whole lot of rubble, and surely, if one wall had fallen and landed on Ned, then there must've been other unstable ruins on the bomb-site that could've fallen on Mr Wyngate too. He was a quiet sort of hero; he would never have told anyone how dangerous it had been to rescue Ned, just as he never told anyone how hard it must've been to pull Connie and Jack out of the water-filled crater.

'He's hungry and dehydrated, and he's got scratches and bruises – but he'll recover,' Dr Salter went on. 'His hearing, however... when the wall fell on him, it must've been incredibly loud, and it's severely damaged his ears. In other patients I've seen with the same damage, they can hear very loud noises, but everything else is very muffled, and I'm afraid Ned's not able to understand speech at all – he simply can't pick out the words. Now, ears are clever things in some ways, and with time parts of the ear can fix themselves. But the damage was so bad that I'm afraid for Ned to have any chance of hearing properly again he'll need to have surgery.'

Jack nodded. 'And you'll do it?'

'Then it's really not so bad as we feared,' Lisette said.

Dr Salter lowered his gaze for a moment and shook his head. 'It's not as easy as that, I'm afraid. It's very specialist treat-ment, and not something we can do here. The surgeon who came up with the technique is brilliant, but you see, because the surgery is so new, it's fiercely expensive, and there's a long waiting list – Ned really needs to have the treatment as soon as possible in order for the best chance of success.' He swallowed, before adding, 'And the other problem is... he's in New York.'

Connie's heart sank. 'That's like saying he's on the other side of the moon!' she retorted furiously, her hands clenched. How could the doctor give them hope, then dash it?

TWENTY-THREE

CONNIE

They only had one chance to get Ned's hearing fixed, and it was impossible. The cost of the surgery itself was one thing, because Connie couldn't imagine how they'd ever raise the money. They'd already put on a show to save Jasper's nightclub. Would anyone want to come to another, for Ned? And would they raise the money in time?

But even if, by some miracle, they managed to raise the money, there was the huge expanse of the Atlantic Ocean between London and New York. It wasn't safe; German U-boats and battleships patrolled it, searching for ships to sink.

New York and the surgeon who could save Ned's hearing were impossibly far away.

'We can bring the surgeon here!' Jack insisted. He turned to Wyngate. 'Can't we? For Ned?'

'Mr Wyngate, we can!' Elsie grabbed his sleeve. 'You can make anything happen, can't you? You can get that doctor on a ship to London!'

Ben had climbed onto the edge of the bed, and was holding Ned's hand. 'He's our mate. We've got to fix him up!'

Lisette glanced at Wyngate, then said, 'But it's a very long way. We all want Ned to get back to his old self, but...' Her voice trailed off. Connie could guess what she couldn't bring herself to say: *there's a war on.*

Wyngate's jaw tightened and he glanced towards Ned.

'What's goin' on?' asked the little boy. 'What're they sayin' about me?'

Connie realised they'd forgotten to keep Ned in the loop. It was difficult adjusting to the fact that he couldn't hear them, when he always had before. She passed the notepad and pencil to Mr Wyngate.

Wyngate scribbled down an explanation and Ned, stoic as ever, nodded.

'It's all right,' he assured them. 'Maybe it'll come back on its own, eh? And if it don't, well I always get by, don't I? It ain't nothing.'

Dr Salter had watched Mr Wyngate write in the notepad, and he seemed to approve. 'You'll need to adjust. Ned can learn to lip-read, and, when you talk to him, make sure you're looking at him. Don't mumble, don't talk too fast. Just speak clearly. And when you're all talking together, make sure Ned isn't left out. Write it down, if you need to. And maybe all of you could learn sign language. Watch this.'

Dr Salter gave a wave, then he pointed at himself, before dancing the index finger of his right hand around the fingers on the left. 'There – I've just said, *hello, I'm Dr Salter.*'

Susan mimicked the wave and aimed it at Ned. 'That's easy! I've just said *hello!*'

Ned waved back and Wyngate stooped to pick up Pippa and put the little dog on Ned's bed. He put his arms round her and buried his face against her fur, murmuring softly as Wyngate told them, 'Whatever Ned needs, I'll make sure he gets it. He's going to see that surgeon.'

Connie stared at Mr Wyngate. How could Ned go, even if they got the money? He couldn't head off on such a long voyage to a completely new country by himself; he was only a boy. Who would go with him?

Then he looked to Elsie and Connie and added, 'I promise.'

TWENTY-FOUR
LISETTE

Lisette still had to go to work, even though her worries circled around Ned while the telephones jangled and her colleagues tapped away at typewriters and hurried between desks with messages. Every time she took her focus off her translations, she pictured Ned in his hospital bed, the bandage wrapped round his damaged ear.

She had been so relieved that Wyngate had found the boy, but she wasn't sure where to begin with his deafness. Dr Salter had given them some leaflets, and they'd been waiting for her in her handbag all day while she'd been at work, but she couldn't bring herself to read them, even if there was hope of a cure. If she did, it would all be too real.

She had come across another message that mentioned the *Amfortas*, the ship that Capitaine Ardouin had been so keen to hear about. And this time it said that it was carrying a prototype weapon.

Ardouin had got on the telephone within seconds of Lisette passing the message to her. It made the ship a prime target for the RAF and USAAF. It astonished Lisette that she was in the inner circle, that her work was so important. She had watched

Ardouin as she'd spoken rapidly into the receiver, her heart thumping as she pictured the aeroplanes waiting on the tarmac, that would be prepared to attack. And all because of a message that Lisette had translated.

But her shift was over. She tidied her pencils and notepads into the drawer of her desk, ready to leave the world of secret messages and weapons and head to Whitechapel to look after the children. She'd need to put aside her devastation that Wyngate had ended their relationship so that she could talk to him about Ned, and what they could do to make sure his lost hearing wouldn't make his life too hard until they could get him treated.

She looked over at Marie, who seemed to lead a simpler existence. She was reapplying her red lipstick in a small, tortoiseshell mirror. 'What are your plans for tonight? Are you going to go dancing with your boyfriend?'

'One of them,' remarked Marie mischievously, patting her carefully curled hair. 'My Frenchman tonight. I told my American that I have to wash my hair!'

Lisette chuckled. If only her problems began and ended with having too many men chasing after her. 'Marie! Well, why not? I hope you have a lovely time with your Frenchman, but don't lose your American – or else, where will we get our nylons?'

'We are Frenchwomen,' Marie reminded her. 'We will never struggle for nylons!'

Lisette laughed, and was about to push back her chair when the tall figure of Capitaine Ardouin appeared at her desk. There was never a crease or a speck of lint on her uniform, and her shirt looked stiff with starch. Her grey hair was styled with precision to the point that it was so perfect, it almost looked like a helmet.

'Thank you for your hard work today,' she said, but she wasn't smiling. Lisette wasn't sure she ever did. 'I'm sure you will have noticed that there is a lot happening. I can't say anything, but there's something I need both of you to do. When any messages come through about Nazi activity around the ports – in France or anywhere else – you must bring them to me at once. It doesn't matter if I'm on the telephone to General de Gaulle – you must bring me the message. Is that clear?'

Lisette felt an icy finger run down her back. What on earth was going on? She nodded. 'Of course, Capitaine, we'll bring them to you immediately.'

'Good,' Capitaine Ardouin said. Then she sighed. 'I can't wait to finish tonight. I'm looking forward to a long soak in the tub. Or perhaps I should go to the pictures?'

Lisette was surprised. She never heard Ardouin talk about her personal life, but perhaps, with so much happening in France, the pressure meant that Ardouin needed a break from her usual stiff persona.

Who would she go to the pictures with, Lisette wondered? Was there a Monsieur Ardouin? She must live in a billet some-where, Lisette suspected, a hotel commandeered by the War Office for the Free French staff. There wouldn't be a cosy flat under a sloping roof for her like Lisette had.

'What will you see?' Lisette asked, curious where her ques-tion would go as she'd never spoken to Ardouin so casually.

'I will see *Quiet Wedding*, I think,' Ardouin replied. There was something almost dreamy in the way she said it, as if her professional life wouldn't let her have a real wedding, quiet or otherwise. The door opened and the evening shift arrived. Ardouin looked at her watch. 'It's time you two headed home – go on, *allez-y!*'

Lisette picked up her gas-mask box and her handbag, and she and Marie wound their way out of the office and through the War Office, heading past men and women in the uniforms of so many countries, all united in the fight against the Nazis.

She had never got used to how grand the building was, with

its white marble stairs and banisters and huge oil paintings of battles on land and at sea. She glanced up to look at one that showed tiny planes in the Great War circling above the ruined French countryside below, and it made her shiver. Why had war come back to Europe so soon? How had it managed to spread across the world?

Marie was full of gossip and chatter, and Lisette tried her best to listen as they made their way to the front door, but she kept thinking about Ned and seeing the bandages over his ears. Was there nothing they could do to help him here, without that dangerous trip across the ocean?

She came out of the huge double doors, which wouldn't have looked out of place on the front of a grand hotel, and was heading down the steps when she turned back and spotted Wyngate inside the building. She hadn't had a chance to apologise to him for what she'd said only the day before.

He was striding through the lobby towards the doors, his gaze set straight ahead, dressed as usual in a smart suit, his fedora at an angle that shielded his eyes. She saw him then as he wanted everyone to: an island, alone and strong against the tide of war. But Lisette and the children knew better now; they'd seen the soft heart that he hid so well.

'Mr Wyngate!' she called as he came outside into the sunlight. As far as anyone at the War Office knew, they were just friends, not a couple. She couldn't catch his hand and walk alongside him, not until they were out of sight of their workplace. But it seemed as if he was radiating a shield around him that was keeping even her away.

At the sight of Lisette he stopped walking and gave her a nod. 'Mademoiselle,' he said, for the benefit of any of their War Office colleagues.

'I haven't had a chance yet to go through the leaflets Dr Salter gave me,' she told him. She wanted to keep to practicalities – she couldn't reveal her feelings on the steps of the War

Office. But she couldn't keep them in. 'And... oh, Adam, I'm so sorry. For what I said to you. It's not true. You *do* care, of course you do.'

He settled his gaze on Lisette and gave a slight nod. She caught a glimpse of sadness in his eyes before he said, 'I have to go. I've got business at the Admiralty.'

'Oh.' Lisette gripped the handle on her handbag. She'd hoped they could've talked about Ned. 'I'm going to see the children. Perhaps I will see you there later?'

'I don't know,' Wyngate said. 'Maybe at the hospital.'

'If we get an air raid, don't try to come to us,' Lisette said. 'Just stay where you are and take shelter.'

'Lisette.' Wyngate took a deep breath, then set his jaw. 'I don't think— I can't bear the thought of you waiting for me to come home every time I have to go away. It isn't a good idea to care about someone like me. Because one day... my job is very dangerous. You know that.'

'That doesn't matter to me,' Lisette said, trying to keep her voice down so that the War Office staff hurrying up and down the steps wouldn't overhear. 'I can't stop worrying about you. Everyone needs someone to look after them.'

But he shook his head. 'You already lost Tom, I couldn't put you through it again. I couldn't have you sitting at home, waiting for word of me that never comes.' He kissed her cheek softly. 'I'm sorry, Lisette. I'll always care about you, but I can't let you do the same for me.'

And with that, he turned and walked away. There was nothing unusual in his step or his bearing to show that he'd just closed off his heart.

Lisette was too stunned to speak. His kiss on her cheek was already fading. She blinked as he vanished into the crowd.

Tears were threatening to fall, and the warmth of the sun disappeared. She shivered. It was over.

TWENTY-FIVE
LISETTE

Jack had set the radio up on a table in the front room beside his puzzle books, and his friends sat in a row along the sofa staring at it. Pippa had given it a good sniff, and now sat in front of it, her tail wagging. But there was a Ned-shaped absence in the room, and Lisette knew they could all feel it, even though no one would say so out loud.

'Right,' Jack murmured to himself as he knelt down before the wireless. 'Just this morning I've heard stations broadcasting from France and Germany. And there's some strange stuff out there too, signals and noises. I'm trying to make out what I'm hearing half the time.'

The air bristled with anticipation. It'd been Jack's project ever since Wyngate had given him the broken radio, and he'd spent hours and hours on it; cleaning components, finding replacement parts, and finally wiring it all together.

Lisette, leaning against the back of the sofa, clenched her hands tightly at the thought of Wyngate. She didn't even know where he was at that moment, and wished he was there to see Jack unveil the radio. But she didn't want to tell the children that Wyngate had broken up with her; she knew that the two of them together offered them stability in a world that had turned on its head.

At least now that Ned had been found, she wouldn't camp out in the children's front room every night but would go back to her flat. It'd give Wyngate a chance to spend time with them without her being there too. But the thought of being away from him hurt so much that she clenched her hands even tighter, trying to hold in her pain so that the children wouldn't see it.

He'd ended everything for her sake, not his. But it wasn't his decision to make. She was a grown woman, and she knew the risk of giving her heart to him; the loss, the grief. But that was the price of love, especially during a war. And it was her choice, not his. Why should he take that decision away from her?

'I'm going to tell Dad about the radio working in our next letter, and, when Ned's healed, he'll be so excited to listen in,' Jack said, glancing over his shoulder at his audience. 'I was thinking, you know, if we could raise money for Jasper, then why not Ned? If he needs to go to America, we can send him!'

But Lisette wasn't sure it would be that easy. And he needed to get to New York soon, if Dr Salter was right; if they waited too long, then no surgery on earth could bring back Ned's hearing.

Lisette knew that neither she nor the other children would rest if Ned took that journey, but perhaps after the war... perhaps.

Suddenly Connie hopped to her feet, brandishing the latest issue of the *Evening News*. A photograph of Ned, which Esther had taken a few months ago, beamed from the front page, under the headline: *BLITZ KID DEAFENED!*

'Look, Esther's written about Ned already.' She scanned the article and stared in wide-eyed disbelief. 'You'll never guess what she's said, neither!

'After going missing following the fundraiser show to rebuild Jasper's famous Soho nightclub, young Ned Mitchell has been found, but he's badly injured and has lost his hearing. His only hope lies with a specialist surgeon in New York. We can exclusively reveal to our readers that Jasper has pledged all the funds raised from the show for Ned's treatment.'

Connie looked up from the newspaper. 'Blimey, Jasper... what a lovely bloke! He's giving up his club for Ned!'

Lisette swallowed. She couldn't imagine the guilt that Jasper carried; Mrs Dupree was dead, and Ned had been injured. But it wasn't his fault. He hadn't asked for his club to be destroyed, or Ned to run out after the show. What a sacrifice he was making – and yet she thought of Ned, his head bandaged, his hearing gone. What else could Jasper have done?

'Everybody loves Ned,' Susan assured them brightly. 'And won't that mean we'll need another show for Jasper? He can't lose his club, it wouldn't be fair.'

Jack turned the dial on the wireless. There was a blast of music here or a voice there, then the static cleared and another voice emerged, filling the little living room.

'Germany calling. Germany calling.'

Jack's mouth fell open and he turned to look at his friends, eyes wide. It was as though the temperature in the sunshine-dappled room had suddenly grown frigid.

It was Lord Haw-Haw. He always broadcast at just after nine o'clock in the evening, but today he was on air much earlier than usual. Was this a special message? But why?

Lord Haw-Haw broadcast from Germany, pretending, with the plummy voice he put on, to be a member of the upper classes. He sounded like a P.G. Wodehouse character, but one who had become a traitor, because this man was no friend to the people of Britain or their allies.

Lord Haw-Haw bragged about Nazi victories in his

affected, plummy tones, and yet the British listened. Because sometimes it was the only way to know the fate of servicemen who had disappeared.

Hearing that voice reminded Lisette that, despite all the suffering so many had been through, there were people like William Joyce – the man behind the snooty persona – who were willing to betray their own.

Elsie picked up Pippa and fussed the little dog. 'He's a horrible man.'

'The British Ministry of Misinformation has been conducting a systematic campaign of using children to maintain the British morale, encouraging them to return to the city of London, facing all the dangers of a city at war, so that they might enjoy spurious celebrity,' said Lord Haw-Haw in his steady, upper-class tones.

Lisette glanced at the children. So that was it; the children were what warranted an early broadcast by Lord Haw-Haw.

'That's us...' Ben whispered, wide-eyed. He looked at his sister, then up at Lisette, who never for a moment had thought that the Blitz Kids' fame would travel to Berlin. 'He's talking about us, isn't he? That means the Nazis know who we are.'

'Recently, a British bomb fell on the city of London, resulting in the wounding of one of these children,' went on the voice. 'Master Ned Mitchell is now a patient in hospital, a victim of his own regime. British newspapers report today that the bomb was dropped by the Luftwaffe during their devastating air raid. This is not so. British airmen, paralysed by fear in the face of German dominance, discharged their bomb in their blind panic. The British Ministry of Misinformation continues to print lies. The Luftwaffe continues to hold dominion over the skies as the Kriegsmarine does over the ocean. German vessels patrol the North Atlantic, sending British and American convoys to the depths. German domination continues to advance by land, sea and air. Take the matter of El Alamein—'

But Jack had already spun the dial again, replacing the voice of Nazi Germany with the melodic tones of Vera Lynn. He shook his head and murmured, 'Only Ned could get himself onto Lord Haw-Haw's broadcast. And that rubbish about it being our boys who dropped the bomb that injured Ned; we've got Jerry over here night after night!'

'What sort of country would bomb itself?' Susan asked with a shiver. 'No one listening to this nonsense believes him, surely! But he knows Ned's name.'

'You're famous, now.' Lisette sighed. 'I suppose it was only a matter of time until the Nazis heard of you. It's their fault he's injured, and now they're using him to spin their lies.' The face of the dead boy at the morgue floated towards her in her memory. She swallowed down her anger. Children shouldn't get caught up in wars started by adults.

'Well, Ned's not going to give up, is he?' Ben said, jutting out his chin with determination. 'He'll go to New York and he'll get his hearing back.'

'He said they dominate the Atlantic, but that didn't seem to bother Mr Churchill when he went to America and back not so long ago. They didn't manage to get him, did they?' Jack pointed out optimistically, then glanced up at the clock. 'I make that visiting time. Wait until our Ned hears that even Radio Hamburg's talking about him.'

TWENTY-SIX
LISETTE

They took the Underground to the hospital. The other passengers came up to speak to the Blitz Kids, who were recognised across London now, offering their kind words about Ned.

'If there's anything we can do to help that lad, you let us know,' a man in an army uniform told them.

Lisette wondered how many of them had heard Ned being mentioned in Lord Haw-Haw's broadcast. Not many people wanted to admit that they tuned in to hear the words of a traitor. What would Wyngate make of it?

Once they arrived at the hospital, they made their way to Ned's ward. They passed other patients who had copies of the *Evening News* and were excited to find out that one of the Blitz Kids was being nursed back to health in the same place as them.

Lisette spotted a familiar figure. It was Jasper, wearing a pinstriped suit and a swirling yellow and purple paisley tie with a matching pocket square. He was smiling.

'Don't suppose you'd mind if I come in with you? I want to have a quick word with Ned,' he told them brightly. The way he was so pleased at the prospect of giving up the chance to resurrect his club spoke volumes about the man. This was why so many people had wanted to help him. He never put himself first.

'Of course,' Lisette replied warmly. 'You know, we saw it in the newspaper, Jasper. I can't begin to find the words.'

'It's what anyone would do for a kid,' Jasper assured them as they headed into the ward.

The ward was busy, even for visiting time. And Lisette noticed something different. The children were showing their visitors comics, and toy boats and aeroplanes. One of the girls was proudly dancing a teddy bear on her knee.

Lisette knew where they had come from as soon as she spotted Ned sitting up against his pillows with a box on his lap, handing out even more toys. They'd been sent to him by well-wishers, and Ned had decided to share his gifts. As he exchanged a thumbs-up with a boy to whom he'd just handed a stack of comics, Ned called to his new visitors in the voice that sounded ever so slightly unlike his own, 'Still can't hear bobbins! But look at all this gear folks've sent!'

'I hope you're not selling it,' Jack teased, then scribbled the message on the notepad Ned kept beside his bed and held it up. Ned shook his head.

'No way,' he said. 'I ain't making a penny from this. I'm the hospital Santa these days!'

He never stopped smiling, never complained, but Lisette knew that even Ned had to be struggling. He might never admit it to his friends, but his smiles were always the way he coped.

'Right, before you even open your mouth, I've got some-thing to say to you.' Ned was addressing Jasper, businesslike now. Still the words came more slowly, and Lisette wondered if Ned had been rehearsing what he had to say, going over the words in his head because he wouldn't hear them when he spoke. 'I saw what you was saying in the paper and I never thought I'd say this to anyone, but I don't want the money. That's for the club. That's for London, that is.'

Lisette glanced at Jasper and saw the colour drain from his face along with his smile.

'A-are you sure, Ned?' he gasped. Then he tutted at himself and reached for the notepad. He wrote down his next words and showed the page to Ned. 'Your hearing is more important than a nightclub!'

But Ned was shaking his head. 'Mate, I'm going to say thank you and I mean it. It's right kind, but it ain't my money. Build that bloody club so I've got a place to flog baccy and nylons when I'm out of here!' Then he gave Connie a nod. 'And so I've got a place to hear Connie sing again once my ears are right!'

As surprised as Lisette was, she reminded herself that Ned *was* London. He knew every street, every alleyway. He had arrived on the doorstep of the orphanage as a baby, as if the very pavement had brought him into being. When he turned down Jasper's offer, it was as though he was speaking for the city that had given him life.

'I'm stunned,' Jasper said as he wrote in the notepad. 'I'll see you all right, Ned.'

Ned nodded and smiled, then held out his hand to Jasper. Without saying another word they shook hands, the decision made.

'We got the radio working,' Jack informed Ned. 'Lord Haw-Haw sends you all the very best from Germany!'

Susan helped Ben climb onto the bed to sit at Ned's feet, while Connie and Elsie perched on the edge, close to Ned, and Pippa licked Ned's face in greeting. Lisette glanced round, relieved that the nurses were too busy to notice.

'How are you feeling?' she asked, writing on the pad at the same time.

'Like a bloody building dropped on my 'ead.' Ned laughed,

the sound rasping in his throat. 'But I'm alive and that's got to be something, ain't it? Fancy them old Nazis knowing my name, eh? They'll know it right enough when I parachute into Germany and kick Adolf up the arse!'

Susan chuckled, then she wrote on the pad, *That's a rude word!*

But Lisette didn't tell him off. After what he'd been through, he was more than entitled to say *arse*. Instead, she poured him a glass of orange juice from the jug beside the bed. As she was about to hand it to him, she saw Wyngate walking towards the bed, holding a box wrapped in brown paper.

Her smile disappeared and she tried to pretend that she hadn't spotted him. But she couldn't say anything to him in front of the children; she would have to swallow down her anger and hurt.

As he came closer, the air seemed to grow thicker and too hot, filled with the crackle of static. She couldn't reach him, couldn't force her way through the wall of thorns that surrounded him. She would have to harden her heart against him, but it hurt her deep inside.

'Mr Wyngate!' Elsie called, waving across to him. She glanced at Ned and did what seemed to be her own invented sign for their friend, miming touching the brim of an invisible hat. Ned returned the gesture and gave Elsie a little wink.

'Hello, troops,' Wyngate said as he reached the bed, and returned Elsie's wave. Jasper stood aside for him. He settled his gaze on Lisette and said, 'Lis.'

Lisette pressed her lips together. Her heart was full of so many words, but they couldn't come flowing out here. And would he even listen? Wouldn't he just turn on his polished heel and walk away?

Instead, she nodded to him and greeted him with a good evening in French. 'Bonsoir.'

Wyngate put the parcel he was carrying in Ned's lap, and

the boy excitedly untied the string and tore away the wrapping. 'A camera?' He blinked up at Wyngate. 'And it's a good one an' all. Like the one Esther uses for her news reporting!'

Wyngate nodded and flipped a page in his notebook. He showed what was written there to Ned as he said for the benefit of the others, 'So you can photograph your journey and share it with your friends.'

The children instantly clamoured around Ned. A camera was a novelty that they didn't see every day. Connie pouted and posed as if she was a pin-up painted on a plane, Elsie was pleading him to photograph Pippa, Susan tried to get a closer look, and Ben squared his fingers and peered through them at Ned.

'Pew-pew! Ned's taking photos!' Ben cheered.

Lisette smiled at the children and their excitement, but it touched her deeply that Wyngate had bought Ned such a thoughtful present. A camera was just the perfect gift for someone who had lost their sense of hearing. Wyngate was telling him, *show us what you see with your eyes on your journey through life.*

'Thank you, Mr W!' Ned grinned. 'I'll take plenty of snaps.'

And Wyngate flipped the page in his notebook, so Ned could read as he spoke.

'Last night, Mr Gray got hellish drunk with Mr Winant, the American ambassador, and they toasted your name,' Wyngate explained, unable to capture the little smile that escaped as he mentioned his superior's misadventure with the American statesman. 'This morning, Mr Roosevelt telephoned Mr Churchill. The Americans would like to invite you to New York as their guest, for the surgery you need to restore your lost hearing. You've officially been bumped to the front of the queue.'

Ned blinked as he reached the end of the written explanation. Then he gasped, 'Bleedin' 'ell. First Adolf and now Franklin D! Tell them from me, Mr W, that I would be delighted to accept!'

Lisette was overwhelmed by the kindness of the Americans, and Jasper looked stunned all over again. 'Well, doesn't the universe have a funny way of making sure everything works out all right?' he said with a chuckle.

Lisette sighed with relief. But then she thought of Lord Haw-Haw and what he'd said about the Atlantic came back to her. 'But... what about the voyage to New York?'

'Mr Churchill went to America and was safe,' Jack reminded her again. 'Besides, he'll be on a civilian ship; they'd leave that be, wouldn't they?'

Wyngate nodded. 'And I'll be with him,' he said. 'I've been asked to conduct some government business while I'm over there, so Ned won't be let loose on the unsuspecting Americans.'

'And I'll come too,' Connie declared, patting Ned's shoulder. 'Someone needs to look after Ned while Mr Wyngate's havin' meetings and all that. He's like my little brother, after all!'

There was so much excitement in the air that Lisette had to step back and instead quietly tidy the toys that Ned had been given. She tried to disguise the tremble in her hands.

It was difficult enough seeing Wyngate again, holding down her anger and frustration, hiding the fact that they'd split up from the children. Now on top of that, there was her fear of that long journey across thousands of miles where Nazi submarines could be lying in wait.

They had come so close to losing Ned, but now they risked losing him again – and Connie and Wyngate too. But how could she tell them, in the face of their joy, that it was too dangerous to go?

She picked up a toy ship, painted gaily in red with gold rims around the porthole windows, and swallowed. She thought of the *Lusitania* in the Great War, sunk by the Germans only a few miles from the Irish coast; almost as many lives had been lost as on the *Titanic*.

Then another memory took its place. The SS *City of Benares*, which had been taking evacuees to Canada at the beginning of the war. It'd been sunk by the Nazis, and over half the people on the ship had died – including nearly eighty children. And then, only a few months earlier, there was the MV *Struma*, carrying nearly 800 Jewish people to safety in Palestine. All but one of them had been killed when the ship was attacked by a German submarine.

She knew Ned needed treatment, but was it worth risking his life, and Connie's and Wyngate's too?

TWENTY-SEVEN
CONNIE

Connie and Jack were going shopping together, just the two of them, as Mr Gray had taken the other children on a trip to the Tower of London. Connie wondered if Mr Gray had done it on purpose, but how could he know? Ben had been excited, telling everyone that Mr Gray was going to show them heads impaled on spikes at the Tower, and had been disappointed when Susan told him they didn't do that to traitors any more.

Connie didn't get the chance to be alone with Jack very often. There were always the other children to look after; although Susan was thirteen now and could help, Ned was only just ten, and Ben and Elsie were a year younger than him. Connie didn't expect the younger ones to work out how to stretch what food they could find into decent meals for so many. And they'd forget to tidy up, or they'd wear odd socks, or walk muddy shoes across a freshly mopped floor. There were lessons that Connie and Jack taught, to make up for the fact that none of them went to school any more. Besides, having six people in a small house made it hard to find space. And now that she was going to America with Ned, an internal clock was ticking down the moments.

She was so excited at the prospect of the trip, but her mind kept circling back to Jack. She'd miss him and she'd worry about him, thinking about him clambering over bombsites and rushing to help when he could. And yet, she couldn't let Ned go without her. She blamed herself for him losing his hearing; it was only right she should take the same voyage as him to look after him and be the big sister she'd failed to be on the night he'd run away.

It was another sunny day, and the dusty high street was busy with shoppers, who were moving slowly through the summer heat. The green tops of carrots were wilting outside a greengrocer's, but they wouldn't have to wait long before they were bought. She wondered what the shops would be like in America, and whether maybe she wouldn't have carrots every day for dinner.

Connie had never eaten so many carrots before the war, and she wondered if she'd ever want to eat them again once it was over. But maybe, she thought to herself as she watched a woman balance her baby on her hip as she examined a cauliflower, that would depend on who won. And she hated speculating about that. She forced herself to believe that the Nazis would be defeated. Somehow.

The shops that hadn't managed to find enough stock had signs cheering everyone on: *THREE CHEERS FOR CHURCHILL!* and *WHITECHAPEL SHOPS FOR VICTORY!*

'You sure you'll be all right, looking after everyone when I go off to America with Ned?' Connie asked Jack as she swung her shopping basket as she walked. Lisette would still come to stay with them sometimes, she knew, but Connie was worried that Jack might think she was abandoning him.

'We'll muddle through.' Jack smiled. 'But we'll all miss you both.'

He'll miss me. Connie was worried she was blushing from

the force of that thought. She glanced away from him, looking into the window of a grocer's. There was a precarious stack of tins in the window, but she wondered if they had anything in them or if they were just for show. The *Dig for Victory!* poster pinned up on the door didn't make her feel confident; it was as if the grocer was telling his customers, *I don't have anything in my shop, so you'll have to grow everything yourself.*

She glanced back at Jack. 'I'll miss you, too, Jack. You and that great big brain of yours.'

Jack flushed red and gave a shrug. 'We'll have to have a heck of a party when you get home.' Then he gave her another smile. 'I bag the first dance with you, though!'

Connie could hear the orchestra in her head again, playing a swooning melody. *He wants the first dance with me!* Even so, she still wasn't sure if he *really* liked her, in the way Wyngate liked Lisette. And if she tried to kiss Jack, it'd just be really embarrassing if he winced and shoved her away.

'Too right, we'll have the best party anyone's ever seen,' Connie said. 'And once I get dancing with you, I'm sorry, but I'm not letting anyone else dance with you!' She thought she might've said too much, so quickly changed the subject. 'We need some bread, don't we, but there's a massive queue outside that baker's.'

'We're used to queuing these days,' he reminded her with a warm smile. 'And I wouldn't want to dance with anyone else.'

Connie grinned. But would he still want to dance with her, and her only, if he met another girl who didn't have a scar down her face? She couldn't chase the doubt away.

'But we're famous now – even that Lord Haw-Haw knows who we are,' she reminded him. She tried to sound cheeky and teasing as she asked him, 'What if loads of girls come knocking on our door while I'm away, looking for that handsome and clever Jack Taylor?'

He widened his eyes in surprise. 'And what if one of those

Americans sweeps you off your feet? I don't know if a London lad like me's much competition for them!' He gave her a cheeky wink. 'I mean, they've got chewing gum and nylons and ice cream... all I've got to offer a girl is a wireless set that picks up weird noises off the dial.'

'I can get by without nylons and all that,' Connie assured him.

As Connie spoke, a familiar woman in the queue for the baker turned and glanced over her shoulder. At the sight of the two teens, Ma Mahoney called, 'Here's a sight for sore eyes. Two of our lovely Blitz Kids!'

The sun glowed off Ma Mahoney's dyed, copper-coloured hair. Connie assumed that she was hiding the grey, and why not? Her son made a lot of money and could send her to the hairdresser's every day if he chose. She was very well dressed for a day of shopping, especially on such a hot day with a fur stole around her shoulders. Her buttoned-up silk dress battled to stretch across her large bosom, and diamonds dangled from her ears.

Other people in the queue, which wound its way from the door of the baker's past three other shops, turned as well, and smiled to see Connie and Jack. There were women in cotton frocks, and summer hats that had seen better days, but which they'd trimmed with new ribbons and wax fruit. Older men in suits wore their ties loosened against the heat. They would only take them off if they set foot on the beach at Margate or Southend.

Connie waved. 'All right, Ma Mahoney! What've they got in stock that everyone wants to buy?'

'Some lovely rock buns,' she said. Then, the mother of the East End's fearsome gang boss, Toe, clapped her hands together and called out, 'Let's bring these little heroes to the front of the queue, ladies, and get them some rock buns for their pals!'

No one was going to disagree with the word of Ma

Mahoney. The queue parted and the smiling shoppers gestured for Jack and Connie to come past them.

'We won't buy all the rock buns,' Connie said as she and Jack made their way to the front of the queue. 'Promise! We'll make sure there's enough left for all of you too!'

She smiled at Ma Mahoney, and as she did she remembered that the gangster's mother had once had another son, who wouldn't be coming home from the war. While Toe had remained in Whitechapel to run his empire, his brother had joined the navy. His ship had been rammed by a Nazi battleship, and he'd died a horrible death at sea. The same sea she was about to cross with the little boy who had become her honorary brother.

Ever the gentleman, Jack took Connie's arm and escorted her along the line, nodding his thanks to the ladies who had stepped aside. He was already reaching into his pocket for the little collection of ration books when Ma Mahoney held out her hand to Connie. In it, she saw a pound note.

'Get yourself those buns, petal,' said Ma. 'And keep the change.'

Connie stared at the money, before slowly taking the banknote.

'Blimey, Ma!' she gasped. 'I dunno what to say – thank you! I'll get Ned a present with the change.'

They reached the counter and Jack handed over the ration books as Connie put the rock buns, and a grey, wholemeal National Loaf into her basket. She much preferred the white bread they'd had before the war, but everyone ate the National Loaf, even the king and queen. It was full of vitamins, so they said.

Out on the pavement again, Connie's thoughts returned once more to Ned, sitting in that hospital bed with a bandage round his head and dried blood on his neck.

'Jack, I still feel awful about what's happened to Ned,' she told him. 'He could've died when that building fell on him, and Mr Wyngate, too, when he rescued him.'

'It wasn't your fault,' Jack replied gently. 'And Ned hasn't got any grudge about it. You need to be kinder to yourself, Con.'

'But I love that little bloke like my brother,' Connie replied with a sniff. 'We're like a family, and then there's me screaming the place down at him. I made him run away. Goin' with him to America is the least I can do to show him that I'm sorry; really sorry, right down to the bottom of my heart.'

Jack had let go of Connie's arm once they went into the bakery, but now he took it again.

'You just be careful over there,' he said. 'Don't let those American boys turn your head with their chocolate and Coca-Cola!' Then he glanced at his watch. 'Just the butcher left, then home!'

'Oh, it's just London boys for me,' Connie assured him. *One in particular, but I don't know how to tell you.*

They reached the butcher's, where they were faced with another queue, but once again the shoppers parted for them. There wasn't much on display at the counter, but Connie and Jack bought some sausages, which were thinner than the ones Connie remembered from before the war, and some meagre slices of ham. It'd last them for a few days, padded out with lots of vegetables.

They carried on, walking up the high street to head home. There was a busy street market just up ahead, where Connie liked to go from stall to stall, getting the best fruit and vegetables like her grandma used to do.

She could hear the cacophony of market traders calling out their wares. There were all sorts of goods for sale – some stalls sold second-hand bedsteads and lampshades, picture frames and saucepans, but some were rather dubious. Ned came here sometimes, Connie knew, and she could already see a man up ahead with a suitcase on the ground at the edge of the market.

He was glancing about, not just for potential customers but for the police as well, she was sure.

Not far from the market was a bombsite where a wholesale warehouse had once stood. As Connie walked past with Jack, she heard a sound like pouring sand, followed by the thud of falling brick. Her head whipped round. One of the last, charred walls still standing was leaning at an angle.

'Jack, look! That wall's about to go.' She gripped Jack's sleeve. Then she noticed something long and curved, something metallic, lodged in the crumbling brickwork. She knew at once what it was.

TWENTY-EIGHT

CONNIE

'That wall's comin' down and it'll set off that bomb!' Connie gasped. 'We've got to raise the alarm. The market's full of people!'

'Oh, heck!' Jack exclaimed. 'That's going to be a job with just the two of us!'

Connie took a deep breath, then slid her basket down her arm so she could cup her hands round her mouth. 'Everyone back, everyone back!' she shouted. 'There's a bomb in the old warehouse!'

Heads turned. Milling shoppers froze to see where the shouting was coming from. Connie had their attention.

'I'll let the coppers know,' said the man with the suitcase. It wasn't often someone who made their living selling black-market essentials would want to talk to the Met, but Londoners pulled together when it mattered.

Jack took off along the lanes of the market, calling out a warning to the shoppers and stallholders. Unexploded bombs were part of life now, but they weren't usually teetering on the edge of a crumbling ruin.

Connie, clutching her basket, spread her arms and tried to shepherd everyone away. 'Get back, get back! There's a bomb!'

An elderly couple who were shuffling by, arm in arm, looked shocked, and Connie hurried over to them to try to help them out of the way of danger. But as she did, she was still calling out, 'Bomb at the old warehouse! Get back, everyone!'

The crowd was dispersing. Even the stallholders were stepping back from their wares. Piles of potatoes and orange heaps of carrots were left abandoned, along with a stall that was heavy with old books, and beside it racks of second-hand clothes. The lady who had been standing behind the haberdashery stall reached under it to pull out a tin helmet, on which a white letter W was painted. Transformed now into an ARP warden, her voice joined with Jack and Connie's commanding the shoppers and stallholders to retreat to safety.

Connie and Jack saw the elderly couple back to the high street, where they were offered shelter in a café with taped windows, Union Jacks fluttering from its frontage. Then they were off again, back to the fast-emptying market.

The sun still beamed down, as if no one had told it that it had no right to be cheerful in the face of such danger. But Connie barely noticed the warm summer day. She felt cold, right down to her core. They had to clear everyone away.

She cast a glance back at the bombsite, and her stomach lurched. The wall had leaned even further since she'd first seen it, and the bomb shone in the sunlight as if it was as innocent as a ride on the pier.

But at least everyone was moving back to safety.

Suddenly a woman rushed up to Connie and Jack. Her small straw hat had slid on her hair, and her eyes were wide with panic.

'My kids – where are my kids?' she cried. 'I turned my back for a second, and they'd gone!'

Jack nodded sharply. 'Could they have gone onto the bombsite?'

The woman screwed up her face and started to sob. 'I think so! Yes. I had them evacuated, see, but they hated it, so they came back. They'd never seen bombsites before, and they keep wanting to play on them.'

'I'll go and look for them,' Jack assured the worried mother. 'What're their names?'

'P-Penny and Bill,' the woman said. She stared across at the bombsite and Connie followed her gaze. There was so much rubble still left that it was hard to see much, but then Connie saw a flash of red between two piles of fallen bricks. Was that one of the children?

'I'll come with you, Jack,' she said, determined. She handed her basket of shopping to the children's mother. 'Look after this. I'll be back in a tick.'

She knew he would tell her not to even before he shook his head and said, 'You stay safe.' Then he told the children's mother, 'Get back with everyone else, ma'am. I'll find the children.'

The woman retreated with difficulty. Connie couldn't imagine how scared she felt. And she knew, too, that she'd now be blaming herself for the danger her children were in.

Connie went with Jack, towards the bombsite. She could feel all the hairs on the back of her neck standing up.

'Penny? Bill?' she called softly. She didn't dare shout their names in case the sudden noise made the wall – and the bomb – crash to the ground.

'Anybody there?' Jack paused, then resumed picking his way carefully over the rubble of the bombsite. 'First to come out is an honorary Blitz Kid!'

There was nothing at first, then Connie saw the flash of red again. And then she saw a face peering out from behind a fallen rafter. It was a little girl in a red dress.

'Is— Is that a bomb?' the little girl asked fearfully, pointing up to the tottering wall. Beside her, another small figure emerged from behind the rafter. This was certainly her brother, Bill, and his eyes were wide as he peered up at the bomb.

Jack nodded. 'Come on,' he said kindly. 'Just take your time and come over to me and Connie. We'll get you safely back to your mum.'

Bill glanced to his sister and shook his head. 'I'm too scared to move,' he admitted as his bottom lip began to wobble. It reminded Connie of Ned, trying not to cry in the hospital.

Time seemed to slow down as Connie and Jack nimbly headed through the rubble and finally reached the two children. More bricks crashed to the ground from the unstable wall, but Connie didn't look over. She couldn't waste a second.

Connie let Bill scramble up onto her back, and made sure he was clinging on tight. Jack had hold of Penny, who he scooped up to carry in his arms.

'Make a run for it!' Connie said, and they were off like hares across a field.

They kicked up dust, they scraped their shoes, they sent rusty nails flying. Connie stubbed her toe against a lump of concrete, but she didn't register the pain. They had to get away, they had to get to safety.

Connie heard the terrifying crash of the wall collapsing behind her. She knew what would follow, and she dropped to the ground, bringing Bill into her arms to protect him. She curled up tight next to Jack, who was holding Penny, and then the summer day was torn apart by the roar of an exploding bomb.

As the smoke cleared, Connie was aware of approaching footsteps and voices, then of cheers ringing out. She lifted her head to see the crowd they had cleared from the market venturing closer to the bombsite, the terrified mother leading the way towards the children. At Connie's side, Jack sat up, Penny still clutched tight in his arms.

'All present and correct?' Jack asked the children brightly. He must've been as frightened as Connie when the bomb detonated, but he wasn't about to let anyone see that. He looked to Connie with a warm smile and said, 'What would I ever do without you?'

Connie smiled at him, even though it made her heart ache to think that soon she'd be getting on a ship that would take her far away from her brave friend – a friend she had fallen in love with.

TWENTY-NINE

LISETTE

It was Saturday, and Lisette left her little flat in Soho to head off to visit the children in Whitechapel. Before she'd met them, her time had been her own, and on a Saturday morning she'd lounge about in her flat, or while away the hours in a coffee shop. And yet, since the children had come into her life she'd never regretted losing her quiet Saturday mornings. There was always something happening with the children; a dispute that required her grown-up presence to settle, or a hug that needed to be given.

And Wyngate had so often been there with her that she felt a pang at the thought of the distance that had forced itself between them now. But she couldn't say anything to the children. They had enough to worry about, with Ned's injuries and the dangerous journey that he'd soon be taking with Connie, and which was eating away at Lisette's nerves too.

She took the Underground. The buses were still running, but there were so many diversions to get around bombsites and buildings that were on the verge of collapsing that it took for ever, and she struggled to orientate herself in a city made unfamiliar by the war. Perhaps that was why the Underground was so busy. Since the bombings had started, so much of London life had become subterranean. But even down there, the dust and the smell of smoke was unavoidable. It had become the city's own scent.

She was almost on the street where the children lived, passing a large S painted onto the side of an empty house with broken windows, an arrow showing the way to the nearest shelter, when she glanced down and noticed that the gravy browning she'd tanned her legs with had smudged. If only she could've got hold of some new nylon stockings – she didn't like going about bare-legged, even in the summer. But there were none to be had, especially with Ned out of action, unless a girl was dating an American.

She paused and dampened her fingertip to hide the worst of the smudge, then brushed at the mark on her leg. She heard footsteps, and recognised them at once. It was Wyngate: only he had such a brisk and determined step.

She stood up quickly as he came round the corner. 'Adam...' she said, her heart suddenly racing.

Wyngate pulled up short at the sight of her, then answered, 'Lis.' He kicked at a stone on the pavement with the toe of one polished shoe and said, 'I assume we're going the same way?'

'Yes, to see the children,' Lisette replied in French, out of habit. But it seemed too intimate somehow. She swallowed and switched into English. 'Just to see how they are, you know. And I'll take them to see Ned later.'

'He'll be coming home soon,' he replied. 'Then... America. Bit of a headline grab by the Yanks, that one.'

Lisette didn't want to tell him how worried she was about the trip. She nodded. 'Well, if it means Ned has a chance to get his hearing back, we can't really complain about them grabbing the headlines.'

She'd always taken his arm whenever they'd walked anywhere, unless they were at the War Office, and it felt strange not to take it now as they walked through the midsummer sunshine along St Joseph's Terrace to the children's house. The street had seen good and bad luck; most of the houses were still defiantly standing, even though they were old and losing roof tiles. Along the length of the street, though, were houses that had been lost to a bomb, the remains of walls sticking up like broken teeth. The pavement was gritty with brick dust.

She wanted to say something, but she wasn't going to tell him exactly what she thought about his decision in front of the children. She wasn't sure they'd noticed anything different between them; understandably, their thoughts were entirely consumed by Ned and his trip to America with Connie.

Although, it wasn't certain whether Connie was in fact included in the trip. The American offer had been made to Ned, and Wyngate's own journey was for the war effort. Would Connie be permitted to travel with Ned, simply to provide a friendly face for the little boy?

'Connie has decided she's going with Ned,' Lisette told Wyngate. 'But it hasn't occurred to her that she'll need someone to pay for her ticket. I don't want to dash her hopes – but she's right that Ned will be going through a lot, travelling to a strange new country and having his operation. He'll need a friend while you're busy. I don't suppose the Americans will pay for her too?'

She thought of Lord Haw-Haw's smirking broadcast again, telling the world that the Nazis would attack allied ships crossing the Atlantic. It was a dangerous journey, but she tried to push the thought away. It couldn't be more dangerous, surely, than living in London with Nazi bombs raining down on them.

'Gray asked the question,' Wyngate replied as they reached the front door, with its polished door knocker and scrubbed-clean step. 'So far, America hasn't answered. If they won't foot the bill for her ticket, I'll pay it myself. I can scrape that money together somehow; it's not the sort of loose change I have lying around, but my car's worth a bob or two for starters.'

Without thinking, Lisette touched Wyngate's arm. 'Oh, Adam, you're so kind, but you can't sell your car.'

She wondered what she could sell to help as well. There were some small diamond earrings that her mother had given her when she left Paris. Perhaps she could sell them? But she had so few things from her mother, because she hadn't expected to be so drastically cut off from her. She pictured them twinkling in their worn, velvet-lined box, and realised that selling them would be like selling a piece of her heart.

'Money's never been important to me,' Wyngate said with a shrug. 'Probably because I didn't have any for a long time. I'm not exactly rich now, but what I've got I'll put into Connie's ticket.'

Lisette tried to think of something else of value that she could sell. But all that came to mind was a slender gold chain with an amber pendant that had been her mother's as well. What good was jewellery in boxes when Connie should be able to go to America with Ned? And yet the thought of parting with it made her heart ache. Before Lisette could reply, Pippa started barking her greeting from inside the narrow brick house. She saw Ben had lifted the curtains of the front room window, which looked out into the street, and they were draped round his shoulders like a cloak. He was flying a toy plane, and waved hello before darting away from the window and out of sight.

Elsie opened the front door. She was gripping Pippa's collar to stop the dog from leaping up at their guests.

'Morning, you two,' she said. She stepped back to let them into the little hallway with its tiled floor that Connie mopped religiously to keep clean. 'Mr Wyngate, you have to come and see Jack's radio – you haven't seen it working yet!'

'Heard anything good?' asked Wyngate, stooping to fuss over Pippa. He gave Elsie the smile that he so rarely shone on anyone else besides the girl who reminded him of his lost sister. 'No more Lord Haw-Haw, I hope?'

'No, we don't want to listen to him,' Elsie replied. 'He's a liar. But we've listened to lots of other stuff. You know them Americans have got radio stations for their troops? They play jazz, and Connie makes Jack dance around the room to it with her.' She chuckled.

Lisette was instantly reminded of the conversation she'd had with Wyngate where they'd decided they would have to speak individually to Connie and Jack about the birds and the bees. How long ago that seemed.

'I'll stick the kettle on,' Wyngate told Elsie as they stepped into the house. Lisette could hear the other children in the living room and, alongside their chatter, the sound of laughter and voices on the radio. 'Then we'll give that radio a listen.'

Lisette was about to follow Elsie into the front room, but she realised that, if she went with Wyngate into the kitchen, she could speak to him. Even just quickly. Even just in whispers. She had to say something.

'I'll come with you,' she told him. He had opened up now that he was at the children's house, and it seemed like her only chance. Because when he spoke to her anywhere else, it was like speaking through a wall that had been built between them.

Elsie headed off towards the front room, calling, 'Mr Wyngate and Lisette are here!'

Lisette tried to catch Wyngate's eye and smile at him as they went into the kitchen, but it felt like trying to get a response from a statue carved from stone.

'Adam, I want so much to speak with you,' she whispered, switching into French again. 'About... us.'

'I'm sorry,' Wyngate answered in French. 'But we need to keep some distance between us, Lis.'

'You care about me,' Lisette replied. 'That's why you've pushed me away. But it doesn't have to be like this. I know the dangers. And yet, when we're together, none of that matters. What are we fighting for if we ignore our hearts? We can't close ourselves away from each other, because we're scared we might lose the people we love, or we shut out all the joy from our lives.'

Wyngate said nothing, but held Lisette's gaze. She could see the softness there, the affection that they shared, and she held back a tremble that threatened to run through her. But she could see the resolve too, the survival instinct that had protected him and with which he was determined to protect her too.

'Lisette—' he began, but then his brow furrowed. From the living room the sound of voices had been replaced by static and interference that sounded like the rhythmic pattern of Morse code, then static again as Jack turned the dial. Suddenly, Wyngate's head flicked round and he called out, 'Jack, tune into that again!'

Then he was hurrying from the kitchen, heading towards the living room.

Lisette clenched and unclenched her fists, before following him through.

THIRTY

LISETTE

Lisette watched as all the children sat in silence in the living room, staring at Wyngate. The Morse code went on. Somewhere, someone was tapping out a message.

Jack was kneeling in front of the wireless on the table, his ear pressed against the speaker grille. He looked up at Wyngate and said, 'I'm sure I can just about hear voices in the background. I think they're Germans!'

'Make a note of the frequency,' Wyngate instructed. He dropped to one knee in front of the wireless and, as Jack moved to pick up a notepad, pressed his own ear to the grille and listened intently. No one else moved or said a word.

Lisette thought of all the messages that came across her desk for her to translate. They'd all come through a radio at a listening station somewhere and yet here, in a Whitechapel front room, a message was coming through on a child's radio.

'It's not on the dial,' Jack explained. 'When I was fixing it, I did a few modifications here and there, to see if I could get hold of stations from further out. Mr Gray said it was a really good way to hear other languages and music and everything. You get all the way to the left and then give the dial another three turns or so. I've heard signals and noises but you can never find them again, so you can't be sure. But there's not usually anything this far along but interference.'

Wyngate nodded. 'Tell nobody about this,' he said. 'I need to let the office know what you've found. Any movement on that phone installation?'

'Some bloke from the GPO came round yesterday morning to have a look,' Connie told him. 'Said he'd be back next week to install it. Sorry, Mr Wyngate.'

'It's all right,' he assured her as he rose to his feet. 'I need to go.'

'Can we still use the radio?' Jack asked, but Lisette suspected she knew the answer even before Wyngate shook his head.

'Some folks from the War Office will want to come over and take a look and get the frequency,' he explained. 'Once they're done, the radio's all yours again. I've a feeling it'll be today. This is important, Jack, you may've found something here.'

Lisette had gone cold. The war reached its fingers into every corner of their lives.

Connie patted Jack's shoulder. 'That's our Jack, he's a genius.'

Elsie nodded proudly towards her brother. 'No more dancing until the radio people have been, though.'

'I promise it won't be too long,' Wyngate told Elsie as he headed for the door. He paused to assure them, 'And I'll make sure that the War Office throws in a few extra rations to thank you all.'

With that, he was off to the front door.

Lisette didn't go with him. Whatever it was that he'd heard, it was more important than what she wanted to say to him, even though it bruised her heart to have been robbed of the chance to talk.

Just as Wyngate left, Pippa ran to the window and started

barking again. Elsie went over to see who had attracted her dog's attention, and then she turned back to announce to the room, 'It's Jasper and Mr Dupree!'

She ran off to the front door as Jack, at the news of visitors, turned the volume down to silence the messages that were somehow coming through from the enemy. Lisette settled on the arm of the sofa. Wyngate was heading off to the War Office, only for two figures from Soho's nightlife to arrive after him, as if they were from a different world.

'Hello everyone!' Jasper said, striding into the room. He was holding a parcel wrapped in blue and orange paper. 'Mr Dupree very kindly gave me a lift over to see you all. I've brought Ned's get well soon present and a card from all of us lot at the club. Don't suppose you'd mind giving it to Ned when you next see him?'

Jasper had tried to give Ned the biggest gift of all by sacrificing the rebuilding of his nightclub for him. But a parcel wrapped in paper was one that even Ned wouldn't refuse, Lisette was sure.

He passed the present and a card to Connie, then stood aside so that Mr Dupree could come in. Soho's gang boss walked a little taller than he had at the funeral of his beloved wife, but the grief was etched on his face. At the sight of the children he gave a smile and told them, 'You've got a proper little home here now; snug as bugs, my Mo would've said.'

'Would you like to sit down?' Jack asked the new arrivals, every inch the proud man of the house. 'It's nice to see you.'

Connie urged Ben and Susan off the sofa. Lisette glanced at Mr Dupree again as the two men sat down. His pale, drawn face, the blankness in his eyes and the heaviness in his step spoke of the grief that Wyngate was trying to spare her from. But Lisette was no stranger to such tragic loss; Tom's death still haunted her, and every day was coloured by background anxiety because she didn't know what was happening to her mother.

She didn't want to cut herself off from her emotions just to be spared heartbreak, and she wished Wyngate would understand. If she'd asked Mr Dupree if he'd wished he'd never married his wife so that he'd never have to grieve her, he would've said no. Why couldn't Wyngate understand that his urge to protect her was the death of love?

'How are you, Mr Dupree?' Lisette asked him gently instead. 'You're looking well.'

'Better than I was,' he replied with a sad smile. 'The family have pulled together.' Then he looked at the assembled children and said, 'You'll all know about that.'

'Yeah, we do,' Connie replied. 'Family's important, ain't it? Even if you're not exactly related by blood. You have to stick together.'

'Soho's full of families like that,' Jasper said. He smiled and patted Mr Dupree on the arm. 'After all that fundraising – and now we know Ned's going to get that treatment – we've started to rebuild the club. Mr Dupree's really thrown himself into it, and we've found a new place. It's a little bit bigger than the old one, so as well as the main bar with the stage, it's got a snug. And we're going to call the snug Mo's, after Mrs Dupree.'

'That's perfect,' Lisette replied. 'She would have loved that.'

She was so glad that the new club was coming together, but the fact that the old one had been lost at the same time as Mrs Dupree had died would always have made the new incarnation bitter-sweet.

Mr Dupree nodded. 'Now, Scotland Yard'll tell you that nothing happens in Soho without my say-so,' he teased. 'So I was very pleased when a perfect little bolt-hole on Silver Street came available; I was able to secure it for my friend here. That's where you'll find the new Jasper's, once the work's finished. And that's where you'll all be welcome.'

Connie could sing on the stage again, Elsie would have her piano lessons once more, Susan would help with the costumes, Ned would wheel and deal, and Jack and Ben would have their jobs back.

The children all cheered, and their joy was infectious; she could see it in their visitors' faces. The club had always been more than just a nightspot. It had been a community, and welcomed everyone.

'Lisette, you'll come back and sing, won't you?' Jasper said hopefully. 'It wouldn't be the same without you, although I know you're busy now.'

'We'll work something out,' Lisette assured him. She longed to return to the stage, but there was her work at the War Office, too. She'd find time for both, somehow. 'We have some news for you, too. The Americans are going to pay for Ned to go to New York for his operation. It's the only way to bring back his hearing, you know.'

'And I'm going with him,' Connie announced. 'Well, if I can get the money for a ticket on the boat.'

Jasper and Mr Dupree exchanged a look before Mr Dupree explained, 'Well, that's torn it!' He gave a chuckle. 'We read in the paper about young Ned needing to go to America. He's done a lot of work for me and a lot for Londoners. I came here today with an offer to foot the bill for his trip to America, but the Yanks have beat me to it.'

Jack gave Connie a glance. Then he suggested, 'They haven't offered to pay for our Con to go, Mr Dupree.'

'Ned's like a brother to me,' Connie explained. 'He needs someone to look after him on the trip, and keep him company while he's getting over his operation. It doesn't seem right to send him on his own. Mr Dupree, I don't suppose...?'

She glanced shyly at the gangster who ran Soho.

'First class all the way,' he said with a smile. 'Connie, you're going to America.'

Connie's shyness vanished completely and she rushed at Mr Dupree and gave the bereaved man a huge hug. Lisette suspected it was just the sort of unbridled, innocent show of affection that he needed at the moment.

'Oh, thank you, Mr Dupree! Thank you!' Connie said, breathless with excitement, and the other children cheered.

Lisette couldn't help but smile. Connie would be going to America after all, and Lisette wouldn't have to part with her mother's jewellery for it to happen. But all the same, she shivered at the thought of so much ocean, empty save for Nazis intent on destroying everything in their path.

THIRTY-ONE
CONNIE

Connie held Ned's hand tightly. She was being the big sister and keeping an eye on him, not wanting him to vanish into the crowd of people who were waiting at the dock.

Some were passengers, with trunks and suitcases ready to be loaded onto the ship that reared up before them like the side of an enormous hotel. Others were seeing off their loved ones. They were all wearing their best clothes, or at least what passed for their best with all the shortages. Shoes were polished, suits brushed, hat trimmings refreshed. It was an occasion.

Even though the docks along the Thames had come in for a beating from the Luftwaffe, ships still came and went. Nissen huts, with their curved, corrugated roofs, had been set up where bombs had hit, and warehouses that had been damaged had been patched up, as if they were held together with sticking plaster and tape. Cranes stood wonkily where they'd been damaged, but still others were busy, unloading the cargo ships that were waiting in the river. A warm breeze sent dust blowing in from the nearby bombsites, and Connie wondered what it'd be like to see America, which hadn't known the Blitz.

She'd never been abroad before. In fact, apart from when

she'd been evacuated to the countryside, she'd never been further from London than Margate, and the only boats she'd ever been on were rowing boats at the park, and the little ferries that ran up and down the Thames. She kept thinking of the poem about the ancient sailor tormented by an albatross, but she shook the image away.

She and Ned had had their first ever passports rushed out to them courtesy of Wyngate and Mr Gray, and now they were standing at the docks with a suitcase each.

Bunting flapped in the warm breeze and the well-wishers seeing off friends and family waved and cheered, while Connie, Ned and Wyngate stood by the door to the passport desk to say goodbye to their friends. There was a party atmosphere, although Connie had never been this nervous at a celebration before. And she wasn't sure her friends looked happy, even though they were all smiling, and Pippa was wagging her tail.

The days had flown by since Dupree had offered to pay for her passage. Ned had come home from the hospital and immediately packed his suitcase. And now here they were, ready to set sail.

'I'll look after Ned, don't you worry!' Connie assured everyone. 'Me and Mr Wyngate will keep an eye on him.'

'You wait until Ned Mitchell hits New York!' Ned told his friends, his voice bearing the customary loudness and measured care that they had come to expect since he lost his hearing. 'Once I'm out of hospital, I'm getting myself off to Broadway. Just like the pictures, our Connie's coming back a star!'

Connie chuckled. As much as she liked the idea of that, it wasn't why she wanted to go to New York with Ned. And besides, what were the chances of anyone getting off a ship from England and walking straight onto a Broadway stage?

And yet, she had a feeling that Ned wouldn't let the chance slip by.

'Yeah, I'll come back a star and bring all my famous friends with me!' Connie grinned. 'And they'll want to perform at Jasper's, so you just tell him and Mr Dupree to get the club ready for them!'

Elsie's smile faded. She wrote down a note for Ned and read it out loud. '*It's amazing over there in America – will you really come back to see us?*' She glanced from Connie and Ned up to Wyngate.

'Of course they'll come back,' Lisette promised. Connie noticed that she'd looked at Wyngate, then stared off at the side of the ship that was waiting for them.

Ned read the note Elsie had written and furrowed his brow. Then he shook his head. 'Not come back?' he asked, incredulous. 'Mate, you cut me and I bleed River Thames. I'm London to my bones; I'm like them ravens, ain't I? London'd fall down without Ned!'

Elsie smiled at him. She evidently liked the sound of that, and gleefully wrote another note for him. '*So don't be out there too long. Get your ears fixed and come back on the next boat!*'

'We'll come home,' Wyngate assured Elsie gently. 'I always do, don't I?'

Elsie nodded. Connie could see the effort it took her to smile. 'I'll write everything down in my journal for you so you won't miss anything. And I'll look after the house, too, while you're not here, Connie.'

Connie swallowed, thinking of how she'd become a big sister to all of the children and in some ways like a mother too. She'd miss them. She pictured her apron, which she'd hung on the back of the kitchen door for the last time that morning, and imagined Elsie wearing it; it'd come down to the floor on her. 'And you'll look after them, Jack Taylor, I know you will,' she said, catching his eye. There was a tremble in her voice as she turned to the other children. 'Everyone'll be all right as long as Jack's with you.'

The line moved along. In just a minute or two they would

pass the desk and board the ship. Jack gave Connie a smile and said, 'Good luck, Con. Have the best time ever.'

Connie was standing near to Jack, and she could smell the fresh tang of soap on his skin. If only she didn't have to leave him. If only she could tell him how she felt. She'd just have to remember how it felt to see his smile whenever she missed him.

'I'll miss you so much, Jack...' she said.

'Come home soon,' he whispered in reply. 'Please.'

Connie wondered if there was a chance he didn't think of her as a substitute sister, but as a girlfriend. She hoped so. She made a pact with herself then. When they returned from America, she'd run down the gangway from the ship and into Jack's arms, as if they were in a film, and tell him how she felt.

'I will, don't you worry about that,' Connie promised him.

The queue moved again, and they took a few steps forward. She could still feel the warmth of his smile.

Ben and Susan both looked downhearted. Ben kicked a small stone away, and it looked as if Susan was blinking back tears. They'd all become a family, after losing their own, and now it was breaking up. But not for ever, Connie was sure of it. They'd be home soon.

'See you soon, Ben, Sus.' Ned grinned as the children all exchanged hugs. 'We'll get that radio cranked and have a dance.'

'Adam,' Lisette said. There was something in her voice. Something urgent. She held Wyngate's gaze. 'Look after the children, and yourself. Sois prudent.'

He gave that characteristic sharp nod. 'I'll look after them,' he promised.

The queue shuffled forward but, before they could move along, Lisette rushed forward and wrapped her arms round Wyngate's shoulders. Then she kissed him on the lips.

For a moment Wyngate was still, then he took Lisette in his embrace and returned her kiss.

Connie blushed, but she couldn't look away at this display

of devastating love. She wished Wyngate could stay behind, so that he and Lisette wouldn't be separated. And yet, war was full of partings, and maybe that made love all the more precious. All the more intense. She'd miss Jack horribly, and she'd think about him every day.

Their kiss ended and Lisette whispered, 'Je t'aime.'

'You shouldn't,' Wyngate replied in a murmur. Then he put his hand gently against Lisette's face, his eyes studying her. Connie saw his throat bob as he swallowed, then he whispered, 'Je t'adore, Lisette.'

Connie bit her lip. She suddenly realised that she'd never heard Lisette and Wyngate say these words to each other before. Perhaps that was why they'd seemed a bit awkward lately, as if in their hearts they were building up to the moment when they'd finally say it out loud. And then be parted.

'But I do, Adam,' Lisette said softly. 'I can't help it. Come back quickly, won't you, mon cher?'

Wyngate nodded, then kissed her again. It was the sort of kiss Connie didn't often see away from the cinema screen, filled with longing and love. When he finally stepped back, he took Lisette's hand and held it tight.

'I'll come home,' he promised. 'We all will.'

The ship's whistle blew and it was so loud that Connie had to clap her hands over her ears. She wasn't sure if Ned had heard it. But that was why they were going on this journey, to give Ned a chance to hear again, even though it meant that their little group would be split up. It wouldn't be for long.

'Bloody 'ell, even I 'eard a bit of that whistle!' Ned laughed. 'And my ears're buggered!'

'All passengers this way, please,' said an officious-looking man in a blue suit with gold bands on it. He looked like a ship's officer. 'All passengers to the passport desk, please.'

Jack glanced towards the uniformed man, then dashed forward and threw his arms round Connie. He held her tight for a long moment, saying nothing. Connie wrapped her arms round him too, stiffly at first because his sudden embrace had taken her so much by surprise. He really did like her too. She loosened and rested her head on his shoulder. A sob was building up inside her. She didn't want to go. She'd miss Jack too much. How would she survive if a piece of her heart was still in London?

But she had to leave; she had to look after Ned. She released Jack from her embrace.

'This is it, then,' she said. She held Ned's hand again, and picked up her suitcase. It suddenly felt heavy, even though she hadn't packed much. 'Goodbye everyone, bye!'

She glanced at Jack, and already missed him, and she could see tears in Lisette's eyes. Ben and Susan were waving, Elsie held Pippa and waved the little dog's paw. At the last moment before he passed through the door, Ned raised his camera and took a photograph of his friends, then gave them a thumbs-up.

Connie's mind was in a whirl as they went to the desk. Their tickets were checked and passports stamped, then they headed up a ramp to the ship. She smiled at Ned, hoping he wasn't nervous, although she knew him well enough to know that he could be hiding it. They were welcomed aboard by the captain, and the sun caught the double row of shiny buttons on his uniform.

They headed up a flight of metal steps that smelt of salt and oil, then through a heavy door complete with a porthole, which led them out to the deck. They leaned against the metal railings, a crust of brine under their hands, then waved along with the other passengers to the people on the dockside below. Connie shielded her eyes with her hand and caught sight of the pink of Lisette's sundress and saw their friends waving up at them.

'There they are, look!' she called, pointing to their friends. 'Giving us a proper send-off!'

Ned stood up on tiptoe to wave over the railing, holding his camera up high to snap a photograph of the dock far beneath them. Wyngate put his arms round Ned's waist and hoisted him up, the better to take his photographs and wave goodbye to his friends.

Wyngate glanced down at Connie and smiled. Then he said, 'We'll be back before you know it.' He set Ned down again before adding, 'And Ned'll be good as new.'

The ship's whistle blasted again, and the crew shouted orders to each other. With a tremendous clanking noise, the anchor chain rattled up. The heavy ropes that kept the ship close to the dock were flung clear of their moorings and the gangway withdrew. Connie's heart was in her throat as the ship's engines began to thud and the ship moved away from the dock.

But she wasn't going to stop waving. Her friends grew smaller and smaller as the ship pulled away, heading for the mouth of the Thames, Lisette's dress now little more than a pink dot. Even when her friends were completely out of sight, Connie still waved to them; she felt like she'd left half of her heart behind in London.

THIRTY-TWO

LISETTE

Late that afternoon, Lisette decided to take the four quiet, preoccupied children to catch the last of the sun in Victoria Park, in an attempt to keep them cheerful – and, she silently admitted to herself, to keep herself smiling, too. But she kept losing her smile as every few moments, despite the heat of the day, she shivered and thought of steely grey waves. She wished she could reach through the distance with both arms and wrap them round the three travellers.

She could still feel Wyngate's kiss, the touch of his lips lingering. And she wanted to hold on to that, because it felt like a promise that he'd come safely home. If she closed her eyes, it was almost as if he was still there, his quiet presence by her side. She already missed him so much it ached.

Victoria Park was a welcome patch of space and trees in the crowded East End of the city, but much of it was now home to allotments full of vegetables, and the anti-aircraft guns that pounded away every time the sirens went off. There were still winding paths they could walk along, past rhododendrons in bloom, and it was good to be under the dappled shade offered by the trees.

There were large ponds carved into the lawns that had once been swimming pools, but they were turning green with algae. The lido, with its art deco design and large pool with triple diving boards, would've been great fun in the hot weather, but it'd been damaged by the bombing and had been closed.

Ahead, at the edge of the park where Regent's Canal ran, a narrowboat was chugging slowly past, with young women in loose overalls, their hair tied up in spotty handkerchiefs, balancing along the edges. They were called the Idle Women, but they weren't idle at all. Keeping goods moving through the country was war work for women too, alongside the Land Girls and nurses and pilots, the women in uniform at the War Office, the munitions workers, and every other woman called on to do essential work. Lisette wondered what it was like to work on the canals; long days of hard work and sleeping somewhere new every night.

The sight of the canal boat made her think of the ship again, and her heart twisted as she pictured Wyngate, Connie and Ned standing in a row against the railings, staring out to sea. Theirs had to be a safe journey. She couldn't lose them. She couldn't lose Wyngate.

'Where do you think they are now?' Susan asked, as they stopped to admire the allotment beds and their impressive rows of vegetables which meant food on the table for many London homes. The canal boat had made Susan's thoughts travel the same way as Lisette's, she realised. 'Do you think they've gone past the Isle of Wight yet?'

'They must have,' said Jack. 'We'll have a look at the map later and put a pin in it.'

The children had a map on the kitchen wall, where they were following the route they assumed the ship would take. It had been Gray's idea, and had given Jack a new angle for the geography lessons he gave the younger children in their little living room.

Jack had become a teacher to his young friends alongside Connie, with other lessons coming from Lisette, Gray, Lucien, the club's pianist, and even, sometimes, Mr Wyngate. It seemed easier than trying to convince them to go to school, which Ned was particularly reluctant to do. For the children who had already fled the places they had been evacuated to, being put back into the system was something that all viewed with suspicion, even Jack himself.

And there weren't many schools left open in London. At the start of the war, many children had been evacuated by school group; almost all of the pupils and some of their teachers had arrived in villages safely away from the Blitz, but miles from home. Now the school buildings in the city were either bomb damaged or used as ARP posts and ambulance bases.

'What do they do for fun on the ship?' Elsie asked, although the tremble in her voice told Lisette that the little girl was worried about them too. Not just about them getting bored, but whether they would arrive safely with the German submarines lurking in the depths. 'Do they have parties and play cards and have tea dances? Although I can't see Mr Wyngate dancing without you, Lisette.'

'No, I don't think he's dancing either,' Lisette replied. 'But he'll have taken some work with him. And he has Connie and Ned to look after, remember. They'll keep him busy!'

She tried to chuckle, but she felt the pain of Wyngate's absence as keenly as a wound. He'd been away before, on what she knew were dangerous assignments to who knew where. She'd had sleepless nights and the constant sense of a gap; she always seemed to be glancing over her shoulder even though there was no one there. But there was so much left unspoken and unresolved between them this time, and she knew exactly what dangers he faced out at sea, with the Kriegsmarine prowling after allied ships. She'd never felt the fear of losing him for ever quite as badly as this, as though she was walking the city with nothing inside her; just a hollow shape of a woman moving from the shadows that fell between the buildings.

'I got a letter from the War Office this morning,' Jack said excitedly. 'From Mr Gray, thanking me for the radio signals I picked up. The men who came to see the wireless didn't say much, but they seemed very happy that they could listen in to the code.' He exchanged a proud smile with Elsie. 'I'm going to tinker with it again, see if I can widen the range even more. I want to tell Dad, but I know that would count as careless talk. You never know who might read it!'

Lisette nodded. He was a sensible boy, and had evidently taken in the message that shouted from so many government information posters around the city. *Careless talk costs lives. Loose lips sink ships.* She suppressed a shudder, thinking of the messages she translated that were still coming in from the resistance, about all those Kriegsmarine ships lining up in French harbours. Wyngate, Connie and Ned had passed the Channel already, and must already be out in the Atlantic. But the danger still remained.

'You're quite right, you mustn't write to your papa about the signals,' Lisette said. 'And you mustn't tell anyone else, either. That goes for all of you. Not a word – it's our special secret.'

She hoped she didn't sound severe, and she smiled at the children as she tapped the side of her nose.

Jack nodded. 'Not to a soul,' he replied.

They walked on, and watched a group of soldiers as they cleaned their guns, which had been set up on the football pitches. The turf had been churned up by the wheels on the guns, and Pippa, on her lead, sniffed the air with interest. The goals stood empty, without any nets, and the white lines that had once marked out where the matches were held had long grown out. Most of the children who had played here were in the countryside now, playing on other pitches.

'Do you reckon them soldiers have a kickabout with a ball when no one's looking?' Ben asked. 'I know I would!'

Even though it was sunny, no band played on the bandstand. Instead, some soldiers stood under its shade, sharing a cigarette. There were no ice cream stalls either, but here and there, where the lawn had been spared the anti-aircraft guns, there were people taking a break from their jobs in nearby shops and factories. Young women lay on the grass in twos and threes, sunbathing and reading magazines. An older woman sat on a bench, knitting. Normal life went on where it could, like dandelions growing up between cracks in the pavement.

Lisette and the children headed out of the park and walked down dusty streets until they arrived at the imposing Victorian gates of Bow Cemetery. Elsie and Susan were both carrying bunches of bombsite wildflowers, mixed in with roses Elsie had picked from the garden.

'Mum'll like these,' she said with a gentle smile. Pippa looked up at her and wagged her tail.

The cemetery wasn't an obvious place to take four children who needed to be distracted and cheered up, but Lisette knew that deep down it made the children happy, because it meant they could still have some sort of connection with their late parents. She didn't want them to be taboo subjects that no one would talk about.

Jack nodded. He turned to tell Ben, 'You're an ace in the garden, Ben. The roses are lovely!'

Ben beamed with pride. 'They like old tea leaves, that's the key with roses. And I don't let those aphids get hold, neither.'

He held up his hands and gleefully mimed squashing the bugs. Laughing, Susan scrunched up her face in mock disgust.

'Wait until Ned and Connie get home,' said Jack, but his smile looked a little sad at the thought of his absent friends. 'The garden will be more glorious than ever by then. It feels funny without them, doesn't it?'

Elsie nodded. 'The bed feels really big without Connie in it, and the house is really quiet without Ned. I keep thinking about them bobbing about on the sea. And I keep thinking about Mr Wyngate.' She looked up at Lisette. 'I imagine him on the deck, sitting in a chair, with his hat over his face! Except he's not asleep, because he's got to listen out for Ned and Connie.'

Lisette chuckled. She could picture that too. But she wondered, was he missing her as much as she missed him? 'I'm sure that's exactly what he's doing.'

They picked their way along the path towards the grave. The headstones were crowded, and it was easy to lose your way. And it wasn't just years of Londoners being buried here that made the cemetery so untidy; it'd been hit during air raids and there were roped-off areas full of smashed stone, and memorials damaged by shrapnel.

They arrived at the grave where Ben and Susan's parents were buried, in a plot with other generations of their family. Ben and Susan tidied the grave, picking out weeds, before Susan carefully laid her bouquet down for them.

'I grew the roses,' Ben said proudly, standing with his hands neatly clasped. 'They smell really nice and look like silk!'

'And I've been sewing, so thank you, Mum, for teaching me how to do it,' Susan said. 'I've been making new costumes for Lisette and the others at the club, seeing as they lost a load of them when the bomb hit. It's not easy finding the fabric, but I do my best.'

Jack shook his head. 'She does brilliantly,' he said. 'And when the new club opens, Lisette and Connie will be the belles of the ball in Susan's frocks!'

Susan smiled. A warm breeze rustled through a nearby tree, and she said, 'That's Mum, that is. She's saying she's pleased!'

Ben and Susan said their goodbyes, patting the headstone. Lisette held their hands as they all headed off to the newer graves in the cemetery where Jack and Elsie's mother lay.

The bomb damage to the cemetery made Lisette shiver. Even after having their lives taken from them by the bombings, the dead were still not allowed to rest. Some headstones had lost their inscriptions, and angels had lost their wings. But at least they were buried somewhere. She shivered as she pictured the grey waves again and thought about how many who were lost at sea could never be found.

Mrs Taylor's grave was against the cemetery wall, and the headstone was new. Wyngate had made sure that her children would have somewhere to come to when they needed her.

A blackberry bush was growing on the grave, the branches full of blossom and tiny green spots of new fruit. Elsie had told them that one of her last memories of her mother was a day out blackberrying, so the blackberry bush had seemed more appropriate than a vase for hothouse flowers.

'Hello, Mum,' Elsie said, and waved. Then she glanced up at her brother.

'It's your favourite sort of day today, Mum,' Jack said. He knelt beside Elsie and put his arm gently round her. 'Not too hot, but just right. Bees buzzing everywhere and Elsie still being my favourite little terror.' And he kissed his sister's cheek.

Elsie grinned, then she said, 'And Jack's been really clever. He fixed a wireless, and we have dances at home. And— well, I can't tell you everything about it, but you know what a clever-clogs he is. We've got another letter from Dad, too. Would you like to hear it?'

She rummaged in the canvas bag that hung over her shoulder and produced an envelope bearing the Red Cross symbol. She passed the letter to Jack to read.

Elsie and Jack's dad's letter was full of news about the prison camp choir, which he'd joined with his friends. The envelope was bigger than usual as he'd included a piece of music that they sang.

Elsie took the sheet of music from the envelope, as if her

mother could see it. 'I've tried singing it, but it's really hard. They must be amazing singers in that choir. But I reckon Connie could learn it when she gets home and sing it in Jasper's new club. And I want to sing it for you, too. Dad told us to show it to Connie or Mr Wyngate if we couldn't follow it. And Lisette had a look too, but she couldn't work it out neither! Connie'd know, I bet, she's got such a natural way with music.' She looked thoughtful for a moment, before grinning up at Lisette. 'I dunno why Dad told us to show it to Mr Wyngate – he's not very musical!'

Lisette smiled back at her. It was true, Wyngate wasn't musical, but perhaps their father didn't realise that.

Jack and Elsie brushed their fingertips against their mother's headstone and said goodbye. They'd be back again, with more flowers, and more letters to read. But as Lisette walked with the children back to their home in Whitechapel, they were talking about Jasper's club again.

Maybe they should sing the prisoners' song to raise money for the club. They hoped it would be ready to open to welcome Wyngate, Ned and Connie home.

Lisette had to chase away the lingering spectre that warned her they may never come home at all.

THIRTY-THREE

CONNIE

Connie had slept well in her cabin. She hadn't had her own bed for ages. In fact, she hadn't had her own space for ages, and it'd been novel to close the door last night and be on her own. She'd never travelled first class on the train before, let alone on a ship.

She had her own double bed, and all the furniture was made from polished walnut, and there were dark red curtains. She'd felt like a film star when she'd sat at the dressing table brushing her hair. She'd got used to the sound of the ship's engines too, and decided that they sounded like its heartbeat.

But she wasn't sure she liked travelling first class on her own that much. She felt lonely.

After getting up the next day, she left her cabin and knocked on the door of the neighbouring cabin where Wyngate and Ned were staying.

'Hey, what are you two lads getting up to?' she called through the polished door. A moment later, the door was opened by Mr Wyngate, dressed as usual in one of his smart suits, his hat already on his head.

'He never stops talking, does he?' he asked as he stood back so Connie could enter. Ned was sitting cross-legged on the bed, reading a book that Jack had given him as a going-away gift. At the sight of Connie though, he threw *Biggles Defies the Swastika* onto the bed and hopped down.

'Con!' Ned exclaimed. He put his Home Guard cap on. 'You'll not believe this. Mr W says I can't go in the smoking room where the blokes all play cards. I'd rinse 'em at poker, an' all. A lad's got to make a living!'

'I'm not surprised Mr Wyngate said no,' Connie said, folding her arms. 'You're not on this ship to make a living, Ned Mitchell. You're a patient!'

Ned tapped his finger to his ear and said, 'Can't 'ear what you're saying. But I know I'm getting a telling-off!' Then he sat on the end of the bed. 'Tell you what's weird though, I can hear the ship right enough. Like this rumble I can feel?'

Connie smiled. She was glad that he hadn't lost all of his hearing. She didn't like the thought of him missing out. She was doing her best to remember to tap him on the shoulder when she wanted to get his attention, rather than speak to him when his back was turned. And if he could hear the sound of the ship, didn't that mean there was still something left, something the doctors could fix?

She spotted the notepad and pencil by the bed and went over to pick it up, before writing down her reply.

She held it out to Ned and at the same time said, 'Yeah, I can feel it through my feet. Can't you too, Mr Wyngate?'

Wyngate nodded. 'Last night, Ned could hear the music in the dining room in the same way,' he said. As he was speaking, Ned picked up his camera and fired off a shot of Connie and Wyngate. Then he went over to the window, to photograph the bright sunshine that danced on the surface of the ocean. 'When he wasn't fighting off the adoring American wives, that is.'

They left the cabins and headed upstairs to breakfast,

where the American wives appeared again. As Connie and Ned ate their toast and marmalade – so sweet and sticky and a taste of the world before the war – the women with perfect hair and pearl necklaces came by and patted their heads.

'So adorable... so cute... and this little guy looks like an angel!' they said as they went past.

But as soon as the ladies walked away, Connie noticed their expressions change. This wasn't a pleasure cruise, after all. No one was crossing the Atlantic Ocean these days unless they had to. The wives, Connie knew, were married to diplomats and officials, some of whom were on the ship. Or their husbands were officers in the American military, stationed in Britain, and were heading for the safety of home. Even though that safety may as well have been on the other side of a minefield.

After breakfast, Connie and Ned went out onto the deck with Wyngate. It was sunny but cold, with a blast of wind from the north. Around them were the other ships in their convoy, and Connie had mixed feelings about their presence. At least they weren't travelling all that distance alone, so there was comfort in seeing them, but then what if a big group of ships made them easier for the Nazi submarines to find?

If the Nazis tried to attack from the air, the ship was prepared. There were anti-aircraft guns on the deck, mean-looking things like the ones she'd seen dotted around London.

She noticed Ned's usually sunny expression was strained. Connie did her best to write in the notebook, even though the wind was determined to ruffle the pages.

'*Are you all right? Penny for your thoughts, mate!*' she wrote, then showed the words to Ned. At their side, Wyngate was looking out to sea, his gaze far away as he rested against the railing. Connie was sure he could only be thinking about Lisette, the woman he loved.

'I been thinking,' Ned said with a sigh, 'if they can't put my ears right... it's going to be a right weird world, ain't it? I'll never hear you sing again, for one thing.' He glanced towards Wyngate, then blinked up at Connie. 'And I try not to be scared, but I am. A little bit.'

Ned almost always hid his vulnerability, but it didn't mean it wasn't there.

Connie put her arm round him, then reluctantly let go so she could write down her reply. *The doctors will do their best. But if they can't fix you up, you could learn to read lips, and that sign language.*

Connie had tried to learn some phrases in sign, and it'd fascinated her, but she knew that, if she didn't practise and actually use it, she'd never remember it. It was a new language to her, after all. But if Ned needed to use it, she'd learn it with him.

Ned smiled and rested his head momentarily against Connie's arm. Then he said with his usual mischief, 'But now I can't hear so well, it means I can see like a hawk. Bet I see America before you and Mr W!'

Wyngate, who Connie suspected had remained silent deliberately, to let Ned think his vulnerability had remained between just him and Connie, now glanced down at Ned. He scribbled something in his own pad and held it up to the little boy as he said aloud, 'Not a chance.'

'Tanner says I will!' Ned laughed. He looked from Wyngate to Connie. 'Who's on for a bet?'

'Me!' Connie said. She pointed to herself exaggeratedly, because she knew that was sign language. 'I bet Ned.' And she pointed to her friend. Then she shrugged. 'Sorry, Mr Wyngate, but it's them eyes of his. Unless you've brought binoculars with you!'

Ned took a photograph of the convoy ship that was visible on the horizon, then asked, 'Oi, Mr W, can I go off and take some pictures on the boat?'

He was used to going his own way without having to ask

permission from anyone, but perhaps there was something in Mr Wyngate that made him a little less likely to do so when he was around. Wyngate nodded and wrote down a note. He held it up for Ned to read and said aloud, 'I'm not having you flogging nylons to American girls or tricking the captain out of betting his ship on a game of cards. I'll come with you.' Then he asked, 'Do you fancy it, Connie?'

Connie thought for a moment, then shook her head. It was nice for Ned and Wyngate to spend some time together. And she was happy where she was. She was sure that, if she looked in the same direction Wyngate had been, she'd be staring back at home. And home meant Jack.

'Nah, it's all right, you two go off and Ned can carry on like Cecil Beaton,' she said, chuckling as she thought of the famous photographer.

On her own at the railing, Connie felt tears in her eyes, but she told herself it was just the cold wind. It was strange being on the boat. She felt suspended, neither here nor there. And the constant unspoken fear of the submarines meant she couldn't entirely relax. It was hardly a voyage to enjoy. The presence of the American passengers reminded her that she would be arriving in a strange new land where everyone would speak differently, and where she and Ned would be the novelty.

And then there was Jack. She thought of how it'd felt when he'd wrapped his arms around her, and his scent of soap. Sensible, kind, affectionate Jack. He was the sort of boy she'd have liked if they'd met at school, but she was sure that he wouldn't have taken any notice of her – or, if he had, he would've found her loud and silly like other boys did. And yet, he seemed to like that about her. She made him laugh, and the way he looked at her when she used to sing on stage at Jasper's had made her feel almost giddy. And it wasn't just then, either.

Sometimes she'd be mopping the tiles in the hallway at home, and she'd realise he'd been watching her, and that look would be in his eyes then, too. It made Connie clumsy, and she'd drop the mop, or trip over the bucket. He'd insist on taking over the task, and she'd watch him from the bottom of the stairs, blushing as she admired the way the muscles in his arms tensed as he worked. And her dreams were always full of him, coloured by her memories of all the risks he'd taken to save people during air raids. He'd be carrying someone from a burning building one moment; guiding people into a shelter as bombs fell the next.

'I don't like this at all.' The voice belonged to a woman who had come to stand beside Connie at the railing. She was swathed in a heavy fur coat against the cold wind, her hair elaborately styled beneath a hat on which it seemed the contents of a whole fruit bowl had been modelled in wax. She glanced towards Connie and smiled. She looked like a film star in her fur and immaculate make-up, but her face was pale beneath the powder. 'I get frightened at sea even when we don't have Nazis chasing after us. And they call it the Black Pit, you know. My husband talked about it before I sailed... oh Lord, how I wish he hadn't!'

A shiver ran through Connie from head to toe. The Black Pit. It sounded so odd coming from a woman who sounded like she had escaped from *Gone with the Wind*. Connie had seen that film at the cinema three times, and the film's theme tune played in her head as she imagined the American woman in a huge dress held out by a crinoline.

'What do you mean, the Black Pit? That sounds horrible!' Connie exclaimed. But then what was it her grandma had said, about the *Titanic*? That they'd never be able to raise that tragic ship, even if anyone could ever find it, because it was miles and miles down to the bottom. She thought of the ancient sailor and his albatross again, and shivered.

'He's flying bombers for Uncle Sam. Right up at the top of

the tree with a chest full of medals,' the lady explained. 'He told me to stay back home, but... well, I guess I always have to look for an adventure. Just like you and your little buddy. So I've been over in England, doing my charity bit here and there. I kind of wish I'd stayed there too, there's so much more that I can do than I can at home.' She shivered again. 'The Black Pit. It's the place in the Atlantic where we're just too far away from land to have any support from the air. And we just sailed right into it.' Then she attempted a fearless smile. 'But I don't think even Adolf Hitler would have any interest in a whole bunch of wives and a couple of real British heroes like you two, do you?'

Connie thought of that broadcast by Lord Haw-Haw. News of Ned's trip to New York had appeared in the papers, so maybe Hitler knew where they were headed. But he wouldn't know which ship they were on.

And yet, that hadn't stopped the Nazis from torpedoing the *City of Benares*, which had been carrying all those children to safety in Canada. The poor things never made it. What was worse, dodging the bombs in London, or clinging to a lifeboat in the wide, empty ocean?

'Nah, he doesn't give a monkey's about us,' Connie said, hoping she sounded confident. But she glanced at the lifeboat a few yards away on the deck, the canvas tarpaulin that covered it flapping in the wind. She made a mental note of where it was. 'I reckon he's got other things to think about, like how he can get right up Stalin's nose.'

The lady laughed. 'What a pair, huh?' She chuckled. 'I'm Abigail Franklin; I saw you at Drury Lane. You knocked my socks right off, honey. I'm a little star-struck right now!'

'Of me?' Connie laughed. She felt so untidy, compared to the well-groomed Abigail Franklin. Connie's dress was a bit too short and there were lines across it where it'd been taken down to keep up with her growth spurt. And the fabric was patched, and her shoes were too scuffed for any amount of polish to hide.

But Abigail hadn't said a thing about Connie's scar, and that made her smile. 'Pleased to meet you, Abigail Franklin. You know, I ain't been to America before. Never left England, to be honest. I think you might be a useful lady for me and Ned to know!'

Abigail beamed. 'Well then, why don't you and I go and find ourselves some refreshment,' she suggested. 'And I'll give you a crash course on the US of A.'

Connie beamed at her new friend. They might now be sailing through the Black Pit, but, if Connie listened to everything that Abigail had to tell her about the country she was headed for, the fear of everything that lurked in the deep, cold water would recede. For a little while, at least.

Lisette travelled on the Underground to work from the children's house in Whitechapel. It was always stuffy and hot as a sauna in the summer; travellers with loosened ties fanned themselves with newspapers, ignoring the headlines about the latest actions in the war. Lisette's khaki uniform was heavy, but she couldn't take off her jacket in public and look scruffy, so she had to look too warm instead.

She barely saw her flat any more, even though it would've been far more convenient to stay there, near the War Office, than all the way over in Whitechapel. Jack was more than capable of looking after the children, but Lisette worried. Without Connie there, she slept in the double bed with Elsie and Susan curled against her, rather than on the sofa, where she usually slept when she stayed over. She felt lonely without Wyngate, too, and sleeping in the double bed, and hearing the children's chatter that filled the house, helped. He had ended things between them, but then just as he was about to disappear across the globe they'd said *I love you*. Were they a couple again? Lisette hoped so, but wasn't it possible for two people to love one other, yet not be an item? Missing him was a physical ache, one that Lisette couldn't cure.

She wouldn't hear anything from him until they reached dry land. At least she had her work to distract her. As soon as she'd arrived in the office and sat down at her desk, still feeling hot and gritty from her journey on the Underground, there was a flurry of messages from Paris, about the Nazis using railway yards for their supplies. She was relieved that the messages from the ports had calmed down.

At least, they had for a while. But then Lisette drew another buff-coloured file across her desk towards her and a lump formed in her throat as she read.

OVERHEARD IN LE HAVRE. ENEMY OFFICER REPORTS ACTIONS TO BE TAKEN AGAINST ALLIED MILITARY VESSELS ASSUMING CIVILIAN DISGUISE. CONVOY TO BE TARGETED AND DESTROYED.

Lisette froze. She reread the message.

In her mind, she saw again Wyngate, Ned and Connie waving from the deck of the ocean liner. She saw the bunting flapping in the breeze. She saw the people on the dockside dabbing their eyes with their handkerchiefs. She thought of the waves, rolling on and on to the horizon. She heard gunfire and the roar of a torpedo. And she saw blood on the water.

Lisette got to her feet. Her heart was pounding. She was unsteady, as if she was drunk. It was like trying to run in a dream when her limbs just wouldn't work.

'Capitaine Ardouin!' she called urgently, turning to the officer's desk. But she wasn't there.

'She's on the telephone to the general,' Marie called to her from her desk. How casually they discussed General de Gaulle these days, as though he was just any other caller. But for the capitaine, he was. 'What have you found?'

'I think the Nazis are going to attack civilian ships.' Lisette swallowed, her throat dry with panic. 'I've got to raise the alarm – I'll go and see Monsieur Gray!'

She hurried out of the room, gripping the folder that contained the message. It felt as if everyone in the War Office was in the corridors, and she struggled to get past them. Perhaps she should've rung Gray from the office, but her thoughts were in a hectic spiral.

Finally, she reached his office. His secretary wasn't at her desk outside, so Lisette strode to the door and banged her fist against it. She called in French, 'Monsieur Gray, it's urgent, please!'

The door opened a second later, but it wasn't Mr Gray who Lisette found herself looking at. To her surprise, it was Mr Fluke, the illusionist who had entertained the children in the basement of the Theatre Royal as the Luftwaffe attacked the city after their fundraising show for Jasper's.

Lisette blinked at him, as if trying to clear a dream. She switched to English. 'Mr Fluke? Why are you here? I must see Monsieur Gray!'

Mr Fluke stepped aside and there was Gray, standing over his desk. On it was a small stack of slips, which Lisette recognised as similar to those she filed her own translations on. He looked up at Lisette and asked, 'Mademoiselle?' Then he glanced towards Fluke. 'You may speak in front of Mr Fluke.'

'A message has just come in from Le Havre. It's the same place where the *Amfortas* is docked,' Lisette explained, glancing from Gray to Fluke. She struggled to speak steadily. Hadn't she read a message saying that the *Amfortas* was carrying a proto-type weapon? Was that what they were going to use on civilian ships? 'It sounds like they're going to start attacking civilian ships. Look!'

She went over to Gray and passed him the file with the original message in French and her translation.

'Where it is *currently* docked,' Gray murmured. 'It will be at the bottom of the harbour by dawn, complete with its cargo of weaponry.'

Gray exchanged a look with Fluke, then opened the file and looked over the message. When he closed the file again, he tapped one fingertip against the message slips on his desk.

'Mr Fluke's team are working on the frequency that young Jack found,' he explained. 'It's leading us a dance, but we think we may have cracked the code. This bears out what we've been hearing.'

Clever Jack, Lisette thought. And she'd had no idea that Mr Fluke was working with codebreakers; yet it made sense. Who better to have on the team than a man who created illusions?

'But Wyngate, and Ned, and Connie...' Lisette heaved for breath and gripped the edge of the desk. The *Amfortas* couldn't reach their ship, she knew that, but what about this new message? What if there was a ship or a submarine already hunting them down? 'I knew it was dangerous for them to go, but... but now it's critical. What are we going to do?'

'Please, mademoiselle,' Gray said gently. 'We have excellent intelligence on the convoy the Kriegsmarine are intending to target.' But he shot another one of those looks at Mr Fluke. Gray was worried too, Lisette knew it. 'And we have cover in place. When they ambush our boys, they'll find a reception committee ready and waiting and armed to the teeth.'

Fluke nodded. 'We're listening to every word.' Then he reached for the door handle as he told Gray, 'I need to get back to the radio. We can't risk losing the frequency when it bounces.'

Gray dismissed him with a nod. 'They don't stay on one frequency,' he explained. 'But we can keep up with them.'

'You must.' Lisette gripped Gray's sleeve. Even though it was another convoy that was being targeted, she still couldn't stop herself from worrying about her loved ones who were so vulnerable out at sea. What if another attack was launched, on a different convoy? She felt entirely helpless in the face of such an indomitable threat. 'For the children. And for Wyngate. Please, Monsieur Gray – please do what you can.'

She could only pray that the British had provided cover to the right convoy, whether it was the ship carrying her little family or not. Somewhere out there, somewhere on that enormous, fathomless ocean, were ships filled with people who had no idea what fate awaited them. As they stood here in London, in Gray's grand office, in Berlin plans were being made to sink a convoy filled with innocent people.

THIRTY-FIVE

CONNIE

Connie and Ned were guests at the captain's table. Abigail was there, too, and she and the captain quickly adjusted to 'talking' to Ned via his notepad. Connie tried her best to join in, but she kept thinking of the Black Pit and the evacuees on the *City of Benares*. She hadn't breathed a word about it to Ned, because she hadn't wanted to frighten him. All she'd done was tell him about Abigail's stories from America – the big cars and the skyscrapers and the roads and railways that went on and on.

But that all seemed a distant dream. They had to pass through the Black Pit first.

Connie laid down her knife and fork. She pressed her hand to her forehead and excused herself from the table with a headache.

She went out onto the deck. No one else was around, apart from some of the crew, who were chatting and smoking. Maybe if she stayed outside, watching the waves, she'd spot the Nazis and they could raise the alarm before there was any time for them to launch a torpedo at the ship. Maybe the crewmen were watching out too?

The wind was colder and stronger, and Connie's hair

whipped around her face. She walked along the deck, away from the crewmen, and, as she reached the stern, she saw a solitary figure leaning against the railing, his back to her, watching the churning water fall away behind the ship.

It was Mr Wyngate.

He looked lost in thought, and Connie wasn't sure if she should approach. But then, she didn't like the thought of leaving him on his own. He might be there to look after her and Ned, but she got the impression that he needed looking after sometimes as well.

'Mr Wyngate?' Connie said cautiously as she walked towards him against the wind. 'You all right?'

She had the sense that she had startled him as he stepped back from the railing and turned to face her. He was as unreadable as ever, but Connie knew precisely who he was thinking of. Just as she was longing to see Jack, he was longing for Lisette.

'I'm not going to win that bet looking back towards Blighty, am I?' Wyngate asked.

Connie chuckled. 'Nah, you won't – you're lookin' in the wrong direction.'

She wasn't sure how to talk to Mr Wyngate. He got on so well with Elsie, in such a natural way. But she'd never found it as easy. He wasn't rude to her, or cold, exactly. It was just that he seemed to wear an invisible suit of armour and didn't want to waste his words.

Maybe the best way to talk to Mr Wyngate was to just be direct. Like he was.

'Bet you're thinking of Mamzelle Lisette, aren't you?' Connie said. 'I know you are, 'cos I'm thinking of Jack.'

For a long moment, he said nothing; Connie wasn't sure if she'd offended him somehow, but she had the feeling he'd tell her if so. Then he sighed and nodded.

'I'm not used to having anybody to miss,' he admitted. 'And

suddenly, here you all are. But...' And he shrugged. 'I'm *always* thinking about Lisette lately. Just like you and Jack, I expect.'

Connie blushed. 'It was so hard to leave him at the docks,' she said. 'I keep thinking of the way he smells, you know. He smells of soap! I know that sounds silly... I haven't told anyone how I feel... even Jack doesn't know. But then you and Lisette are in love. I'm not surprised you're always thinking of her, too. And she's back in London thinking of you too, I know it.'

'I told her not to,' Wyngate replied. 'But she's not the sort of woman who does as she's told.' Then he smiled. 'Thank God.'

'I think you two make a lovely couple,' Connie told him.

'What about Jack?' Wyngate asked. 'Have you two talked about it?'

Connie shook her head. 'Dunno how to, Mr Wyngate. We're friends, but I don't know if he likes me in the same way I like him. Y'know, does he want to be my boyfriend?'

Wyngate drew in a breath, his expression growing thoughtful. 'If you want to know what I think, I think he likes you. Lisette agrees. She wants me to tell him about the birds and the bees.'

Connie gasped and hid her face behind her hands. 'Oh, heck, no! I don't want to have Jack's babies. Not yet, anyway!' Then she lowered her hands and looked out to sea. 'Maybe I need to get my courage up and tell him... when we get back.'

'Your first date's on me.' Wyngate smiled. 'I'll send you to Lyons' Corner House if you like.'

'Oh, Mr Wyngate! Would you? You're the best!' Connie excitedly flung her arms round him and gave him a hug. 'I'll save you a peach melba!'

Wyngate laughed and returned her embrace. The armour seemed to have fallen away, here in the middle of the Atlantic Ocean.

As Connie hugged him, she glanced over his shoulder. Something had moved at the corner of her eye, to the north of their ship. She blinked and now she saw it more clearly. Far away on the horizon was the dark grey bulk of a ship. It looked top-heavy, with stack upon stack of structures rising up from the hull.

Night was falling and the cloudless sky was full of stars, but she could make out the ensign – a huge flag – flying on the stern. And it was red, with black and white across its centre.

Wasn't that a huge swastika?

Connie drew back from Wyngate's embrace. Without saying a word – because her throat had closed up with fear – she pointed away to what she had seen.

Wyngate turned to look at the vessel on the horizon. He narrowed his eyes and peered into the dying sunlight as he murmured, 'That's the *von Schönerer*. She's supposed to be bound for Norway, not here—' Something changed in Wyngate's face then, a look of dawning realisation. 'They've been feeding us false information. The intelligence is wrong.'

Connie thought of Jack's radio and the frequency he'd found. Perhaps the real information was to be found there, hidden away at the edges of the radio waves.

She gripped the railing, trying to still the shiver that ran through her. She thought of Jack, of the way he smelt of soap, and how kind and clever he was. Would she ever see him again? 'They're comin' to get us, aren't they? What are we goin' to do, Mr Wyngate?'

'We'll let the bridge know. They can get on the radio and let our people know,' Wyngate said. 'She's heading away from us, but, if Jerry's feeding us false information about naval manoeuvres, there's no telling what other rubbish we've fallen for.'

The invisible threat that Connie had felt ever since Abigail had told her about the Black Pit now had a face, and it was a massive battleship flying a swastika. She'd been up against Nazi bombs in London, but at least that was her home, and at least she knew where to run to.

Here, out in the lonely ocean, there was nowhere to hide.

THIRTY-SIX

LISETTE

Lisette's thoughts were spiralling. She'd done what she could to protect Wyngate and the children out at sea, but it wasn't enough. Once she got back to Whitechapel after work, she battled with herself to keep her anxiety reined in, because she didn't want the children to think anything was amiss. But she suspected they had noticed the smile that didn't reach her eyes, and her jumpiness at every sound. She'd tried to keep things steady and normal, encouraging the children to get ready for bed, but they were reluctant to go upstairs. It wasn't their usual alertness in case the air-raid sirens went off. They were worried about their friends at sea, and she knew her nerviness had put that seed there.

'Do you think Ned's all right on the boat?' Ben fretted. 'I know he's got his notepad and all that, but there'll be all them new people who won't know he can't hear them.'

'If I know Ned, he'll have all the ladies eating out of his hand and all the men wondering how a ten-year-old cleaned them out at the card table,' Jack said and chuckled, fastening the screws on the wireless that he had once again been tinkering with. 'And Mr Wyngate will make sure people know what's going on. Ned will probably be the captain of the ship by the time it docks!'

Ben chuckled, but he still looked uncertain.

Elsie stroked Pippa as she said, 'I don't like the thought of them being so far away. And in the middle of all that sea, as well! What if something happens to them?'

'The ships sail in convoys,' Lisette said, trying to reassure her. 'They're not out there alone. There's little chance that anything will happen.'

But she thought of what Gray and Mr Fluke had been talking about. The Nazi navy were focusing on one convoy in particular, and, although the information they had made them certain it wasn't the one that Wyngate, Ned and Connie were travelling in, it reminded her of just how vulnerable they were.

Lisette had tried to make the children go to bed, but Susan was sitting under the light from the standard lamp, still sewing even though it must hurt her eyes. Lisette knew she was determined to recreate at least some of the lost costumes from Jasper's before the new incarnation of the club reopened. Elsie should've been in bed as well, but she couldn't settle and was still clutching her father's sheet music. She picked up one of the china dogs on the mantelpiece with her other hand, put it down again, then came to stand beside Susan. She tried to catch some of the lamplight so that she could read the sheet music.

'I still can't make out this song.' Elsie sighed. '*We are the men of Stalag Luft*... it's such an odd tune, and it uses hardly any notes. It just goes *la-la, lah, la-la-la, lah*... short, short, long... short, short, short, long...'

Jack was nodding along as his sister went on sounding out the tune, but Lisette had never heard a song like it. Musically, it made no sense at all; she wasn't sure how anyone could ever sing it.

Suddenly, Jack's head jerked upright and he exclaimed, 'It's not just a song. It's Morse code!' He leapt up to his feet and snatched up the Morse code alphabet sheet he kept beside his radio. Then he hurried to where Elsie was standing and peered over her shoulder at the sheet music. 'Sing it again, Els, from the start.'

Elsie sang the oddly staccato melody again. It really didn't fit the words. But now they knew why. The song was made up of short and long notes, and each set represented a letter in Morse code.

'Jack!' Lisette whispered. 'You're right, it *is* Morse code. Your father has hidden a message in the music!'

She thought back to the letter that Mr Taylor had written, telling the children to show the music to Connie or to Wyngate if they needed to. She hadn't understood why he'd mentioned Wyngate, who wasn't a musician, but now it made sense. Mr Taylor had picked up clues from the children's letters to him, and had worked out that the Mr Wyngate they kept mentioning would know exactly what to do with a message disguised in code.

'But what does it say?' Susan asked, curious enough at last to put her sewing down.

Jack was following the message, his fingertip moving along the Morse code alphabet as he listened. He and Elsie went through it a second time and then a third as he painstakingly jotted down each letter in turn, before casting his eyes over the note once more.

'If I'm right,' he said, 'It's about prisoners.' He glanced back at the sheet music, then settled his gaze on the notepad again and read, '*Amfortas* is a Nazi trick. Prisoners of war on board. No weapons.'

Lisette couldn't let on what she knew from her translations. But there it was, the name of the ship that Capitaine Ardouin had been so interested in. The *Amfortas*, with its prototype weapon, sitting in the dock at Le Havre with the united strength of two nations' air forces ready to strike before dawn.

Lisette had to stop them.

'Your telephone still hasn't been installed, has it?' she said. There'd been some hold-up; a lack of the right supplies.

'Not yet,' Jack replied. As he spoke, the air-raid sirens began to wail. 'And the box at the end of the road went out of order with the last raid. Most of them did; must be on the same exchange.'

'We need to go to the War Office,' Lisette said, buttoning up the jacket of her uniform. She could've told the children to stay at home, but there was no point; she knew they'd follow her if she did. 'We'll be safe from the raid if we're travelling through the Underground. We have to get your father's message to them, right now.'

THIRTY-SEVEN
LISETTE

The air raid had sent everyone out into the street, as they hurried for the nearest shelters with prams and suitcases. Lisette told the children to stay close on the crowded pavements, and they ran along together in a group, holding hands. Each time their chain broke, Lisette shepherded them together again.

Pippa was in Elsie's arms. The dog was an old hand at air raids now and didn't look afraid. She snuggled against Elsie as they headed through the tide of people. Like them, most people were heading for the Underground station.

An ARP warden was standing at the entrance with a shielded torch, guiding everyone in. The huge crowd was moving urgently, and all it'd take was one person slipping on the steps for hundreds more people to fall as well. Lisette chased the thought away; she had to focus on getting to the War Office and somehow passing on the message. *Don't bomb the Amfortas!*

They headed down to the platforms. The escalators weren't turned off yet, but once they were there'd be people sleeping on each step. Anywhere was preferable to being above ground in the raid.

Lisette led the children past people who were setting up camp on the platform, to the area left clear for passengers. She'd long ago ceased to find it odd; it no longer felt as if she was walking through complete strangers' bedrooms each time the siren went off.

They only had to wait three minutes for the next train, yet it felt like hours to Lisette. She let the children on first, and checked and double-checked that no one was left behind. Then, once the doors closed and the train moved away from the platform, she allowed herself to be calm. Who would be around, who might listen to her? If Gray was still at the War Office, or Capitaine Ardouin, then they had a fighting chance. But it wasn't as if they lived there; everyone was allowed to go home sometimes.

The children had barely spoken and Lisette was now aware of their anxious glances, which they had fixed on her. And she knew what Jack and Elsie would be fearing. If there were prisoners of war on the *Amfortas*, could their father be among them?

As soon as the train arrived at Westminster, Lisette shepherded the children onto the platform, and then they zigzagged their way past people seeking shelter to get out onto the street. As soon as the way was clear, they all ran along the pavement, without Lisette needing to give them any signal.

The War Office rose up in front of them, standing out like a huge wedding cake on Whitehall, and they rushed up the steps and through the doors.

The building was busy despite the late hour and the air raid, but as they stepped over the threshold into the lobby a shout rang out from the street.

'Get your children into the shelter, miss!' It was an ARP

warden, who had followed the little party off the street. 'Come on, now!'

'Non!' Lisette replied, whirling round. 'I have an urgent message that I must pass on – lives are at stake, monsieur!'

He frowned, then looked at the children, and Lisette saw recognition dawn on his face. With a nod, he shouted across the bustling lobby, 'Clear a path for the Blitz Kids! Reception, please! Everyone else into the shelters!'

Behind the desk, a woman in uniform acknowledged the ARP warden's summons with a wave of her hand. She was putting the strap of her gas-mask case round her neck as she called, 'Can I help?'

'Thank you, sir,' Jack told the ARP warden, who was already heading back towards the doors and the raid outside. 'Good luck tonight.'

'I need to speak to Mr Gray, or Capitaine Ardouin – or Churchill himself!' Lisette told the receptionist. She hoped that her Free French uniform would give her an official air. She wasn't a random civilian who had run in from the street, making crazed demands. 'We have vital intelligence, and it must be passed on at once.'

The woman shook her head and, outside, Lisette heard the unmistakable sound of aircraft soaring overhead. The raid was on.

'They're not available, I'm sorry,' the woman said, casting a nervous glance upwards. 'You need to get to shelter, all of you. Capitaine Ardouin and Mr Gray will be available tomorrow, I'm sure.'

Lisette felt Elsie tug her sleeve. Their father was the only family she and Jack had left in the world, and Lisette wasn't going to put his life on the line. And what about all those other men who would be prisoners of war? Sons, fathers, brothers, husbands?

'Non, it won't wait until tomorrow. They have to be told *now*.'

'Someone must be able to help!' Jack protested. 'It won't wait until tomorrow!'

Wyngate would know what to do. He'd square his shoulders and push through any door that stood in his way.

Then she remembered something: he'd told her his codename.

'Corbeau,' Lisette said. 'Raven.'

The receptionist glanced down at something on her desk, something that Lisette couldn't see. Then she said, 'Just a moment.' She turned her back to the lobby and picked up a telephone, on which she dialled a single digit. A few moments passed before she conducted a short, hushed conversation with someone on the other end of the line, glancing back at the little party as she did so.

'It's all right,' Jack whispered to the younger children, resting his hand on Elsie's shoulder as he spoke. 'There's a big thick slab of concrete under this building, and a whole lot of offices and things safe beneath it. I bet that's where Mr Gray and Mr Churchill are.'

Susan was biting her fingernails, but Lisette didn't tell her to stop. Ben watched the receptionist, his eyes wide and frightened. The floor shook; a bomb had dropped somewhere. If they didn't get the message across, bombs would soon be falling in Le Havre and who knew how many prisoners of war would be killed.

Lisette clenched her hands. She thought of planes on a runway, the ground crew busy making final checks, the pilots climbing up into their cockpits. How long did they have?

The receptionist put down her telephone and opened a drawer, from which she took a large bunch of keys.

'Follow me,' she said.

Lisette took a steadying breath. The seconds were ticking past. Were they too late?

THIRTY-EIGHT
LISETTE

Lisette felt like the Pied Piper as she followed the receptionist, with the children in a crocodile behind. They went through a door and down a staircase and saw women in uniform, with perfect hair, hurrying by clutching cardboard files. The trill of telephones fought with the rattle of typewriters from corridors that led away into the distance. Lisette and her band of children attracted curious glances, but everyone knew them from the newspapers and they didn't stop to quiz them.

Down they went, further and further. The elegant cast-iron banister on the stairs gave way to a more modern version, plain and functional. And even here, in a building full of government employees, the information posters still appeared. *LOOSE LIPS SINK SHIPS.*

Lisette glanced away; lies and misinformation could sink ships too.

She recognised uniforms from the army and navy, as well as the air force. There was an official-looking man with a patch over his eye, no doubt injured in the war but still carrying on. She heard American accents echoing along the corridors, too.

The future didn't seem so bleak now, knowing they were fighting alongside them.

Then she spotted a flash of vivid blue, and glanced up to see Mr Gray, who was dressed as brightly as ever. He was striding towards them along the corridor, weaving nimbly through the tide of uniforms.

'Monsieur Gray!' she called.

Gray waved a greeting. As he reached them, he told the receptionist, 'Get to the shelter now, please. The desk can wait.' Then he addressed Lisette and the children. 'We'll be perfectly safe under the slab. I understand you've something urgent for me? And I will have to tick off our mutual, stone-faced friend for telling you his codename.' With that, he spun on one heel and reached for a polished door handle. 'We can talk in here.'

Lisette followed Gray inside with the children. It was a staffroom, currently vacated, with some armchairs arranged around a table. Copies of *Life* and *Woman's Own* magazines were waiting for the next person who came here on their break, along with a tea urn and a packet of biscuits.

'Don't bomb the *Amfortas*,' Lisette told Gray immediately. 'Jack and Elsie's father has sent them a message. There are prisoners of war, like him, on the ship.'

Jack nodded. 'Show him the music, Elsie,' he instructed his sister. Then he reached into his pocket and took out the sheet of notepaper on which he had written down the decoded message. 'It's Morse code, you see?'

Susan was holding Pippa now, while Elsie reached into her canvas bag. She held out the sheet music to Mr Gray.

Gray took a pair of tortoiseshell spectacles from his jacket and slipped them onto the end of his nose. Then he looked down at the sheet music and, to Lisette's surprise, began a note-perfect sounding out of the melody. His rich tenor seemed out of place as they discussed bombing and code, but as he sang his eyes scanned Jack's translation.

'By George,' Gray murmured. Then he pushed the spectacles up into his hair and glanced up at the clock on the wall. 'We must stop the bombers. In twenty minutes, the *Amfortas* will be at the bottom of the dock.'

They followed Gray through more corridors. The bustling staff parted for him as though he was Moses and they were the Red Sea. The children and Lisette were all struggling to keep up with his pace as he strode the corridors on his long legs. But they couldn't lose a second.

Lisette kept thinking of the men who'd been crammed onto the *Amfortas*. They must've wondered what on earth they had been moved there for. And what would they think when they heard the throb of the bombers' engines overhead?

Gray took them through a door, and they found themselves on a gallery. Down below was an enormous map, surrounded by women in uniform wearing headsets as they pushed models of aeroplanes and ships around with long poles. A large speaker was mounted on the wall. There was silence in the tense room, apart from the scrape of the models being pushed across the map, and a buzz of static from the speaker.

Lisette glanced at the figures, some in suits, others in uniforms, who were leaning against the railing, looking down at the map. She saw a cloud of cigar smoke rising up from a rotund man, and she knew at once who it was.

Churchill. The prime minister himself, who everyone in the country had pinned their hopes of victory on, was overseeing the operation. He was the most famous man in the country, a hero who hadn't flinched as he'd accepted his duty as a leader during wartime.

Just his presence told Lisette that this wasn't being taken lightly. Of all the different actions going on at that moment across the world in this war that spanned continents, Churchill was here.

Beside him was an older man in an RAF uniform, with an upright bearing and an air of importance. He had grey hair and a neat moustache, and granite determination in his gaze.

'They're leading us a bloody dance!' Gray bellowed as they strode into the room. He brandished the sheet music like a banner of war. 'The ships are full of prisoners. It's a bloody propaganda trick so we kill our own boys!' Without waiting for any of the assembled group to speak, he embarked on an explanation of what they had found, from the letter Elsie and Jack's father had sent to the message they had decoded in his music.

As Gray went on, Jack stood on tiptoe and cupped his hand to his mouth. 'That's Bomber Harris,' he whispered to Lisette, nodding towards the moustachioed man. Harris was frowning, as though he didn't quite believe what he was hearing. 'He's in charge of Bomber Command.'

Lisette stared in amazement. This man was responsible for the bombing raids on Nazi Germany, and she was standing in the same room as him. She wondered what went through his mind each time the air-raid sirens sounded and the Luftwaffe took their revenge on Britain for the raids that Harris ordered. But this was a war and the Nazis had struck first. Britain had to retaliate.

But not now. They couldn't bomb the *Amfortas*.

'You've got to call off the attack,' Lisette said, her voice cutting through the tense silence that had descended. She saw heads turning to face her and heard murmurs run through the men who were gathered along the gallery. But she needed to be heard. 'Those prisoners of war survived being shot down, or torpedoed at sea, or never left the beach at Dunkirk. They have families at home. You must call it off!'

'Our dad might be on that ship,' Elsie told them, her young voice so out of place in that operations room. And yet, wasn't it a reminder that wars weren't just about maps? They were – most importantly – about people, too. Elsie glanced up at her brother. 'If he dies, me and Jack'll be orphans.'

Harris looked at Churchill, shaking his head in a warning. 'They have sowed the wind. Now they reap the whirlwind,' he said firmly. 'The mission must go ahead. Prime Minister, this story of prisoners is the decoy. There are weapons on board that ship. The only people who will die are Nazis.'

'What if you're wrong?' Jack asked him, drawing his shoulders up high. 'If Dad says it, it's true. He's hardly going to be part of a Nazi plot to fool you!'

Churchill listened silently, chewing thoughtfully on his cigar. Wordlessly, he held out his hand to Gray, who passed him the sheet music and Jack's handwritten translation.

'We cannot afford to let children set the policy,' Harris urged, earning himself a fierce glare from Gray. 'No matter how well-meaning they are.'

Churchill nodded, then folded the papers and put them into his pocket. He made his way towards the children and held his hand beneath Pippa's nose, letting her catch his scent before he scratched the little dog beneath her chin.

'She has some poodle in her. One of Rufus's kind,' he observed. Then he nodded to a desk, beneath which Lisette saw a small brown poodle curled up atop a cushion, without a care in the world. 'Fiercely loyal and very intelligent.'

'She's the best dog there ever was,' Elsie replied. 'And I

want my dad to meet her one day. Please, Mr Churchill; please, Mr Harris... you must believe us.'

Lisette anxiously watched Churchill's face, trying to work out what he was thinking, but he was giving nothing away.

The radio speaker crackled into life and an American voice said through the scratchy connection, 'This is Brigadier General Franklin. It's good to have you on the line with us at last, Mr Churchill; this connection is a little iffy. We estimate five minutes to target; skies are clear and the flight's been smooth.'

The words cut out into static and Lisette realised that Brigadier General Franklin was somewhere over the sea right now, leading his men towards the docks where the ship waited.

Gray glanced towards the speaker before he said, 'If we are wrong, Prime Minister, we lose nothing.' He flicked his gaze to the speaker again, where static sounded once more. 'The weapon will still be on the ship, the ship can still be destroyed.' He looked at Harris and gave a gracious nod of acknowledgement. 'With respect to the commander-in-chief, if we are right, we prevent the needless slaughter of hundreds of brave Allied men, our men, all prisoners of Nazi Germany.'

Churchill drew in a steady breath, casting his gaze across the assembled faces. Then he gave a nod – decision made – and walked back to the railing. There he looked down onto the busy scene below.

'Group Officer Underwood,' he said in a voice loud enough to silence the bustle of activity from around the map. 'Get the brigadier general back on the radio. The raid is off.'

The women looked up. One of them, with neat dark hair, was urgently tapping the earpiece on her headset.

'I've been trying to, Prime Minister,' she called up to the gallery, 'but we've lost radio contact.'

'Then get it back, Group Officer!' Churchill barked. 'Now!'

Lisette put her arms round Jack and Elsie's tense shoulders, watching as Group Officer Underwood turned towards a huge bank of lights and dials.

There was nothing more that they could do.

Just off the coast of Normandy, a fleet of bombers were nearing their target, and there was no way to stop them.

FORTY

LISETTE

Nothing but static came through the speaker on the wall. Every eye was on Group Officer Underwood as she turned the dials. She wasn't frantic – but then she needed to be calm to find the frequency again.

Lisette glanced at Jack. He was completely absorbed, as if he was thinking through each step Underwood took, working out which one would finally reconnect them with the bombers heading for their target.

Just then, there was a loud squeak from the speaker, and Underwood turned round to give a thumbs-up to the anxious crowd on the gallery. The static had gone, and been replaced by what sounded like the purr of an engine and the beat of propellers. They had made contact again.

'We have target in sight,' Franklin said, his voice utterly calm. 'Estimate sixty sec—'

'The raid is off, Brigadier General,' Churchill told him, earning himself a look of disapproval from Harris. 'For the time being, at least. Return to base.'

For a moment there was nothing but the sound of the engine, then Franklin said, 'Roger Wilco, sir.'

Static cut into the conversation again then, but Franklin's voice came through once more. 'Adolf's boat's still floating and we'll see y'all soon. Out.'

The tension in the room broke at once. Lisette suddenly felt so light, it was as if she might float up to the ceiling. Jack and Elsie hugged each other, and Ben and Susan piled on to hug them too. Pippa barked, and Rufus joined in. Around the map, the women with their poles and headsets beamed at each other.

Lisette held her hand out to Churchill to shake. 'Thank you, monsieur,' she said. 'Thank you from the bottom of my heart!'

He took her hand and replied, 'If the young lady's father is correct, we will all owe him a debt.'

Lisette smiled, even though she knew that it could be a long time until they were able to tell Mr Taylor that he'd saved all those lives. But perhaps he'd find out soon – if he'd been able to discover the *Amfortas* plot to begin with, surely he'd hear that it'd been foiled? She just hoped that none of the Nazi officials would discover that he'd sent the message that had warned them off the attack.

The whole room seemed to have relaxed, uncoiling like a spring. Yet Lisette couldn't celebrate yet, not with the knowledge that a convoy was under threat. Even though the prisoners of war were safe, there was more danger out there in the darkness.

The Nazis had successfully misled the massed officials of the War Office on the cargo being carried by the *Amfortas*. What if they had achieved the same feat with the identity of the convoy that they intended to attack?

Lisette looked over the railing, down at the map. It showed the British Isles, with part of the French, Belgian and Dutch coasts. But the whole of the vast Atlantic couldn't be captured on it – wherever Wyngate, Ned and Connie were after so much time at sea, it must be off the map by now. She thought of the endless waves and the cold wind blowing down from the north.

And she knew they were too far from land for help to reach them if something went wrong.

She touched the Cross of Lorraine insignia on the lapel of her jacket and whispered a silent prayer for them.

'They're broadcasting Kurzsignale like there's no tomorrow!' The door flew open and a man rushed in, already speaking before Lisette had a chance to register his sudden arrival. 'Bring up the Jack frequency. They know something's up!'

It was Mr Fluke, Lisette realised, the illusionist who had become a fixture at the War Office, although he looked so different out of his vivid stage costumes.

Group Officer Underwood was at the dials again, this time aided by two other women. Lisette looked over at Jack again, and wondered about this bright boy who had modified a domestic radio to find a frequency that took three RAF staff to locate.

The speaker on the wall burst into life. Morse code poured from it, and Lisette wondered if that was what Kurzsignale meant – Morse in German. She couldn't imagine what message was beeping from the speaker, or where it was coming from.

'Mr Fluke—' Churchill began, addressing the new arrival. But Mr Fluke held up his hand, his attention all fixed on the speaker.

'Shh!' he told the prime minister. Still watching the speaker, he took a small, well-thumbed book from his pocket. The cover was red and, printed on it in black, Lisette saw the eagle and swastika of the Third Reich. He listened intently, then looked down and opened the book.

Gray was at Fluke's shoulder in an instant and Lisette could guess why. From his lessons with the children, she had learned he spoke more languages than she could count, and, together, the two men studied the book as the dots and dashes sounded.

Were the Nazis reporting on their foiled plan? But then she

thought of the convoy out in the ocean, and she tried to swallow down her panic. Were they sending a message about the vulnerable ships out at sea instead?

'It's not automated,' Gray murmured, furrowing his brow. He dropped his spectacles down from his hair onto his nose. 'They're reporting calm seas and skies in the Atlantic... I think this is the convoys, Prime Minister.'

Churchill nodded. 'And our welcoming committee is in place?' The question was directed to a man in a smart uniform that Lisette recognised as that of the Royal Navy, gold braid glittering at his cuffs. The man nodded.

'Ready and waiting for Jerry,' he confirmed.

Jack was chewing at his lip, as though he wanted to say something. He glanced towards Lisette, perhaps seeking her permission, then spoke up.

'They hoodwinked you all over the *Amfortas*,' he said. 'They might have you lined up to defend the wrong convoy too.'

Lisette remembered how confident Gray had been that the convoy that Wyngate, Ned and Connie were travelling on wasn't a target. But if he was wrong, then it meant that the *City of Newcastle* ship, ploughing at this moment through the waves towards New York, might already be in the gunsights of a Nazi submarine.

'Mr Gray, do something!' Lisette gasped. 'Jack's right, they've been filling our ears with lies.'

'I've already got the huff-duffers working on the location,' Fluke told Lisette, as if that might mean something to her. He looked down at the book again, as the sounds from the speaker continued. 'They'll put a call in as soon as they have it.'

'The huff-duffers can pinpoint the location of the enemy vessels,' Gray explained. 'It's a telegraphy trick.'

And as he finished speaking, the telephone rang. Churchill crossed and picked it up as Gray and Fluke exchanged a look.

'Sir,' Gray said urgently. 'Our people have intercepted the

attack order. The Germans have just given their subs the command to fire on the convoy.'

'We have to stop them!' Lisette shouted desperately, her voice hoarse with terror. She couldn't explain it, but she knew something was wrong. She felt it deep inside her.

She pictured Wyngate at the docks, where she had last seen him, and heard again those words of love they'd shared at last. She felt the memory of their last kiss. The thought of him so far away, facing down the inhumanity of the Nazi warships and submarines, tore at her heart.

Churchill hadn't even replaced the receiver before he was reeling off coordinates to Group Officer Underwood. Something in his manner told Lisette that she was right: the welcoming committee that was waiting to meet the Nazi attack was in the wrong place.

'Which of our convoys is it, Group Officer?' the prime minister asked urgently. The Nazi code signals seemed to be coming thick and fast now, their sounds echoing around the room.

Underwood took scribbled notes from the women who were at the radios. Then she looked up and said, in an even voice, 'It's not the one we thought it was. It's merchant marine, and includes a liner. The...' She turned back to her notes, then said, 'The *City of Newcastle*.'

Jack gave a cry of dismay as Fluke lifted his head from the pages of the code book.

'They've launched,' he said, his face pale. 'Torpedoes away.'

FORTY-ONE

CONNIE

Night had fallen and it was chillier than ever, but Connie had refused to go to bed and instead was standing on the deck. She didn't want to be asleep in her nightdress if the ship was going to sink.

Perhaps she shouldn't have told Ned what she'd seen – he already had a lot on his plate, after all – but she thought it was better that he knew. And once she'd told him that she'd seen a Nazi battleship on the horizon, there was no chance of either of them going to bed.

Wyngate hadn't protested, and Connie had been surprised to discover that he wasn't as strict as she had expected. Then again, he'd suffered at the hands of the nuns in the orphanage too, so perhaps that made him more relaxed when it came to looking after children.

'If any of us spot them Nazis again, Ned should take a photo!' Connie said, as they stood in a row against the railing. 'Then we can show people when we're back home just how hairy it is to go sailing over the sea!'

She'd made sure they were standing near a lifeboat. There

was an anti-aircraft gun nearby, but she knew they were too far from land for an attack to come from the air.

It had become second nature to Connie and Wyngate to write down their words as they spoke now. In fact, Ned had managed to make plenty of other friends on board the ship who were willing to do the same, too. They all wanted to meet the Blitz Kids, and the Americans seemed so excited at having them in their midst that Ned had been in his element. He regaled them with stories of their heroics in London, earning gasps of wonder. Reporters travelling back to the USA scribbled down his tales to carry Ned's adventures back to readers on the other side of the world.

They were the only children on the ship, which wasn't surprising. The wives who were travelling back to America hadn't risked taking their children to Britain. They were surrounded entirely by adults, and as so many children had been evacuated from London it wasn't all that different from being back at home.

'When we get home, Lisette doesn't need to know we were out on deck at all hours,' Wyngate told them with a half smile, writing as he spoke. 'And in return, Ned, I won't tell her that I caught you sipping a Martini.'

Ned nodded. 'Fair swap.' He grinned.

Wyngate was very relaxed for a chaperone, but then Connie suspected that he'd never really been around children until he'd met her and her friends. He treated them like small adults. And besides, Connie had felt tense from the moment she'd set foot on the ship, and Wyngate must've known that being strict would only have made her feel even more on edge.

'At least he wasn't smokin' a bifter!' Connie said, miming smoking a cigarette. Ned laughed and snapped her photograph, the flash on his camera lighting up the night. 'Mind you, you can't go smokin' out here on deck. Them Nazis'd use the light to take aim, ain't that right, Mr Wyngate? That's what they said about smokin' in the trenches. Three lights and…'

She glanced along the deck, just in case she spotted anyone who was stupid enough to provide the enemy with a cigarette target. But there was no one else around.

Her hands relaxed round the railings for a moment. No one would give them away. That was something, wasn't it? That was—

A huge explosion ripped the air and the ship, which had been travelling so steadily, suddenly lurched to one side as if it'd been punched.

Connie grabbed hold of Wyngate's sleeve, her heart pounding as they were hurled back from the railings to the other side of the deck. The night sky was suddenly full of light and an emergency siren blared on the ship. There were shouts and yells.

The other ships in the convoy, which had been a quiet but distant presence, were suddenly alight. Flames blasted from the side of one ship, and thick, black smoke billowed across the water towards them.

Connie could barely see through the smoke, but with her other hand she reached out blindly, feeling desperately for Ned.

FORTY-TWO

CONNIE

The ship was listing to one side, and Connie knew through her panic what must've happened. The Nazis had attacked and blasted a torpedo into the hull. It'd be taking on water and would eventually keel over on its side. What if the Nazis struck the ship again? It was like being circled by sharks.

'The lifeboat – we're right near the lifeboat!' Connie shouted.

'It's all right!' She felt Wyngate's hand close over hers in the choking cloud of smoke that billowed up into the night. Ned was calling Connie's name but his voice was close by, even as it filled with panic. 'I've got you both. Keep hold of my hand!'

Connie held tight. She heard doors slam open and people running.

'Life jackets!' a voice shouted. 'Everyone put on a life jacket and get into the nearest lifeboat!'

Connie squinted against the smoke and saw a sailor in a jumper with *City of Newcastle* stitched across it open a locker on the deck, then hurriedly empty it of cream-coloured life jackets, their strings coiled like tentacles.

Wyngate scooped Ned up with one arm while still holding

Connie's hand. Ned clung to him, suddenly the child he had always tried so hard not to be.

'Lifeboats,' Wyngate said. 'Come on.'

A younger sailor, who couldn't have been much older than Connie and Jack, was already tying on his life jacket. He picked up three more and staggered towards Connie and her friends. 'Put these on, quickly. Then we'll get you down in that lifeboat.'

Everything was happening so fast that Connie barely remembered putting her life jacket on. It felt cumbersome, but she wasn't going to protest. She was bracing her feet against the leaning deck, trying not to slide back. The deck was filling fast with passengers, their faces illuminated by the light from fires blazing on the other ships of the convoy.

The cover was yanked off the lifeboat and the young sailor scrambled into it. He held out his hand to a woman who was shaking with fear.

And Connie suddenly recognised her. It was Abigail Franklin.

The older woman stepped back, recoiling from the help the sailor was offering her.

'There are two children on this ship,' she said, her voice shrill with panic. 'We have to find them! We can't just go!'

'They're here!' Wyngate shouted, carrying Ned towards the lifeboat as Connie ran alongside, holding his hand tightly. 'I need you to take care of them for me. People on the ship need help.'

Connie stared at Wyngate in terror. She knew what that meant. He wasn't going to get into the lifeboat with them. 'You can't leave us, Mr Wyngate! You have to come too!'

But before her words had left her mouth, she felt the sailor's hand grip her arm and pull her up and into the lifeboat. She didn't dare look down at the huge drop beneath her to the sea below.

Wyngate bundled Ned into Abigail's arms, as the little boy

shook his head, tears welling in his eyes as he shouted, 'Where're you going? Get in the boat! Please!' But Wyngate's reply was to shake his head. Then, to Connie's surprise, he embraced first Ned and then Connie, holding each tight for a moment.

'You'll both be fine,' he told Connie. 'You're bloody brilliant, the both of you.' He put his fedora on Connie's head, then stepped back and addressed Abigail. 'Thank you, Mrs Franklin. I'll see you all soon.'

'What about Lisette?' Connie shouted, but it was too late. They were in the lifeboat now, which had rapidly filled, and a sailor on the deck was turning the crank. Another explosion ripped through the night and Connie gripped Ned's sleeve as the lifeboat began to unsteadily descend. 'Lisette loves you, Mr Wyngate! You have to come too!'

But it was no use. He'd made up his mind. She thought of him on countless bombsites, hurling aside bricks and fallen girders with his bare hands to pull complete strangers from the rubble. And he was going to do the same now; he was giving up his chance of safety to rescue lives even though it meant putting his own at extraordinary risk.

The cold wind blew wisps of smoke around them, and Connie took in the faces of her fellow passengers. One woman had cold cream on her face; some of the others were wearing hairnets. They were all in their nightwear, with coats hurriedly pulled on, and life jackets haphazardly flung on over the top. Abigail was wearing a fur coat, and Connie could see elaborate silk frills poking out from her nightdress, which looked like the sort of gown that Ginger Rogers went dancing in.

'It's okay,' she murmured softly, as Ned sobbed against her. Then she reached out and took Connie's hand. 'I promise nothing's gonna happen to you two. I swear it.'

Connie squeezed Abigail's hand in reply. She was trying not to watch the sailor in their lifeboat, who was pushing them away from the side of the listing ship with one oar. Then there was a splash; the lifeboat had hit the water.

The sailor whistled up to the deck, then grabbed the oars and with surprising strength rowed them away from the ship. It felt like madness to leave the safety of the ship in the middle of the ocean, but it was useless now.

Connie looked up and saw smoke rising from the vessel. She thought of her fancy cabin with the walnut furniture, and the bunting at the dockside when they'd left. How could it end like this? She thought of Wyngate, fighting against the angle of the deck. He'd get into another lifeboat, wouldn't he?

All around them, lifeboats were dotting the sea as passengers and crewmen fled the sinking ships that had made up their convoy. Ned was still clinging to Abigail's fur coat, his body shaking with sobs, but Connie couldn't take her eyes off the stricken liner that had been their home these past few days. Flames licked from deep within and the enormous ship seemed to be listing more than ever, tilting drunkenly towards the waves and exposing a dark expanse of its underside.

They were a distance away now, the young man having rowed valiantly until they were clear of the *City of Newcastle*'s looming shadow, and Connie thought suddenly of Jack, not much younger than this terrified sailor.

As she pictured him and the warm little hearth in Whitechapel where she and her new-found family gathered, there was a sound like the very earth itself opening up, a thunderous roar as a second torpedo thumped into the liner and tore a ragged hole in the exposed steel of the ship.

As Connie watched, the *City of Newcastle* seemed to shudder, then it collapsed onto its side and was swallowed by the Atlantic.

FORTY-THREE
LISETTE

Lisette held her breath. A scream was lodged in her throat, and if she opened her lips it would escape. It would echo and echo through every room in the basement and up into the War Office like a banshee's wail that would go on for ever. She couldn't let it out. She clenched her hands, trying to hold herself upright, trying not to dissolve onto the floor. She had to show the children a face of calm. The worst thing she could do would be to show that she was falling apart inside.

The speaker on the wall gave only static as the women working at the radios turned dials and flipped switches.

But what might come out of that speaker once the radios made contact?

The four children were looking up at her, as if she was the only person who could tell them what was going on, even though she knew nothing more than they did. So she made a decision.

'Let's go back to that staffroom and wait,' she said to them, hoping they couldn't hear the tremble in her voice, hoping the scream in her throat wouldn't escape.

. . .

In the staffroom, she tried to make the children comfortable. Ben curled up on an armchair, his head tucked tightly against his grazed knees. She knew he was crying but trying to hide it, and she stroked his hair, before Susan caught her glance and took over. Like Connie, she was stepping in and being a grown-up before her time.

Lisette plumped up the cushions on the sofa for Jack and Elsie. The little girl's eyes were shining with tears, and Pippa was on her lap, keening. The dog had picked up on the emotions in the room.

'Sit down, that's right,' Lisette said gently. There was nothing she could do but swallow her anxieties and look after the children. She patted Jack's shoulder. He was trying to be strong, just like she was, but Lisette passed him her handkerchief anyway, as if giving him permission to cry.

She wasn't surprised when Jack shook his head and handed the handkerchief back to her. She balled it tightly into her fist, her hand locking up with fear round it.

Jack swallowed and told them all, 'They'll be all right. I just know they will.' He went over and sat beside Ben, where he put his hand on the little boy's shoulder and told him, 'You know Ned and Connie, they're not going to leave us. And Mr Wyngate neither. No chance!'

Despite his confident words, Lisette could hear terror in Jack's voice.

She held her breath again; the scream was trying to get out. She swallowed in an attempt to keep control, to hold on for the children and be courageous for them. Her hands were shaking and she slipped them into the pockets of her skirt to keep them out of sight.

Ben had uncoiled himself. He glanced at Lisette, then up at Jack. Hope battled in his expression with fear. 'I know they'll be all right,' he said, his voice tight. 'But I'm worried about Ned.

He can't hear anything – how's he goin' to know to run to the lifeboats?'

Lisette closed her eyes, pressing her eyelids tightly shut for a moment, trying not to see what her mind's eye was showing her. A deaf child surrounded by panicking adults, and not knowing what was going on.

'Connie and Mr Wyngate will make sure he knows,' Susan told him. Then she glanced up at Lisette. She wanted to be reassured too.

'Yes, yes, Susan is quite right,' Lisette replied, determined, even though her voice was trembling with the effort, not to scream. She pictured Wyngate and Connie now, getting Ned to safety, caring for him. And she felt so guilty that she wasn't there with them. 'They'll tell him, and they'll be in a lifeboat right now, I'm sure of it. They might even have been picked up by another ship and they're on their way again.'

Shudders were running up and down her body with the effort of keeping her panic inside.

Jack squeezed Ben's shoulder, then returned to join Elsie and Pippa. He put his arm round Elsie and she snuggled against him. Very softly, Jack kissed Elsie's hair before he said, 'Mr Wyngate will make sure Connie and Ned are safe. There's nothing he can't do, is there, Elsie?'

'He brought Lisette back from the dead,' Elsie said. Her voice was wavering, and she wiped the back of her hand across her eyes. 'And he rescued me, too, and lots of other people! Maybe he even fixed the ship, and shot the Nazis, and everyone's safe?'

'H-he'll have done everything he can to make sure the people on that ship are safe,' Lisette told her, trying to keep her voice steady. 'I know it.'

Even though she knew – and she couldn't bear to put it into words, especially in front of the children – that he'd have done it at enormous risk to himself.

There wasn't any chance of anyone sleeping as they waited for news. The night crawled on, and Lisette did her best to keep the children upbeat, while battling with her mind's horrific images of fire at sea and the shouts of drowning passengers.

With a trembling hand she wiped away their tears, and reassured them. But inside she felt hollowed out, stretched as taut as wire. Tears prickled her eyes, but she couldn't let them fall, or else she'd fall apart completely in front of the children, and they needed her to be calm and keep them safe.

She kept thinking of Wyngate's words when he'd called things off between them. He hadn't wanted her to get hurt again, to grieve. But he had to come through this. He had to come home, and she had to feel his arms round her again. She loved him. And nothing would make sense ever again in this world if she lost him to the sea.

She didn't know how long had passed before the door opened gently and Gray slipped into the room, his arms laden with blankets.

'Monsieur Gray,' Lisette said, speaking in French to disguise her question as best as she could. 'Have you heard anything? Is there any news... any news about...?'

Gray lowered his voice to reply, in his own fluent French.

'It was a comprehensive assault on the convoy,' he explained. 'Every vessel was hit. We have royal and merchant navy ships in the area now and they're already picking up survivors from lifeboats. It'll be a while before we get any names, I'm afraid.' Then he glanced over her shoulder at the children. 'I'm so sorry, mademoiselle; we had no idea that they were misleading us.'

Lisette closed her eyes for a moment, trying to take on board what Gray had told her. *Every vessel was hit.* How many hundreds of people were imperilled by that attack? She thought of the dockside, and the families and friends waving their loved ones off. How many would see them again?

He went around the children, distributing blankets and kind words in equal measure. Each of them also received a little beige-wrapped rectangle bearing the familiar blue writing that identified it as a ration of chocolate.

'Don't tell anyone,' Gray told them in a confidential whisper. 'I pinched them from the stores.' Then he took out a little brown paper bag and passed it to Elsie. 'Some treats for Miss Pippa, courtesy of Master Rufus Churchill.'

Lisette could see that Elsie was doing her best to smile. 'Thank you, Mr Gray,' she said as she took the treats from him.

Gray had been like an indulgent uncle to the children as soon as they had entered his life, and despite the shortages he always tried to source what he could for them. Thank goodness he'd still been at the War Office when Lisette had arrived with the children.

'You must not apologise, Monsieur Gray,' Lisette said to Gray, in French again to avoid upsetting the children. 'This war is full of evil games. But you say they're already picking up the lifeboats? Then Connie and Ned and Wyngate... They might already have been rescued.'

Gray nodded. 'I was on board the *Titanic*, you know,' he replied. 'Mr Fluke too, though we didn't really know one another then. Neither of us left the ship in a lifeboat, but we both lived to tell the tale. There is hope, mademoiselle. It would seem that a good many lifeboats were launched this time.'

Lisette gasped. 'The *Titanic*? I had no idea.'

She thought of that famous ship, lost all those years before on the same route that Wyngate, Ned and Connie had taken.

So many people had been killed, and yet here was one of the survivors, and another had been in the operations room with them only a few hours before. Warmth suddenly bloomed inside Lisette; her fear began to ebb.

'You're right, there *is* hope,' she said. She tried to picture a younger version of Gray making his escape from the ill-fated ship. 'And we must all cling to it as tightly as we can.'

FORTY-FOUR
CONNIE

It was so dark at sea, but it was surprising how much light the stars gave out, and the moon, too, when it appeared from behind scraps of cloud. Every so often a flare would go up from a lifeboat, and the sailors would call to each other. Another lifeboat found, more lives saved. They were their own convoy now, of rowing boats and life rafts; a scrappy collection of survivors shivering on the sea.

At some point they heard a voice calling for help close by, and in the light of a flare Connie saw a figure in the water, reaching up towards their lifeboat. The sailor who was rowing their boat pulled back his oars and, with the help of two of the women passengers, hauled aboard a terrified young sailor. He was shivering and incoherent, but he'd been saved, hadn't he? The women on the boat helped to revive him, trying to warm him as they rubbed his limbs and wrapped him in their coats. And maybe Mr Wyngate had been pulled into one of the lifeboats too?

Or maybe he was on a life raft with some of the sailors? They couldn't really shout from boat to boat; there were too many of them and they were spread out. He had to be there, though, somewhere. And besides, Connie was still wearing his hat. Because if he wasn't in one of the lifeboats, wouldn't that mean that he hadn't left the ship in time? Connie didn't want to think about that, but the bleak possibility hung over her like a dark cloud.

Connie and Ned were snuggled together under Abigail's fur coat, which she'd insisted they have to keep warm. Abigail had become such a good friend to them in only a short time.

'Let us repay you,' Connie said. She glanced at Ned. She knew he'd agree. He'd calmed down now and seemed to be back to his cheeky old self. Connie knew better though. She could see the anxiety in his eyes, which continually scanned the horizon for any sign of their lost friend. Nobody else would've guessed he was worried though. Just as he did in London when the bombs rained down, he was doing his best to keep everyone smiling. 'I'll sing you a song!' she said. She knew Ned wouldn't be able to hear her sing, but it was what she did best.

He read the note she'd written, then nodded and said, 'Give 'em something cheery, Con.' Then he told the other passengers, 'You're lucky tonight, because Miss Connie is in talks with Noël Coward to star in his spring revue, but she's giving you all an exclusive!'

'Ned!' Connie nudged him, embarrassed. But then it was true, wasn't it? 'Yeah, Mr Coward wants me to sing in his show, which can't be bad. So I better sing one of his songs, hadn't I?'

There were plenty of Noël Coward songs that were cheerful, but Connie decided to sing 'A Room with a View'. It made her think of being back in the house in Whitechapel, sitting beside Jack.

As she sang, she felt a tear run down her cheek, but only because she missed Jack and the rest of her friends so much, and their home that they'd created together. She thought of Mr Wyngate and Lisette and their je t'aimes. The other survivors in the lifeboat smiled as Connie sang; even the young sailor, who was leaning on his oars, his head tipped to one side. He seemed to be thinking of someone far away, too.

Eventually, morning came; a flush of rose on the horizon in the direction of home. Connie hadn't realised she'd dozed off with Ned's head on her shoulder. She blinked against the morning light.

The sunrise glowed on the pale face of the young sailor who they'd pulled into the lifeboat last night. He was lying so still and was staring glassily at the sky. Connie knew straight away that he hadn't made it, and the sailor who'd rowed them to safety whispered a prayer as he closed the dead boy's eyes.

He was so young. He could've been Jack. Connie felt a sob rise up inside her.

Then her heart jumped.

There, in the distance, she could see the dark grey shape of a ship. Not just one, in fact; there seemed to be loads of them. It couldn't be the Nazis again, could it? Would they attack survivors in lifeboats? Or would they be rounded up and sent to a prison camp, like where Jack and Elsie's father was waiting out the war?

Connie wrote a note in Ned's notebook. She didn't want to say it out loud and scare the wits out of everyone else.

BOATS! FRIENDS OR FOES?

Ned blinked away the sleep from his eyes and read the note. Then he squinted into the horizon and said with a dawning smile, 'They're ours.' With that, he leapt up to his feet and started waving his arms above his head. 'Oi,' he shouted, 'Over 'ere!'

As one, Connie heard Ned's call echoed across the open ocean, from the survivors who were still awaiting rescue.

Despite the early morning sunlight she saw a bright light illuminate on the deck of the first ship, and then its beam swept the surface of the waves, arcing back and forth.

'This is Captain Draper aboard HMS *Nemesis*.' The voice was loud and echoed from the ship's loudhailer. 'Sailors from *Nemesis* and USS *Neptune* will recover everyone in this area.'

And from that same horizon, a second amplified voice could be heard.

'The cavalry's here,' said an American voice from the *Neptune*. 'And just an hour ago, we blew a couple of U-boats halfway to the moon. USS *Neptune* out!'

Cheers rang out from the lifeboats and life rafts. Maybe it wasn't the kindest reaction to the news that all those German submariners had met a horrible end, but the survivors from the convoy could've died themselves. Connie tried not to look at the dead sailor; not everyone had made it, and the thought of it made her feel cold.

But rescue had come, and the tension and fear was flowing out of her. She hugged Ned tight. She didn't need to say anything or write it down. He'd know; he was just as relieved as she was.

'Bet they've already got Mr W on board,' he told Connie. 'And if they ain't, one of the other ships will have!' Then he rested his head on her shoulder, clinging on to her as though for dear life.

'As soon as we're on board, we'll find your friend,' Abigail promised Connie. 'And don't you worry, because you're staying with me until we do.'

The *Nemesis* and the *Neptune* came alongside, dwarfing their ramshackle convoy. They were enormous battleships, casting huge shadows like the biggest buildings in London. There were guns on every possible surface, and Connie didn't fancy the chances of any enemy ships that came their way. They smelt of fuel and oil and the tang of the sea. And all along the decks, she saw young men smiling down at them, ready to bring them aboard.

There was shouting from the ships, and ropes were lowered down. Some of the sailors from the life rafts clung on and shimmied up the ropes like monkeys, even though the ones who'd fallen into the sea were still soaking wet. More ropes came down, and their own young sailor attached them firmly to the prow and the stern of their lifeboat, and they jerkily made their way towards the deck.

Connie clung on to Ned. She was scared he'd fall out; she was scared *she'd* fall out. She reached for Abigail's hand and held it tight, as the huge wall of the ship slowly went by.

Finally, they reached the deck, and the crew helped them all climb off the lifeboat and onto their enormous ship. Connie's legs were wobbling and she was still clinging to Ned and Abigail. Even though they were safe now, she didn't want to let go. And as she watched survivors getting out of the other lifeboats, she peered at them, trying to spot Mr Wyngate. Where was he?

'There's going to be a lot of confusion right now,' Abigail explained gently, scribbling the message down for Ned. 'It may take a little time for us to find Mr Wyngate, okay? He may be on a different ship. But we'll do our best.'

'But we have to find him,' Connie told her, as she wrote down her words for Ned. 'He's looking after us. And we're looking after him too, see? I've got to give him back his hat!' She tapped the brim of his fedora. It felt like a lucky charm. As long as she had it with her, they'd find him.

Before they could do anything, they were given breakfast and something to drink. Connie and Ned both had cocoa and porridge, and Connie hurried hers down. She wouldn't rest until she'd found Mr Wyngate.

Then, with Abigail, they started to make their journey around the enormous ship, from one cluster of survivors to another. Every huddled figure in a blanket, every sailor telling a tall story, they stopped and asked.

And the more they asked, the more they heard from people who *had* seen Mr Wyngate. But they'd only seen him on the *City of Newcastle*, where he'd helped other passengers get to safety before it sank.

Not one person they'd spoken to had seen Mr Wyngate leave the ship alive.

FORTY-FIVE
LISETTE

Lisette hadn't been to work for three days. She couldn't have concentrated even if she'd tried. Her mind was full of images of sinking ships and survivors drifting in lifeboats. She tried to picture Wyngate pulling powerfully on the oars, and Connie and Ned, frightened yet hopeful, their arms round each other, in the lifeboat with him.

If she could think of that, then she could hold on for the children, who she couldn't leave. She needed to be there to look after them until news came, and she kept telling them it would be all right.

And when Pippa barked, and Ben announced that the telegram boy was riding up to their house, a stone dropped into the pit of her stomach. This was the news she was both hoping for and dreading. She opened the envelope with a shaking hand. And there it was.

The best news. And the worst.

ME AND NED SAFE IN NYC STOP MRS FRANKLIN
LOOKING AFTER US STOP V V SORRY SAD NEWS
MR W LOST AT SEA STOP SAVED LOTS OF PEOPLE

STOP ENQUIRED EVERYWHERE NO SIGN OF HIM
STOP DEVASTATED STOP SO SORRY CONNIE
XXX STOP

Her voice cracking with shock, she read Connie's telegram
out loud to her audience of four tired, worried children.

It didn't hit her immediately. There was a moment when
she felt that, if she read it again, the news would be different. It
would say that Wyngate was safe, that he was with them in
New York.

But as she reached the line about Wyngate, the words
hadn't changed.

She couldn't read any further, and tears took over, huge
racking sobs that shook through her body. Trembling, she
leaned back against the wall, because she couldn't hold herself
up, as if the shock had made her bones forget what to do.

She couldn't fight against the force of the utter despair that
was forcing its way through her, tearing apart every joy and
dream she'd ever had with Wyngate, blotting out his face from
her memories, and trampling its leaden heels across her heart.

The telegram dropped from her hand. Through her tears,
Lisette was aware that one of the children had picked it up.
There were whispers, hushed and shocked. Someone was crying.

Then, the children she had done so much to look after were
looking after her. They led her, blinded with tears and helpless
with shock, from the hallway to the lounge. They guided her
down to the sofa.

He'd gone. Wyngate had gone. Lost, for ever, to the waves.
The bravest man, the man she would always love.

'But if he's lost, doesn't that mean someone just has to find
him?' Elsie asked innocently, but Lisette heard tears in the little
girl's voice.

'Elsie, it's a lot of sea to be lost in,' Susan reminded her, her tone kind. 'Connie and Ned are safe, though. Mr Wyngate made sure of that, I'm certain, even though he— Oh, heck, Lisette... I'm so sorry. He was such a lovely bloke.'

Lisette nodded in acknowledgment, but she couldn't speak. Her throat was choked with tears.

Jack was kneeling on the floor in front of the table where his wireless stood. The back was off it again, a collection of parts and tools neatly laid aside until he and his little family were ready to begin work on it again. He bowed his head, then shook it and murmured, 'I just— I can't believe it. I *know* he'll have found a way. He will.'

'Our dad was alive all along,' Elsie reminded Lisette. She placed Pippa on Lisette's lap, and the little dog licked the tears from her cheeks as they fell. 'You mustn't give up hope, Lisette. Maybe he's on a desert island somewhere, like Robinson Crusoe.'

Ben patted Lisette's hand. It was an oddly mature thing for a boy of his age to do, and yet Lisette knew only too well that she was surrounded by children who had endured far more than their fair share of loss.

'Maybe he is,' Ben said. 'With his fedora keepin' the sun off his face. And he'll find a way to come back to you, to all of us. Elsie's right, Lisette. Don't give up.'

She wished she could believe them. And she envied them their ability to hope. But she knew the realities of the war well enough.

Tom, poor Tom, her boyfriend, reduced to a lifeless figure on a stretcher after being caught in a raid.

She thought of her friend Sidonie, too, who had disappeared from Hamburg.

And now she had lost Wyngate. She saw him drifting down through the depths, the sunlight fading away the deeper he went. He'd turn into pearls, Lisette told herself, and she would

think of him that way. Not lost, just transformed beneath
the sea.

Lisette lost track of time. She couldn't move from the sofa.
She kept thinking of Wyngate, gliding along the ocean currents,
his smart suit soaked through, the name on his identity card too
blurred to read. He would never be found.

Susan brought her food, and the others took it in turns to
stay with her, never leaving her alone. Her heart had been
shredded to pieces and she had no idea what to do. She couldn't
find any strength, but the children were there, bringing her a
blanket, handkerchiefs, sweet tea.

She needed air. Her body was trying to knit itself back
together again. She needed to reply to Connie. She couldn't let
the girl's message go unanswered after what she and Ned had
been through. Lisette forced herself to her feet, with the children helping her to set one foot in front of the other until she
remembered how to walk again.

She headed off with trembling steps, the four children there
to guide her, to send a telegram to New York. One for Connie
and Ned, to tell them she was so relieved they were safe, and to
pass on her thanks to Mrs Franklin – whoever this mysterious
lady was – for looking after them. And then she decided to send
another.

Should she really send a telegram to a dead man? And yet,
the children wouldn't give up hope. So perhaps Lisette
shouldn't either. She sent the telegram in French, via Connie at
her hotel, to Wyngate:

PLEASE COME HOME SAFE STOP I LOVE YOU I
LOVE YOU XXX LIS STOP

FORTY-SIX

CONNIE

Connie had never seen anything like New York before. It was one thing seeing it in films, but actually being on the streets and tipping back her head to look up at the very tops of the enormous skyscrapers made her head spin. They had three days before Ned's operation, and they spent them exploring the city.

There were no bombsites, but buildings were going up everywhere she looked, as if the city would burst if it didn't keep growing. The cabs were yellow and honked angrily in the traffic, and everything looked new and shiny, even the people.

The shops were full, and Abigail bought Connie and Ned new clothes and shoes to replace what they'd lost on the boat. Nothing was darned or patched; there was no make-do-and-mend in New York. Abigail bought comics for Ned, and *Calling All Girls* magazine for Connie. She absorbed the fashion tips, movie star gossip and agony aunt advice about boyfriends.

Ned was a Londoner to his bones, as he was always so fond of telling people, and in New York he told them even more loudly. Yet he seemed at home here just as he did in the East End, basking in the attention of the Americans who had read about his plight in the press and delighting them with tales of his bravery and that of his friends back home. He told them too of Mr Wyngate, the man they were searching for.

Never without his Home Guard cap, Ned devoted himself to experiencing the culinary delights that Manhattan had to offer. He devoured burgers and hot dogs, sundaes and milk-shakes, and he only stopped smiling when he and Connie were alone and could talk about their ordeal at sea.

Then she saw the vulnerability he masked so well. He stayed close to her, and at night she could hear him crying in his sleep. Perhaps he thought of the poor young sailor who had died in their lifeboat; Connie thought about him sometimes too, the way the sunrise had touched his face even though he'd never see another one again.

Yet Ned was always optimistic: Mr Wyngate would find them in New York, whatever it took.

But they weren't here on holiday. Connie didn't want Ned to have to go to the hospital, where she couldn't look out for him. And yet, he was here to be cared for by experts. She had to trust that he would come through it all right.

Ned was a celebrity patient. He wasn't taken through a side door into the hospital; instead they posed for the press.

Connie smiled for the cameras, standing on the steps outside the vast hospital. Her arm was round Ned's shoulders, and standing on Ned's other side was the impossibly tall Dr Mayer in his white coat, a stethoscope round his neck.

Immediately behind Ned was the British ambassador with his bald head, smiling broadly. Nearby, but out of shot, was Abigail, who had looked after them from the moment they'd stepped into the lifeboat on board the stricken ship.

Journalists with notepads were shouting questions at them, and Connie kept replying, 'Ned can't hear you! That's why he's having an op!'

'Here's a statement from me, Ned Mitchell, to the folks of America!' Ned was every inch the little celebrity, but Connie knew that it was a whole lot of show. Behind closed doors, all he wanted to do was keep on searching, keep on tramping the streets and asking if anyone had seen Mr Wyngate. 'I come over 'ere to see Doc Mayer, thanks to good old FDR. Now let's get these ears of mine fixed, so I can get back home and keep on kicking Adolf's arse until he can't hear himself fart!'

Just to her right, out of the line of the cameras, Connie saw Abigail visibly flinch as Ned made his unexpected statement. When the journalists responded with cheers and laughter, though, she joined in. It was nice to hear her laugh, Connie thought, because none of them really had since that awful night at sea.

Ned held up his fingers in a mimic of Churchill's V for Victory sign, milking the limelight for all it was worth. He even raised his own camera and photographed the enormous crowd of photographers, giving them a taste of their own medicine.

Connie raised her hand, as if she was asking a question at school.

'And can you all tell your readers that anyone who knows where our mate Mr Wyngate is, please come forward,' she implored the journalists. 'We haven't seen him since... since the boat went down, and we don't know what's happened to him. You've got to help us find him, please!'

'Please do support our appeal and the appeals for the other souls who are still unaccounted for after the attack on our ships,' Abigail said. She reminded Connie of Lisette in many ways, so self-possessed and elegant as she glided through life.

Even here, on the steps of the hospital, reflected in the lenses of dozens of cameras, she looked more Hollywood star than rabbit in the headlights. 'We all have loved ones in this conflict one way or another,' she went on. 'If you can reunite these children with their guardian, it'll be one drop of hope in an ocean. And every drop is so valuable.'

The journalists seemed to like that, and started asking even more questions, but Connie couldn't make out what they were shouting. It was like a rugby scrum armed with pencils and notepads and cameras.

Finally the press call was over, and they went into the hospital. It was like a palace inside. But Connie noticed that they had government information posters here, too. A man in a white top hat pointed out of his poster, saying, *I want you for the US army!* And an advert encouraging people to car-share said, *When you ride ALONE, you ride with Hitler,* complete with the ghostly outline of the Führer himself in the passenger seat.

Dr Mayer led the way up to Ned's room – his own private room. He wasn't on a ward full of other children here. There was even a vase of flowers on the windowsill, and it made Connie think of the garden at home. She saw Jack, leaning against a spade, sweeping his hair back from his face. But someone had been prepared for a ten-year-old boy's arrival; there was a stack of Superman and Popeye comics and a large toy aeroplane in USAAF colours beside the bed.

Ned took photos of the room. 'For Mr W to see,' he explained.

Ned's brand-new suitcase, courtesy of Abigail's shopping spree with her new charges, was neatly stored on top of the wardrobe, and someone had unpacked his clothes and hung them. On the bed were the Stars and Stripes pyjamas he had chosen on their trip to the glittering department stores that seemed to be so full of everything under the sun.

Ned had even turned down cosy dressing gowns in favour of a neat silk smoking jacket. After all, *that's what theatre agents wear,* he had pointed out. Abigail had indulged him, but there was a cosy dressing gown on the bed too.

Connie was still getting used to her completely new outfit, including her lace-up shoes. They were in two different colours of leather – cream and dark blue – and were called saddle shoes. She'd never seen anything like them before.

She was wearing a new dress, too, in candy stripes with a lace collar, and back at the hotel she had a wardrobe full of new things. And not just for her – she'd insisted that, if Abigail was buying new clothes for her and Ned, then they should get some things for the others back at home, too. It hadn't taken any persuading at all for Abigail to add the other four children's needs to her shopping list.

Connie remembered Elsie's words at the dockside. She'd been convinced that they'd like America so much, they wouldn't want to go home. And yes, Connie was amazed by New York City at every moment. There didn't appear to be any shortages here, and everything was big and shiny. But she didn't want to stay here. Her home was in London, not New York. Even though it meant crossing that treacherous ocean again.

'Little Ned, you have a little time before the doctor's ready for you.' Abigail knelt on the floor in front of Ned, jotting down her words in the notepad she now always carried. 'So I'm gonna leave you and Connie for a few minutes and go talk to Doctor Mayer. I'm so proud of you. Both of you.' She flung her arms round Ned and held him tight.

Ned hugged Abigail in return, even as he said, 'Yeah, you ain't so bad yourself neither. Now crack on, see the doc. Me and Connie'll be fine.'

Abigail rose to her feet, crossed to Connie and enfolded her in a hug too.

'You and I will be waiting here when Ned comes back,' she promised. 'It's going to be just fine.'

Connie breathed in Abigail's perfume and the powdery scent of her make-up. A memory stirred. Connie thought of her mum, when she'd say goodbye to her before she went off to a dance or down the pub.

She said goodbye to Abigail, then picked up Ned's new toy plane. She flew it at him, narrowly skimming the top of his head, then nudged him playfully.

'Ned, mate...' She put the plane down and started to write her note to him, speaking the words aloud. 'You're the best little brother I never had. I really, really hope your op goes okay. Dr Mayer looks all right, though, don't he?'

Ned nodded. 'You're the best big sister ever an' all,' he replied. Then he gave her a wink. 'And when we get home, tell our Jack that you're sweet on him, all right? We can all bloody see it but him!' Ned smiled. 'I love you, Con. You're the best.'

'I love you, too.' Connie blushed. 'Do you know, after what we went through, I think I should tell Jack. Life's short, ain't it?' But she wished she hadn't said that, or written it down, because now she was thinking about Mr Wyngate. Poor man, wherever he was. Surely he couldn't have died in the sinking? Not Mr Wyngate. 'And you know that Mr Wyngate – wherever he is – I bet he's thinking of you, and crossing his fingers and toes and his eyes as well that you'll do all right.'

Ned's gaze moved over the words and he nodded. 'He's probably swum over to Germany,' he joked. 'He'll pop Adolf between the eyes, then home in time for tea!'

Connie chuckled, but she couldn't help thinking of the telegrams from Lisette that had arrived at their hotel earlier that day. She'd shown Ned the one addressed to both of them, but she hadn't told him about the other one, addressed to Mr Wyngate. She hadn't opened it, but she knew it was from Lisette. The thought of her sending him a telegram when no one knew where he was broke Connie's heart.

'And then he'll go home to Lisette and give her a massive kiss,' Connie said, writing her words down at the same time. She gave Ned a hug. She didn't like to think about him out for the count in the operating theatre. But they'd come so far and risked so much. They couldn't pull out now. 'And when we see Mr Wyngate again, he'll tell you everything he's been up to, and he won't need a notepad to do it in neither.'

She hoped so much that all would be well. She still had nightmares about the sinking; she still clung to the bedsheets as if they were the edge of the lifeboat. She still heard the shouts for help and felt the rough scurf of brine on her skin, and the lurch in her heart as the last of their ship vanished under the ocean's surface. She still thought of the dead sailor.

If Ned's hearing could be saved from silence, then, against all the odds, maybe Mr Wyngate could be rescued from the endless, dark waves too.

FORTY-SEVEN
LISETTE

Susan had made a small scarecrow out of scraps from her sewing. It looked like it was made from a patchwork quilt, and it smiled as it swayed from side to side on its beanpole in the warm breeze. Bees drifted between the blossoms and flowers that filled the small garden, around the crowded vegetable plots and busy flower beds. The flowing green heads of onions and carrots had poked up from the earth beside cauliflowers and cabbages, and lettuces were lined up in a trough beside hardy tomatoes, which climbed the sunny garden wall on a wooden lattice.

Ben was industriously digging up weeds with his trowel, while Elsie was picking pea pods for dinner. Pippa followed her route, sniffing the ground as she went. Susan was showing Lisette how to squash the aphids that were trying to attack the roses again.

Lisette tried to smile. Being out in the garden, close to the earth, made it easier to forget about the deep ocean where Wyngate was lost. And yet his face kept drifting back to her. His dark eyes. The memory of his scent. He'd called things off because he didn't want her to fall in love with him and then lose him. But it'd been too late; she knew in her heart that she'd fallen for him long ago.

In the house, Jack was seeing the engineer who had finally installed their telephone to the door. It was too nice a day to remain indoors though and, once Jack had done his duty, Lisette knew, he would join them outside once again. He'd even moved his lessons for the younger children outside so they could enjoy the sunshine. That morning there had been maths and English. Later in the afternoon, with Mr Gray, there would be more history to learn.

'We have a telephone!' Jack called brightly from the back door. 'I'll be out in a minute, with some of Ma Mahoney's home-made lemonade!'

Susan brushed her hands together and called to Jack, 'A telephone – at last! Do you need a hand with the lemonade?' They were always looking out for each other, this little band of children. Always trying to help.

'I can manage, you enjoy the sun!' Jack assured her, disappearing back into the house. As he busied himself in the kitchen, Lisette heard a car disturb the birdsong of the afternoon, but she paid little attention. It wasn't the throaty roar of Wyngate's sports car, and it never would be again. There was the sound of car doors closing and, a moment later, the door knocker banged in the otherwise empty streets.

'I'll get it!' Jack shouted.

Lisette leaned towards the roses and closed her eyes, breathing in the scent. They needed a way to remember Wyngate. He wouldn't have a place in the cemetery, but she wanted somewhere she could go to and think of him, where she could lay flowers. She imagined his expression if she'd given him flowers in life. He wasn't a flowery sort of man, but she knew he'd have found a vase for them in his comfortable little flat all the same.

'Who is it?' Elsie asked, calling towards the house as she

stretched up on tiptoes to pick a pea pod. As she did there was the sound of skittering paws, and a little brown poodle darted out of the back door and into the garden. Pippa suddenly sprang from her contented stroll into a run, heading straight for the poodle, and the two dogs tumbled and chased around the garden.

'We have guests!' Jack called as he stepped out into the sunlight, followed by Mr Gray. Gray's deep green suit shimmered and he greeted the children and Lisette with a salute. Jack peered back into the house beyond Mr Gray and said, 'This way sir, please.'

Lisette recognised the poodle straight away. It was Churchill's dog. And that could only mean that the prime minister himself had made the journey across central London from Whitehall to Whitechapel.

'Children,' Lisette said gently, smiling, allowing herself to feel joy for this moment, for the children's sake, 'we have an important guest!'

Ben shot to his feet and flung aside his trowel, which hit the stone path with a clang and made Elsie laugh. Susan brushed down her dress, then hurried to smooth down Ben's cowlick and tidy the collar on Elsie's blouse.

'No, no,' Winston Churchill said as he walked out into the garden. He should have looked incongruous in the humble little space that the children had made their own, yet somehow he seemed entirely at home.

Here, away from the uniformed officials and the tension of the room beneath Whitehall, he looked more like a friendly neighbour than the prime minister. Lisette could see the excitement in the faces of the kids, though, as well as the hope that there might be good news. She admired their optimism, despite her grief. 'Please don't stand on ceremony. Rufus certainly hasn't.'

'How are we all?' Gray asked gently. He stooped to

exchange hugs with the younger children, then greeted Lisette with a polite nod. He kept his eyes on her though, his gaze filled with sadness. 'We've come to thank you.'

Lisette thought of their invasion of the War Office with the code they'd worked out from Mr Taylor's sheet music. If only they'd been able to find some other code, too, which would've meant that Wyngate was safe.

'That is very kind of you,' she replied. 'We did our best – I hope we were right.'

Churchill nodded. 'You were correct. The message of the music was as you all believed,' he said. 'A good many people have reason to be very grateful to you.'

Lisette thought of all the men who'd been on that ship. The airmen among them would've recognised the sound of the bombers as they approached. The relief they must've felt when they heard the aeroplanes turn away would have been immeasurable.

Elsie beamed, and grinned up at her brother. 'Our dad helped too,' she said. 'But I s'pose you can't say thank you to him, not until he comes home.'

'Alas no, not until he returns,' Churchill lamented. He held out his hand to Gray, who reached into his pocket and held out a small pile of cream envelopes to the prime minister. 'But I have here a letter of commendation for each of you, to thank you for your good work.'

And one by one, he made his steady way to each of the children, handing them each their letter. The last one he reserved for Lisette.

'And Mademoiselle Souchon, I hope you will accept my condolences,' he said softly as he held out the last envelope to Lisette. 'Mr Wyngate has done a great deal for the country's war effort. We are all so very sorry.'

Lisette took the envelope. Churchill's words had brought tears to her eyes again, and she battled with them, not wanting to cry in front of the prime minister. 'Thank you. I know he's done far more than he could ever tell me. He was such a gallant and selfless man... I suppose just the sort of person we need if we're ever to win this war. I just never thought... I never thought we'd lose him.'

'It will be precious little comfort, I know,' Churchill replied, 'but he has done more than we had any right to ask of him.'

Gray nodded, watching the children as they opened the envelopes and read the letters within. Then he turned to Jack and said, 'Mr Fluke has asked if you would come into the War Office, Jack. He'd like to talk to you about your talent for the wireless and for reading music, if you follow?'

Jack's eyes grew wide and he said, 'Oh yes, I would, Mr Gray!' Then he glanced towards Elsie and said, 'Our mum and dad took us to see one of his shows just before the war. It was amazing. We couldn't work out how he did any of it!'

'That's how I feel when you fiddle around with your radio!' Ben teased him with a grin.

Lisette's threatened tears melted away. Wyngate would've been so impressed by Jack for rebuilding the radio and learning to recognise Morse code.

She would think of Wyngate's proud smile, and that would make her loss just a little easier to bear.

FORTY-EIGHT

CONNIE

A couple of days had passed since Ned's operation. Connie and Abigail had been to see him at every visiting time. His ears were still bandaged as they healed inside, and Connie spent most of her visits crossing her fingers out of his sight, hoping against hope that the surgery had worked.

When they weren't visiting Ned, Abigail was taking Connie to see the sights of New York, but she found it hard to enjoy herself without Ned, and with the looming absence of Mr Wyngate too.

The city was so busy, and everywhere Connie looked she saw men and women in uniform. There was a buzz on every street; these young men and women had travelled from all over the States to come to New York, where they'd set sail for Britain, and they were enjoying themselves while they could.

Abigail took Connie to Times Square, where there were cinemas – *movie theatres*, Abigail called them – and enormous advertising hoardings. She liked the one with the huge cartoon camel smoking a cigarette. Abigail took her to see *Ziegfeld Girl* with Judy Garland, and Connie loved it so much that Abigail took her to see it another three times.

But despite all the excitement of being in New York, Connie felt as if she was full of cracks. When she'd burst into tears in Central Park after Abigail had bought her an ice cream, her new friend understood. Connie wished Mr Wyngate could've been there too, but he was gone.

If only he'd got into the lifeboat with them – Connie dreamed every night that he had, but her dream always ended the same way. Mr Wyngate climbed over the side and swam back to the stricken ship. He had lives to save, but he didn't save his own.

On their next visit to see Ned, Dr Mayer was in the room. He smiled as they came in.

'You're just in time,' he said in his warm tones, which made him sound like a nice uncle. 'I'm just about to remove Ned's bandages.'

'So look out, Manhattan!' Ned laughed. 'Come on, doc, let's get it done!'

Abigail took Connie's hand and gave it a reassuring squeeze.

'God bless him, he's gonna be fine,' she whispered. 'I just know it.'

Connie didn't say a word. She couldn't. She just gave Ned a thumbs-up. He'd understand.

Dr Mayer slowly removed the bandages, untying gauze here and snipping through knots there. He unwound a length of the bandage from round Ned's head, and it reminded Connie of a film she'd seen where an Egyptian mummy had run amok. He removed wedges of cotton wool that had been placed directly over Ned's ears, then he stood to one side, so that Ned couldn't read his lips. He whispered, 'It's good to have you back, Ned.'

'Bloody hell, mate,' Ned said, screwing up his face in a jokey grimace. 'Turn the volume down!'

'Ned, you can hear him!' Connie cheered as she skipped on

the spot with glee. The rubber soles of her saddle shoes squeaked on the polished floor. Then she saw Dr Mayer's good-natured wince and stopped. 'Blimey, I'm sorry… bit loud there, wasn't I!'

Ned opened his arms to Connie. 'Now I can 'ear again,' he said, 'we'll get back on finding Mr W!'

Connie ran into Ned's arms and hugged him tight. 'We have to try, don't we?' She paused, wondering where Ned's notepad was, then remembered he didn't need it any more.

She couldn't help it. She nursed a tiny thread of hope that Mr Wyngate was still alive. It hurt too much to think that he was gone.

Just then, someone knocked at the door, and Connie smiled, because she saw that Ned had heard the sound. A nurse came in, dressed all in white like an angel, and she whispered something in Abigail's ear.

'Excuse me,' Abigail said to the children. 'There's an old friend asking to see me.' She crossed to the bed and scrubbed her hand over Ned's hair. 'I'm so happy for you,' she said with a smile. 'And I'll be right back.'

As Abigail and the nurse left, Ned frowned. 'You didn't tell me she sounded like she went out with Rhett Butler!' Then he looked up at the doctor. 'I don't know what to say to you, pal. Thank you don't seem enough.'

Dr Mayer patted Ned's arm. 'You don't need to thank me, young man. All you need to do now is lead a good life. And I know you will – I've heard all about what you've done for folk back home in England. It's why I wanted to help you.' He drew back his sleeve and looked at his watch. 'Right, I have to go prepare. I've got another surgery in an hour. Take care, Ned – and you, Connie, too.'

And Dr Mayer headed out of the room. Connie wondered what it was like to have a job like his, where he could transform someone's life.

Ned beamed up at Connie, his eyes bright.

'Sing us a song, Con,' he whispered. 'I've missed hearing your voice.'

Connie swallowed. 'Oh, Ned, I was so sad about what you were missing out on. Well, all right, I'll sing for you, but something gentle – you choose. I can't be too loud, or you'll need Dr Mayer to fix your ears up again!'

He shook his head. 'Loud enough for Mr Wyngate to hear,' he instructed. 'So he knows where we are.'

Connie smiled. 'Yeah, I hope he can hear us too, wherever he's gone.'

She stood up straight, and started to sing 'Anything Goes'. Abigail had bought it for her from a record shop, and at that moment Connie couldn't think of any other song that was brash and loud enough to celebrate Ned's recovery.

She treated the hospital room like her own stage, and danced about, ignoring her squeaking shoes, and flung out her arms to emphasise the lyrics. She kept Ned in sight as she sang, singing just for him and his new ears.

Ned reached out and picked up his Home Guard cap from the bedside table. He put it atop his blond curls, restored once more to the familiar Ned she knew as he clapped along, his face lit by a beaming smile. As Connie sang she heard the door open behind her to readmit Abigail, and Ned's grin grew wider. He gave a thumbs-up and pointed to Connie as though to say, *isn't she something?*

Connie spun round on her heel like a tap-dancer, smiling for Abigail. But then she saw someone else standing there too. Someone she hadn't expected to see at all.

It was Gabriel Cooper, the star who Ned had gone to find after the show on Drury Lane. He looked immaculate in his uniform, as if he'd been polished by a wardrobe team on a Hollywood backlot. His toned muscles had somehow been restrained by the sober green of his jacket, but Connie had seen him shirtless on a pirate ship at the cinema, and she blushed furiously.

She stopped singing.

'Oh, flippin' heck, I didn't realise I had an audience!' She clasped her hands awkwardly. 'Mr Cooper, blimey...'

'Ain't you s'posed to be fighting a war?' Ned asked the Hollywood leading man. 'You won't find many Nazis over 'ere, mate!'

Gaberiel Cooper laughed, showing a set of teeth more straight and white than any Connie had ever seen before in her life. 'I'm back home visiting a few of our guys here in hospital,' he replied. 'But then I heard Deanna Durbin singing in a side room and thought I'd look in and say hi to an old friend.'

Ned shook his head, dismissing the comparison to one of the sweetest-voiced leading ladies that Hollywood currently had on its books. 'Not Deanna Durbin, mate. Miss Connie Harrington, the toast of London town. The Whitechapel Sparrow herself!' He sat up straight and pointed at his new visitor. 'In fact, when you was over in England, you missed out on the chance to book her for one of your charity shows. Well, I'm offering you that chance right now, Coop. She's available for Broadway booking during her strictly limited New York engagement!'

Connie was drawn along by Ned's enthusiasm. Her heart was pounding. She wouldn't get a chance like this again. She curtseyed for Gabriel Cooper, a move she had been practising ever since she'd first sung at Jasper's nightclub.

'I'm sure I can fit it into my hectic schedule before we return home,' she said, knowing from Ned that she needed to talk herself up and not sound desperate.

Abigail gave a smile and touched Gabriel Cooper lightly on his arm. 'Coop and I go way back,' she told the children. 'Coop, don't you think Connie would be perfect for your benefit for the war orphans this weekend?' She gave Connie a long-lashed wink. 'And after all, little Ned here *was* looking for you when he had his accident.'

Coop glanced at Ned, who pouted and widened his eyes in a pantomime of cherubic wounded innocence. Then Coop laughed and nodded, and told them all, 'You don't need to convince me, okay? She did that as soon as I heard her voice.' He addressed Connie then. 'We don't have a lot of time, but I've got a feeling you won't need too much rehearsal. You've got the pipes already, Miss Harrington.'

'Oh, I always have my songs at the ready,' Connie replied, hoping she sounded professional. 'You never know when you might need them!'

She'd sing for Wyngate, that's what she'd do. She'd sing as if her songs could bring him back, even though she knew there was little chance of that. Really, it would be her memorial for him; her way of saying goodbye to a courageous, selfless man who had once come out of the night to save her and her friends, and who had given his life to save strangers on a dark and treacherous sea.

FORTY-NINE
CONNIE

Connie stood in the wings, watching Bing Crosby sing. She couldn't quite believe she was seeing him standing there at his microphone only feet away from her. The thought of going on stage immediately after him was terrifying. But then the bill was packed with famous faces. The Andrews Sisters had opened the show, and Connie had bumped into Judy Garland backstage. She'd seen Bob Hope peering at his reflection in the prompt's mirror, his nostrils arched. When a smartly dressed lady had dropped her glove, Connie had bent down to pick it up, then found herself looking up at the sculpted cheekbones and catlike eyes of Marlene Dietrich.

All those celebrities knew who Connie was. And Ned, too. They'd all taken time out from their preparations for the show to shake her hand, and pose for a photograph taken by Ned – and then Abigail had taken over and made sure Ned got into the shots too, before he went off to sit in the front row.

Connie and Ned had been in the newspapers, they'd been interviewed for *Life* magazine, and they'd even been on a radio show. They'd mentioned Mr Wyngate so many times that now interviewers automatically asked them if they'd heard anything about him before they could bring him up.

He still hadn't been found, and Connie's thin thread of hope was fraying. She'd tried her best to be excited about tonight, and had loved going shopping with Abigail, who had furnished her with a shimmering gown for the show, and taken her to get her hair and make-up done on Fifth Avenue. But it all felt a bit hollow, knowing that Mr Wyngate had disappeared.

'Wish me luck,' Connie whispered to Abigail as Bing was approaching the end of his song.

'Go get 'em,' Abigail told her. 'Show these amateurs how it's done, honey!'

'Don't worry, I will!' Connie kissed the air beside Abigail's cheek to avoid smudging her lipstick or Abigail's rouge. She became aware of a man standing at her shoulder and turned to see that there, watching his co-star command the stage, was the show's compère. Bob Hope. The last time Connie had seen them together was at the pictures, when the audience had roared with laughter at their antics in *Road to Zanzibar*, but now she was sharing the bill with both of them.

Bob gave her a nod as Bing was taking his bow.

'You'll knock 'em sideways,' he said, then strode out onto the stage, passing Bing Crosby on his way to the wings. Connie's heart was pounding with anticipation and Bing gave her a polite nod as he passed by.

'I warmed them up for the star of the show,' he said and grinned. 'Good luck, miss.'

'Thank you, Mr Crosby!' Connie said. It was so surreal to be with these people that she felt as if she was floating. 'You was brilliant!'

Bing kissed Abigail's cheek and said, 'I'll watch from here if nobody minds.' Then he addressed Connie again. 'Young lady, you've been through a heck of a thing and you're still smiling. That's a lesson we can all learn.'

'If we don't smile, then them bullies in Germany will've won,' Connie replied. 'So we can cry a bit, now and then, but we've got to keep smiling.'

Bing nodded as, on the stage, Bob Hope took up the microphone.

'Ladies and gentlemen,' he said, 'we're here tonight to raise money for orphans of war. But over in the UK, some of those orphans are keeping the home fires burning. Last week we brought a young man named Ned Mitchell over to the States as a guest of our government, for an operation that restored his lost hearing.'

As Bob spoke, Ned scrambled up and stood on his seat. It was enough to silence the famously fast-talking Bob, who fell silent as the audience rose to give Ned a round of applause. He lapped it up, bowing and doffing his Home Guard cap, until Bob began to speak again.

'Ned and his friend Connie survived a Nazi attack on their convoy – and boy, are we glad they did.' He glanced into the wings, where Abigail put her arm round Connie's shoulders and squeezed. 'Because the Whitechapel Sparrow is here with us tonight and let me tell you folks, this girl can sing. Put 'em together for Miss Connie Harrington!'

The applause was like thunder and Connie took a deep breath in anticipation. She stepped out from the safe shadows of the wings and glanced up at Bob Hope as he walked past her. It was so strange seeing that distinctive face up close. And even stranger to hear him compliment her.

'Thanks!' she whispered to him.

'You'll kill it, honey,' he whispered as he disappeared into the wings.

The stage lights were so bright that it took Connie a moment to adjust to them, and the first place she looked was down to the front row. And there was Ned, roaring with joy to see her on stage. Beside him was Gabriel Cooper himself, the man who'd added Connie to his show. And on the other side of Ned was a seat, empty except for a hat.

Mr Wyngate's hat, on a seat left just for him. The fedora he had left with Connie as he put her and Ned into the lifeboat.

The orchestra burst into 'Anything Goes', and Connie sang with spirit and joy, filling the theatre with her voice. She wasn't standing outside an East End pub now, collecting pennies in her hat. And how strange it was for a whole orchestra to be down there in the pit, when at Drury Lane there'd just been Lucien on the piano. But then, Jasper's club was being rebuilt, and even now, perhaps, Lucien was opening his sheet music, ready to practise in their new venue. Life went on. It had to. And yet, Connie wouldn't forget the people who they'd lost.

Once she reached the end of the song, she curtseyed for the audience.

'Thank you so much for havin' me here to sing to you,' Connie told the vague silhouettes that seemed to go on to the horizon. 'I can't tell you how great it is to be in New York, and to be welcomed by everyone. It's hard livin' in London right now. In fact, the whole of Europe is a right old mess, and the fact that you lot have come along to help us out – well, Europe says thank you to America for being our friend. This next song... I'm dedicating it to Mr Wyngate. He was our mate, see. He was on the ship with us, and...' She sniffed back a tear. She thought of the dead sailor, too, so young to die. But she couldn't cry now, on stage, in front of all these people. 'Well, not everyone made it. He was such a great bloke. The bravest of the brave, he was. So, Mr Wyngate, wherever you are, this one's for you.'

There was silence in the theatre. Connie caught Ned's eye, then she looked down at the conductor, who wagged his baton, and the orchestra started to play the opening bars of 'We'll Meet Again'. She clutched the microphone with both hands.

As she started to sing, her heart filled with sadness for the people they'd lost but, above all, for the man who'd been torn away from her and her new family. Connie longed to go home. She wanted to be with Jack, with the children and Pippa in Whitechapel, and she wanted to hug Lisette. Lisette, who must be going through hell.

A pinpoint of light opened in the rear of the auditorium and an usher came through the door and strode at a clip down the central aisle towards the stage.

There was something in the usher's walk that seemed familiar though and, as the stage lights picked him out, Connie realised why.

It wasn't an usher at all.

It was him. Their Mr Wyngate.

Connie didn't miss a beat or fluff a line of her song, but the whole audience could see where she was looking, and they were all leaning from their seats to see who she was staring at.

She wasn't imagining it, was she? Surely it wasn't just the high emotion of being on this stage with so many celebrities that had made her conjure up their missing friend?

Connie blinked. The man who had suddenly appeared hadn't changed. He hadn't become someone else. It was definitely Mr Wyngate, in a well-cut suit, the light catching his strong jaw.

Wyngate paused before the empty seat and picked up his fedora. He placed the hat at a precise angle on his head, then sat in the seat that had been left for him.

With a cry of disbelief, Ned flung his arms round Wyngate and hugged him tight, as Wyngate hugged him in return.

Connie went on singing, a broad smile on her face, and she filled the song with joy. She bounced on her toes, but she stayed at the microphone; she couldn't stop singing. She had to keep going for Mr Wyngate, and sing the song for him, the man who had come back from the dead.

FIFTY

LISETTE

Lisette was dreaming of dark streets. She was holding a shielded torch that didn't leak any light. She could hear footsteps echoing, and she recognised them. It was Wyngate. She called out, she ran after him, but she couldn't catch up. And then, an air-raid siren began its plaintive wail, and Lisette shook herself awake.

But as she lay there in the dark beside Elsie and Susan, she realised it wasn't the air-raid siren at all. It was the telephone. Why would someone be ringing them in the middle of the night?

She drowsily climbed out of bed and stumbled her way downstairs. Her foot caught against an abandoned shoe, which went thumping down each step to the hallway. But she didn't mind. She loved the chaos that the children brought into her life.

She snatched up the receiver and said in French, because she wasn't entirely awake, 'Hello, who is it, please?'

'Lis,' said a voice that sounded as though it was a long, long way away. Then the voice spoke again, in French. 'It's me. It's Adam.'

The line clicked and purred. Lisette pressed her hand to her mouth. She was still dreaming, wasn't she? Because it was definitely Wyngate, only it couldn't be. He'd died. He'd been lost in the sinking.

'Adam... I wish it was you. I miss you so much,' Lisette replied. Her sleeping mind had given her this chance to speak with him. 'I love you, and I've lost you... oh, Adam...'

'No, Lisette,' he replied. 'I woke up in hospital last night with a bruise the size of a fist on the back of my skull, but I'm alive. I'm with the children in Manhattan. And I love you. I need to say that more often, I know that now. I love you so bloody much.'

Lisette rubbed her eyes and switched on the lamp by the telephone. She wasn't dreaming. But it didn't make sense. Wyngate— but it *was* him. Realisation rushed in, like gushing water.

'You're alive! Adam, oh, you're alive!' She gripped the receiver, she pressed it tightly against her ear as if it would bring him closer to her from the other side of the ocean. 'My God, I thought – we all thought – but Elsie, she knew. Somehow, she knew!'

Lisette was aware then of pattering feet. The light step of a little girl, and the tapping of paws. She glanced around and saw Elsie and Pippa on the stairs.

'She's here now, Adam,' Lisette told him. She smiled at Elsie, who beamed back at her. 'She kept telling us you had survived!'

'Smart girl,' Wyngate said with a sigh of relief. 'I just telephoned Mr Gray and asked him to get a message to you all. That's how I got the new number. We'll be home before you know it. Lis, tell the children that Connie's the toast of New York. She sang a duet with Bing Crosby tonight. I saw her name on the front of a newspaper when I left hospital, and went straight to the theatre where she was playing.'

Lisette chuckled. Everything had come right somehow. 'That is wonderful news. I'll tell them. And Ned? Connie sent a telegram, she told us he can hear again.'

Elsie had come to stand beside her, and Pippa was wagging her tail.

'He's good as new,' Wyngate confirmed. 'And we can't wait to come home to you all.'

Lisette knelt down beside Elsie and shared the receiver with her. The little girl took her cue.

'Hello, Mr Wyngate!' she said. 'It's me, Elsie. I knew you was all right, really! I bet you were just busy swimming to shore, weren't you? It must've been a long way.'

Wyngate gave a soft laugh. 'A bit too far; probably should've waited for a boat,' he said in English. 'Have you been looking after everyone? Making plenty of pies?'

'We got our first blackberries yesterday and I made a pie for everyone,' Elsie told him proudly. She'd stood on a chair to reach the table and baked from memory. 'I used Mum's recipe. There'll be even more blackberries soon, so you'll have to come home in time, otherwise you'll miss out!'

'We sail on Saturday, so save us all a piece,' he said. 'I'll wire the details when I have them.'

'Look after yourself, Mr Wyngate,' Elsie said. 'And make sure you avoid them Nazis this time.'

Lisette squeezed Elsie. 'I'm sure he will,' she said, her voice soft with joy and relief. 'We'll see you soon. We all love you, Monsieur Wyngate!'

Lisette went back to the docks with the children. The bunting was flapping in the summer breeze again, and this time she and the children were armed with paper flags – British Union Jacks and French tricolours.

They clapped and cheered when they saw a huge liner drawing up at the river's edge, and they waved and waved at the figures standing on the deck, leaning against the railings.

Elsie spotted them first. Connie was wearing a candy-striped dress, and Ned was looking smart in a shirt and shorts and, of course, his cap. With his camera to his eye, he snapped photograph after photograph as the boat came into its safe harbour. And there beside them, their own guardian angel: Wyngate.

It seemed to take ages for them to get past the passport desk, but finally the three weary travellers emerged. Lisette couldn't hold back. She ran up to Wyngate and flung her arms round him, holding him tight.

'Adam, oh, Adam!' she gasped. 'I won't let you go – I swear to you, I won't!'

Wyngate said nothing, but instead clung to her as the other

kids clustered around Connie and Ned, hugging them as though their lives depended on it.

'I'm sorry I put you all through this,' Wyngate whispered. Then he kissed her.

Everything was forgiven. Lisette kissed him back, running her fingertips over his cheek to remind herself how he felt. She drew back, gazing at him, drinking in everything she could see. Her man, her Adam. She was in his arms again.

'You have nothing to apologise for,' she replied, breathless with excitement. 'But oh, I thought I'd lost you, mon cher.'

''Ave we got a story for you all!' Ned announced. He patted the camera that hung round his neck. 'And photos every step of the way!'

'Bing and Bob and Marlene and everyone – they all want to come to sing at a little ol' place called Jasper's!' Connie told them excitedly. Lisette thought she could hear a slight American tinge to her accent, which she couldn't have been there long enough to catch. But it didn't matter to Lisette if Connie wanted to display a little bit of American swagger, especially after what she'd been through.

'There'll be plenty of time for stories when we're home.' Wyngate reached down to Elsie, who put her little hand in his. 'After blackberry pie.'

'How did you know?' Elsie grinned. 'I made one especially for you!'

'And I've got a new knock-knock joke for everyone,' Ben said eagerly. 'Just you wait – it's a corker!'

Susan was admiring Connie's new dress. 'That's gorgeous! I'm so jealous. Will you let me borrow it?'

'Of course I will!' Connie replied. She pointed to her large, new suitcase with two luggage stickers on it, for New York and London. 'And don't you worry, because our new friend Abigail has bought you all lots of nice things too!'

Susan gasped. 'Oh, for us? What a nice lady!'

'That's not even the half of it,' Wyngate said. 'We have cases full, courtesy of Mrs Franklin.'

Lisette noticed Connie looking towards Jack. The girl was blushing.

'I missed you, mate,' Connie said. 'And there was something I really wanted to ask you, too.'

'Same!' Jack laughed. 'I mean, I missed you. And I want to ask you something. But you go first.' Then he laughed bashfully. 'You look smashing, Connie. And you're a star now! But go on, ask what you want to ask.'

'Well... I was wondering... and if you don't want to, it's all right, it won't change anything.' Connie swallowed, then asked confidently, 'Will you be my boyfriend, Jack Taylor?'

Jack laughed. 'I don't have to ask my question, after all!' he exclaimed merrily. 'I would love to, Connie Harrington!'

Connie bounced on her toes, then she wrapped her arms round him. 'I thought you'd say no. What a fool I've been! You're the best!'

Lisette smiled. Connie would be even more impressed when she found out about Jack cracking the code in his father's sheet music.

Just then, a woman in a navy blue Wren uniform came over to them. 'I know who you are – you're the Blitz Kids!' she said in a merry Yorkshire accent. She gestured to Ned's camera. 'Would you like me to take your photo for you?'

Ned lifted the strap of the camera from round his neck and held the device out to the Wren.

'Don't mind if we do,' he replied. 'A snap for the family album, eh?'

The Wren eagerly took the camera, and waved them all into position. They crowded together in the bright sunshine, linking their arms together, a family brought together once more, as boats on the river hooted as if they were welcoming them home.

EPILOGUE
CONNIE

Connie stood in the wings behind the thick velvet curtains on Jasper's stage. It was opening night and she could hear the excited buzz of the audience over the sound of Lucien's new piano. Her heart had never beat so fast. What an honour it was to be asked to sing on such an important night. The club was bigger than the old one and smelt of new paint. It was a new start for Jasper's club and everyone connected with it.

Although she'd often been told not to look at the audience through the gap in the curtains, Connie couldn't resist. At the old club, she'd peered through to watch American soldiers in their immaculate uniforms and the Free French energetically flinging their dance partners into the air. It was where the war could be forgotten and people from all over the world could come together to have fun. And those times would come back here, at the new club.

She peeped through the gap and saw Mr Wyngate sitting at a table with Lisette. She'd never seen two people look so in love. They were sitting so close together that Lisette was almost on Wyngate's knee, and they were gazing into each other's eyes as if they were about to fall in. Lisette kept touching Wyngate –

brushing her fingertips against his jaw, his shoulder, his lips – as if she was reminding herself that he really was back. That he hadn't been lost in the wreck after all.

Connie's gaze moved away as she spotted Ned going from table to table, taking everyone's picture and charging them for the pleasure. He hadn't charged Connie, though, when she'd put on the clothes Abigail had made her and Ned had taken her photograph all over London. She'd be autographing them soon, he told her with a bright smile, for all the new fans she was going to have when she was a professional singer.

The audience was full of glamorous people, all wearing their best clothes, among the men and women in their uniforms. Even Noël Coward was there; Ned had already quizzed him about the booking for the revue he'd promised Connie back at the fundraiser and it was really going to happen: Connie was to make her professional West End debut as a leading lady for Noël Coward. Mr Dupree arrived with his family; Connie had noticed that he looked a little brighter these days. He led the way to the snug, which Jasper had named after poor Mrs Dupree. She would've loved to know that a room in the nightclub where she'd spent so many happy times now had her name. If only she had been spared to see it.

Connie's gaze moved to another table, where Mr Gray was sitting with Pippa on his lap, while his wife sat next to them fussing Elsie's little dog. He was wearing a tailcoat and a white cravat that gleamed, and his wife was wearing a silk gown. Connie's other friends were sitting with them. Susan was admiring Mrs Gray's dress, and Ben sipped a ginger beer. Elsie was animatedly telling them about one of Pippa's adventures and Connie could see that Mr Gray was hanging on her every word, his eyes shining with amusement.

But there was an empty chair at the table. Just as Connie wondered with a panic where Jack had got to, Jasper climbed onto the stage and took the microphone. As he welcomed everyone to the opening night of his new club, she could hear the tears in his voice. He'd lost so much, and so had everyone who had ever been welcomed here. And he'd nearly sacrificed his chance to bring his club back for a boy from the streets who almost everyone else had forgotten about. Jasper deserved to see his club rise from the ashes.

'The Whitechapel Sparrow,' a voice whispered close to Connie's ear. 'About to wow her public!'

Connie was glad she was in shadow behind the curtain, because Jack couldn't see her blush as she turned to smile at him. She looped her arm round his waist. What was it that magazine had said about boyfriends?

'I wondered where you were! It doesn't bother me how many people are out there tonight, it wouldn't be the same if I couldn't sing to you,' she told him.

'I wouldn't miss this for the world,' Jack smiled. He put his arm round her waist in turn and added, 'But I didn't want you to go on without me telling you how brilliant you are. Because you are. You're amazing.'

Connie blushed even more. 'Well, I think you're pretty great yourself. I missed you, Jack Taylor. I won't be going off on any more ships without you by my side. I promise.'

Jack beamed, then kissed Connie's cheek. 'You'd better not,' he teased. 'We'd all be lost without you, Con. I would, especially. You mean the world to me.'

For a moment, Connie forgot about the stage and the audience beyond the curtain. All she she knew was that the missing piece of her heart had slotted back into place. She was home in London again, with Jack.

HISTORICAL NOTE

In the early days of the Second World War, hundreds of thousands of children were evacuated from British towns and cities to the relative safety of the countryside. But many returned. One small group of evacuees in London's East End wanted to help protect their city, and risked their lives as the Blitz raged.

Night after night these children, some as young as ten, took to the streets as bombs rained down, putting out fires and rescuing those who were trapped. Two of these fearless children were killed. These brave youngsters, who caught the imagination of a country in its darkest hour, are the inspiration for the Blitz Kids.

Elements of this novel were also inspired by the story of the SS *Cap Arcona*, a German ocean liner that was requisitioned by the Kriegsmarine for war use. The ship starred as the *Titanic* in the 1943 German film of the same name before serving as a prison ship.

Cap Arcona was laden with prisoners from concentration camps when, just one day before the German surrender at Lüneburg Heath in 1945, the RAF bombed her, wrongly believing that she was part of a flotilla carrying senior members of the Nazi regime.

Of the 5,000 concentration camp inmates aboard *Cap Arcona*, only 350 survived.

A LETTER FROM ELLIE CURZON

You may not know it, but Ellie Curzon is actually two authors writing together. Thank you so much for coming along with us on the Blitz Kids' second adventure. To find out more about our books and what's coming next, please sign up to our newsletter and follow us on social media!

www.bookouture.com/ellie-curzon

Aspects of *The Lifeboat Orphans* reflect our own experiences of hearing loss, whether personally or within our immediate families. We really hope you enjoy the book!

www.elliecurzon.co.uk

facebook.com/elliecurzonauthor

x.com/MadameGilflurt

goodreads.com/ellie_curzon

ACKNOWLEDGMENTS

Once again, we'd like to thank the Dead End Kids, the real-life evacuees who inspired the stories of the Blitz Kids.

And a huge thank you to Rhianna, our editor at Bookouture, for everything she does to get the best out of us and onto the page. She helps our stories live and breathe.

PUBLISHING TEAM

Turning a manuscript into a book requires the efforts of many people. The publishing team at Bookouture would like to acknowledge everyone who contributed to this publication.

Commercial
Lauren Morrissette
Hannah Richmond
Imogen Allport

Cover design
Eileen Carey

Data and analysis
Mark Alder
Mohamed Bussuri

Editorial
Rhianna Louise
Ria Clare

Copyeditor
Jacqui Lewis

Proofreader
Elaini Caruso

Marketing
Alex Crow
Melanie Price
Occy Carr
Cíara Rosney
Martyna Młynarska

Operations and distribution
Marina Valles
Stephanie Straub
Joe Morris

Production
Hannah Snetsinger
Mandy Kullar
Nadia Michael
Charlotte Hegley

Publicity
Kim Nash
Noelle Holten
Jess Readett
Sarah Hardy

Rights and contracts
Peta Nightingale
Richard King
Saidah Graham

RAISING READERS

Books Build Bright Futures

Dear Reader,

We'd love your attention for one more page to tell you about the crisis in children's reading, and what we can all do.

Studies have shown that reading for fun is the **single biggest predictor of a child's future life chances** – more than family circumstance, parents' educational background or income. It improves academic results, mental health, wealth, communication skills, ambition and happiness.

The number of children reading for fun is in rapid decline. Young people have a lot of competition for their time, and a worryingly high number do not have a single book at home.

Hachette works extensively with schools, libraries and literacy charities, but here are some ways we can all raise more readers:

- Reading to children for just 10 minutes a day makes a difference
- Don't give up if children aren't regular readers – there will be books for them!

- Visit bookshops and libraries to get recommendations
- Encourage them to listen to audiobooks
- Support school libraries
- Give books as gifts

There's a lot more information about how to encourage children to read on our websites: **www.RaisingReaders.co.uk** and **www.JoinRaisingReaders.com**.

Thank you for reading.